Praise for *Prime T*

"With *Prime Time Romance*, Kate Robb whips up a magical story that feels both gleefully nostalgic and completely fresh. Anyone who's ever spent hours watching their favorite TV couple's best moments on a loop (spoiler alert: it's all of us) will be all-in on Brynn and Josh's love story—it's fun and witty and full of such swoony moments, I had no choice but to devour it in one sitting."

—JESSICA JOYCE, bestselling author of *You, With a View*

"Robb writes the hell out of a romcom. I enjoyed every second of this fast-paced, magical, and electric novel."

—HANNAH BONAM-YOUNG, author of *Out on a Limb*

"Robb delivers all the atmosphere and charm of a small-town Hallmark romance but with a sexy, magical twist. Any reader who has ever rooted for the bad boy to get the girl, or for the girl to get her long-deserved happily-ever-after, will fall for this completely original and binge-worthy book."

—MELISSA WIESNER, author of *The Second Chance Year*

"Sparkling with charm, *Prime Time Romance* cleverly scratches a nostalgic itch. Romance readers will swoon! And anyone who grew up on small-screen tropes will love the dose of reality used to subvert them. This is a magical delight from start to finish!"

—HOLLY JAMES, author of *The Déjà Glitch*

BY KATE ROBB

This Spells Love
Prime Time Romance

Prime Time Romance

Prime Time Romance

A Novel

Kate Robb

The Dial Press
New York

A Dial Press Trade Paperback Original

Published in the United States by The Dial Press,
an imprint of Random House, a division of
Penguin Random House LLC, New York.

THE DIAL PRESS is a registered trademark and the
colophon is a trademark of Penguin Random House LLC.

DIAL DELIGHTS and colophon are trademarks
of Penguin Random House LLC.

Library of Congress Cataloging-in-Publication Data
Names: Robb, Kate, author.
Title: Prime time romance: a novel / Kate Robb.
Description: New York: The Dial Press, 2024.
Identifiers: LCCN 2023058183 (print) | LCCN 2023058184 (ebook) |
ISBN 9780593596555 (trade paperback; acid-free paper) |
ISBN 9780593596562 (e-book)
Subjects: LCGFT: Romance fiction. | Novels.
Classification: LCC PR9199.4.R5735 P75 2024 (print) |
LCC PR9199.4.R5735 (ebook) | DDC 813/.6—dc23/eng/20240117
LC record available at https://lccn.loc.gov/2023058183
LC ebook record available at https://lccn.loc.gov/2023058184

Printed in the United States of America on acid-free paper

randomhousebooks.com

9 8 7 6 5 4 3 2 1

To Joshua Jackson
and whoever knit him that damn sweater.

Prime Time Romance

1

BRYNN

My date has cilantro stuck to his tooth.

A bright-green leaf is clinging precariously to his left central incisor, and I have been trying, rather unsuccessfully, to give him a discreet *you've got a little something,* but so far, all I've managed to do is draw several weird looks from our waitress.

His name is Ford LeClair. He's a hedge fund manager at a rather large Canadian bank here in Toronto. I swiped right because he said he loved labradoodles, a good cup of coffee, and summer nights on the dock of his parents' cottage on Lake Rosseau.

His profile had promise.

The man, however, has spent the last forty-three minutes having a one-sided conversation about cryptocurrency, his predictions for next week's UFC fight, and his recent boys' trip to Las Vegas.

"Have you been? It's fucking epic!"

It takes me a minute to realize he's finally asked me a question.

"Yes." My cheeks flood with heat. "I've been there once before." I don't elaborate.

Thankfully, Ford does not ask any follow-up questions. Even if he did, I'm not sure how I'd manage to navigate around my reason for traveling to the wedding capital of the world.

Something happens to my dates when I toss into a casual conversation that I'm a twenty-nine-year-old divorcée. It's like they assign a "level failed" to my dating scorecard. Seeing as I don't anticipate us even moving this relationship to the dessert course, I don't see a reason to bring it up.

"So . . ." I change the subject, taking the pause in Ford's side of the conversation to sneak in a few of my own questions. "Your profile said you'd love to settle in a small town one day. Is there any town in particular?"

This is my remaining olive branch. One last attempt to connect the man and the profile. However, if I'm to be perfectly honest, the majority of my hope that anything would come of this ill-fated match dissolved the moment the hostess walked me to our table, where Ford ignored my outstretched palm in favor of an obvious once-over and then proceeded to tell me, "You look different from your pictures."

In hindsight, I should have turned right around and pretended it was all some big mix-up, or told him the hostess had accidentally brought me over to the wrong table. But I had made such an effort: new lipstick, my Victoria's Secret push-up bra, and my sale-rack Nordstrom stilettos that make my legs look longer but also cut the backs of my heels because they're a half size too small. So I ignored the alarm bells screaming, *Run, Brynn. Save yourself,* pasted on my best *I am totally into you* smile, and hoped my instincts were wrong.

Fifty-six minutes later, I strongly suspect that they were not wrong.

Ford leans forward, wafting a wave of expensive-smelling cologne in my direction.

"I'm going to be straight up with you. I put that small-town shit in my profile because I know women want to hear it."

His honesty is actually refreshing.

"Oh, okay. I guess I didn't . . ."

"Breanne—" he interrupts.

"It's Brynn."

He ignores me and instead takes a long draw of his locally crafted IPA.

"We both know what is happening here."

I have an inkling, but I want to see where he takes it.

He flicks a glance at his Rolex-esque watch, then inclines his head toward the entrance to the restaurant.

"If you wanna do this, we should probably get going."

I'm not naïve.

It's quite clear that "this" means sex. Sadly, Ford is not the first overconfident Bumble date this year to cut to the chase, although he lacks the *je ne sais quoi* that typically accompanies this delicate dance. And even though I've never been one to ask for what I want in the bedroom, I have no problem telling Ford I have no intention of stepping into his tonight.

"You know what? I'm really tired, I think I'm going to head home." I fake a yawn.

Ford raises his eyebrows as if this fact surprises him. "Not even up for a blowie?"

I should probably be disgusted or, at a bare minimum, annoyed. But my poor little heart has been battered enough that it has formed a protective coating. A thick crust that protects it and keeps my tone even and breezy as I tell him, "Thanks, but I think I'll pass."

Ford stares into his empty beer glass. "I figured I'd shoot my shot. It was pretty obvious this wasn't going anywhere. But a lot of the women I meet on Bumble want a decent bang out of the deal. And I'm more than decent." He winks as if this little tidbit may sway me. When I don't respond, he shrugs and turns his attention to the waitress, who hands him our bill, giving him much more of her attention than I have all evening.

As much as I hate to admit it, Ford is right. Before we even sat down, I suspected that we were a far cry from soulmates. Although he is my type, tall and classically handsome with the deep ocean shade of blue eyes that you could get lost in, he falls short in the most important attributes I look for in a partner: sensitivity, kindness, and actual interest in what I have to say.

I'm not upset we're calling this date early. I'd much rather be home, engulfed in my fuzzy blue Snuggly, comfort-binging the final season of *Carson's Cove* and watching the drama go down instead of . . . well . . . going down on Ford. Therefore, with feigned reluctance, I thrust my Visa onto the table with a "Thanks for this. I had a really nice time."

Ford, however, waves me and my card off, his eyes never leaving the ample crack of the cleavage of our very blond waitress. I watch as he pulls a pen from his suit pocket, writes something down on the back of one of his business cards, then slips both it and his Amex out of his wallet into the black leather folder holding our bill.

The waitress opens it, giggles at whatever he has written, then leans in close to whisper something in his ear.

It's like I'm watching the beginning of a low-budget porno, and I don't know if I should be offended or amused.

The waitress leaves. Exactly three Mississippis later, Ford stands, extending his fist with a noncommittal "So, I guess I'll see you around, then?"

I bump him back, knowing full well that this will be the last I see of Ford LeClair.

I intentionally linger for a few moments in our booth, not wanting to completely contradict my previous thought and create an awkward scenario outside where Ford and I have to make polite conversation as we wait for our respective Ubers. When I'm satisfied that he's well on his way, I swipe open my phone screen and find the red notification bubble on my text app showing eight unread messages.

All of them are from my mother.

MOM: *Thirty years ago, I was in labor, about to have the happiest day of my life*

MOM: *We didn't have the good drugs like you kids have today*

MOM: *You were warm and cozy in your mama's womb. Didn't want to come out. Needed to do things in your own time.*

MOM: *Even back then, you were your own woman*

MOM: *When you finally came, I stared at your pink face for hours. I never loved something so much in my whole entire life.*

MOM: *Happy last day of being 29. Hope 30 is wonderful.*

MOM: *I love you xoxoxoxoxox*

MOM: *You should go out and celebrate! Call up those new girlfriends you told me about and go dancing. You may meet someone. You can't start the next episode of your life if you keep rewatching the old one.*

The last message hits like a sneaky left hook. I've yet to tell my mother that I've gotten back on the proverbial dating horse. Partially because I don't want to answer a hundred personal questions about my dates, but mostly because—with Ford as a case in point—it's not going like I hoped it would.

It's weird to be dating again. Like reading a book where you've already snuck a peek at the last chapter and you know the ending isn't the happily ever after you were always promised. But I will acknowledge that my mother is right in that it's next to impossible to meet a perfect man while bundled up like a burrito in front of my television screen, so unless Uber Eats starts delivering dream dates, I'm once again swimming in this very shallow dating pool.

My thumb skims across the screen, typing back a polite *Love you, Mom.* As I hit send, a new text pops up on my screen from the "Brunch Bitches" group chat.

The "Brunch Bitches" are a group of Toronto girls who, as the name hints, have a regular standing brunch date every Saturday or Sunday at various "it spots" deemed brunch-worthy by *Toronto Life* magazine. I was added to their group chat about six months ago when I met their ringleader, Lainey Evens, at an advertising agency industry mixer at Tequila Bob's. She spilled a margarita down my back and insisted on getting my number to cover the dry-cleaning cost. She never did pay me, but she did christen me a "Brunch Bitch" and started texting me on the regular.

When my ex Matt and I split, I scored our big-screen TV, but he took most of our mutual friends. When I was still in deep grief, I texted someone who I thought was one of my best friends, asking her to meet me for coffee. She ghosted me for three days until I checked in again, sure that there must be something wrong with her phone. But then she replied: *Matt and Billy are so close. I don't want to jeopardize that. I'll call you when things calm down a bit. You understand, right?*

I wrote back that I did.

It's been almost two years, and I still haven't heard from her.

So although I don't have much in common with Lainey, Ashley K, and Ashley T, I join them for their weekly booze-and-bitch sessions and any other random nights they invite me to.

LAINEY: *Ladies, what are you up to tonight?*
LAINEY: *Totally meant to do this earlier, but you know how it is—crazy week! You guys have to come over tonight. We have something special to celebrate!!! (6 party hat emojis)*

I read Lainey's message twice, trying to dissect any other possible meanings.

Two Sundays ago at our weekly meetup, I casually mentioned that my thirtieth birthday was coming up, but we were on our third pitcher of bottomless mimosas, and it was unclear if anyone was paying attention or if they were just bobbing their heads to the Tiesto track blaring through the speaker system.

When I dropped a hopeful "Maybe we can all hang out and celebrate," I wasn't sure if anything would pan out. But maybe I was wrong.

ASHLEY K: *Always down for a party but may have to meet up a little later. Got a thing.*
ASHLEY T: *Catch up bitches! I've been drinking since 3. Summer Fridays!!!!*
ME: *I'm in. Just need to go home and change my shoes. Be there in an hour.*
LAINEY: *Boo Brynn! Just come now. Your feet will be fine. We need you!!!*

I stand, wiggling my toes to see if my feet can take another few hours of pain in my stilettos.

ME: *Okay fine. On my way. We're just hanging out, right?*

Lainey's answer is three party hats and an eggplant emoji.

Exactly three seconds after stepping into Lainey's apartment, I notice that there are dicks everywhere.

They're taped to the walls, morphed into plastic straws in glasses, and even strung into necklaces adorning every woman crammed into Lainey's compact kitchen as she pours cheap prosecco into red Solo cups.

It's not my first choice for party decor, especially since it's been a minute since I've seen an actual dick in the flesh, but it's also not completely off-brand for a Lainey-led celebration.

I glance over at the island again, only now realizing that I actually don't recognize any of the women crowded around it. Wondering if maybe I missed a text on the Uber ride over, I slide my phone out of my purse to check the group chat.

ASHLEY K: *My thing turned into a different thing. Can't make it. Sorry!!!*
ASHLEY T: *I'm drunk. Going to Poutini's. Gonna eat my weight in cheese curds!*
LAINEY: *Boo! You guys suck. Brynn, you're still coming, right?*

I don't answer the last text since Lainey is standing three feet in front of me. She holds out a red Solo cup, beckoning me with the incline of her head. "Come, babe. Meet my marketing bitches."

They widen their circle to let me in, and it feels like a rite of passage. It's almost as if the universe is conspiring with my mother. *See, Brynn? You should be out making new friends. Look how much fun it is.*

"Girls." Lainey's voice takes on a falsetto tone. "This is Brynn. She's the one I was telling you about."

Four girls turn their eyes to me and smile.

To be very honest, in the last few weeks, I've started to wonder if Lainey and I even work as friends. Don't get me wrong, she's fun and outgoing—the kind of friend I feel like I should have. But our conversations don't expand too far beyond weekend plans, food, or her latest dating disaster story. I even thought at one point that she might have mixed me up in her phone with a different Brynn and just kept forgetting to correct her mistake. But as her arm links through mine, a part of me wonders if maybe all this angst about our friendship is just my anxious brain overanalyzing things.

"Brynn, you have to meet Zoe." Lainey points at a woman with long dark hair. "She just got engaged over the weekend. Our beautiful blushing bride."

Lainey leaves me to put her arm around Zoe, but it's me that's left a deep shade of pink as I'm suddenly hit with the realization that we're most definitely not celebrating my birthday. Not even close.

"I am so jealous," says Lainey, letting go of Zoe to give her a light shove. "You are going to look so hot as a bride. I freaking love a good wedding. Aren't they the best?" Lainey turns, her question very much aimed at me.

"The best," I echo, proud that it doesn't sound too forced.

The entire first year after Matt and I split, I dodged every conversation about weddings, marriage, or babies. My wound was still too raw. And though I genuinely wanted to find joy for my co-workers who were stressing out about seating arrangements and what toaster to add to their wedding registries, I was struggling to divide up my assets and fighting Matt for a Vitamix that we got from his aunt Mary, but he never once used. It all felt too hard.

But when Zoe dives into a story about her fiancé and then

turns to me and says, "He is like my perfect soulmate," I smile, and it's genuine. The only semi-negative thought in my head is a note of what different places we are in mentally. I'm happy that she's all optimism and glowy happiness as she thrusts out her hand, wiggling her fingers to show off her beautiful princess-cut diamond ring. I think I'm just sad that I'm a little jaded because I've seen how quickly marital bliss can become marital monotony, and then, one day, "I don't think we work anymore."

I smile awkwardly through twenty minutes of kitchen hangout while the group talks about work people I've never met until everyone but Lainey and Zoe heads to the bathroom to double-check their makeup before it's time to head out.

"I'm so happy you could come, Brynn." Zoe bops completely off time with the Rihanna track blasting from the stereo in Lainey's living room. "This party is so last minute. I was worried we would have to wait forever in line somewhere, so when Lainey said she had a hookup at Devil's, I was like, *Yes! Get her over here!* I absolutely love that place."

I pause mid-sip as my brain turns over her words a second time.

Lainey tosses an arm around my shoulder, pulling our heads together. "It shouldn't be a problem, right, babe? You said your brother used to be, like, the manager."

All of a sudden, I understand my role tonight.

They want to go to *The Devil's Playground*.

It's the bar where my younger brother used to work. He moved in with me after Matt and I separated because I needed a second income to pay my mortgage. When my brother moved out to Vancouver six months ago, he offered his room to a new bartender named Josh, who has been my roommate ever since. I casually mentioned this story last week at brunch. Lainey seemed disproportionately interested in this tidbit of information, and now I understand why.

"Yeah, it shouldn't be a problem," I tell Zoe, acting as if this was the plan all along.

I fully acknowledge that Lainey is using me for my hookup. But I tell myself that awareness of this fact makes me slightly less pathetic. At least she calls, right?

There's no need to text Josh to get us into the bar. I pull out my phone and text the bouncer directly. His name is Little Chuck. I let him feel me up at my brother's birthday party two years ago when I was a newly minted divorcée. It was a dark time, but it earned me a "Call me anytime you need a favor."

Little Chuck texts back almost immediately. It's a simple *No worries. Just come up to the front when you get here. These girls are hot, right?*

I don't respond and instead hold up my phone to the semicircle of eager twentysomethings who have now emerged from the bathroom.

"I got us on the guest list."

The girls raise their glasses for a round of wooing and toasting.

My shoes feel like they're made of razor blades, and I can practically hear the *Carson's Cove* theme song calling to me from my couch. I turn to Lainey, who is now double-fisting drinks, sipping from two separate penis straws, and tell her, "Actually, I think I might skip the bar and head home."

She shakes her head. "You're fine." She presses a cup of prosecco to my lips. "This will help. And you have to come. What happens if they don't let us in?"

I open my mouth to tell her, *You can just text me if there's a problem,* but I'm cut off by someone shouting, "Uber's here," and then I'm swept up into a flurry of activity as Lainey's crew locate their purses and make last-minute bathroom stops.

We leave the apartment in a single herd of stilettos and tube dresses, take the elevator down, and head out to the awaiting Honda Odyssey.

The prosecco does nothing but make me slightly queasy as our Uber flirts dangerously with a string of yellow stoplights all the way down Richmond Street until the driver pulls up to a darkened back alley beside a nondescript redbrick building right in the middle of Toronto's entertainment district.

I wait on the sidewalk, shifting my weight from heel to heel, trying my best to ignore my feet as the rest of Lainey's crew pour out of the van.

"I swear to god, I can never find this place during the week," Lainey says as we all link arms and walk the dark stretch between the sidewalk and the club's front door. "It's like it magically appears on the weekends."

Although she has downed a half bottle of prosecco, she does make a point.

There's nothing that marks the entrance to the Devil's Playground as a Friday-night hot spot other than the long line of twentysomethings vaping outside, decked out in crop tops and vegan leather.

We skip to the front, where Little Chuck gives me a nod and a "S'up" as we approach the door. He's easily six feet tall and built like a linebacker.

I hold up my phone and say, "Thanks for this," referring to our text exchange. But he's too preoccupied with Lainey's proudly displayed cleavage to notice.

Chuck waves us inside through the VIP line, which skips the twenty-dollar cover charge. I follow the girls through a long, dark, narrow hall out into the main bar area and am reminded why I never willingly come to this place. A Top 40 track booms through a speaker system so loud that I can feel the thumping in my chest. The lighting is dimmed in an effort to make everyone seem sexier. There is only one bar. It's made of white Plexiglas and is backlit, which gives it this new-age space-station feel. It runs the length of the entire wall, giving the six bartenders behind it ample room to work.

I watch them for a moment.

Their all-black uniforms stand out against the white bar top. Seeing them all working side by side, it's hard not to notice that they're all unfairly attractive. I'm starting to imagine how an interview to work here might go when one of the bartenders looks up and our eyes catch.

It's my roommate, Josh. The low light has turned his usually brown hair almost black, and his uniform T-shirt highlights his broad chest and toned arms. His stubble is a little longer than usual, as if he's left it an extra day. The effect has turned his normally boyish face into something else entirely.

I almost forgot how attractive he is.

Our paths usually cross in the early mornings, when he's still sleep-crusted and wearing his ratty old sweats, or late at night, when he gets home from the bar and wakes me up because I've accidentally fallen asleep in front of the television . . . again. I don't usually get the chance to appreciate the smoothness of his movements as he picks up a bottle and pours without even looking or notice the air he gives off: casually confident and good with his hands.

"Who is *that?*" Lainey's boobs press into my shoulder. Her eyes are also fixed on Josh, who has turned his attention to a pair of blondes at the bar.

I can practically hear Lainey's brain cranking out a plan for seduction, which absolutely cannot happen. I have, on occasion, run into the odd mussed-haired party girl exiting Josh's bedroom, heels in hand, in the wee hours of the morning. Lainey in my living room tomorrow is not something I need to see.

"He has chlamydia," I tell her, saying the first thing that comes to mind.

Lainey crinkles her nose but continues to watch him. "But that's one of the curable ones, right?"

"No," I lie.

She sighs. "Too bad. He's cute. Come on. Let's go dance."

She takes off without waiting for me. I linger a moment longer until Josh looks up again. He lifts his hands as if to silently ask, *What are you doing here?*

I nod at Lainey's friends, who have already formed a circle, chucking their jackets and purses into a nearby booth. They dance along to a Lady Gaga mash-up, double-fisting vodka sodas that have somehow magically appeared.

Josh shakes his head at them and then mouths a *have fun* to me. I respond with a double thumbs-up, which I immediately regret, knowing it did not come off as carefree or cute as I intended.

I really don't want to be here. And yet I add my purse to the pile and wedge myself into the circle between the bride's twin cousins, who are wearing matching tube dresses.

Lainey hands me a lemon drop. "Drink up, ladies!"

I take the shot glass from her hands. One of the twins turns and hands me hers as well.

"I can't drink this," she explains. "I'm doing paleo and it will totally mess with my diet."

I down her shot, followed by my own. The vodka is cheap and burns my throat, but it also makes the music and the lighting all blur together into this hazy rhythm. Two more vodka sodas later, I find myself thinking, *This isn't so bad.*

Then the DJ takes us back to the old school with that bump-and-grind *Magic Mike* song.

The girls woo wildly. Grinding on one another, they throw their arms up and their heads back. It acts like a signal. Drunk females over here. Things are about to get wild.

An outer circle of dudes is now surrounding us, circling like sharks.

I brace for the first attack.

My bet is on Lainey, with her smoky eyeliner and hypnotic hip sways, or maybe the bride-to-be, whose eyes are half-closed as she sways off-time to the music.

What I don't see coming is the hand that snakes around my waist and the undeniable feeling of a dancing dick at my back.

Nope. Absolutely not.

I drop my drink—only partially by accident. It lands on his black Zara loafers.

He swears.

I dive straight into the booth, combing through the pile of coats, looking for my little black clutch.

There are three almost identical to it. But after some frantic sleuthing, I determine the pleather cross-body belongs to Lainey, the big-buckled envelope-style is Zoe's, and the nondescript leather clutch is owned by the non-paleo twin. Mine, however, is nowhere to be found.

This is a life lesson. One I should have already known. You don't put your purse in the coat pile without repercussions.

With the bass now booming so wildly, I can feel the reverbera-tions all the way down to my toes. The last thread—the one that I've been dangling precariously from all evening—finally snaps.

I want to be in my sweatpants, watching *Carson's Cove,* where everything turns out right. Not here, with my heels in the same shape as my emotional state: rubbed raw and in pain.

I want to go home.

But to get home, I need money.

And with my phone in my purse and my purse god knows where, the only way to get money is to borrow from Lainey, which at best means enduring a lecture about what a wet blanket I am.

Unless . . .

My eyes dart to the bar, where my other option is wiping down the counter and talking to a woman with excellent boobs.

Josh and I aren't really friends.

We occasionally text each other the odd *we're out of paper towels* or *the water bill is high this month,* but it's not the kind of relationship where it's normal to borrow money.

I hesitate, and as I do, a collective cheer goes up from the dance floor and the old-school mash-up morphs into a Katy Perry song interspersed with the sound of shooting laser beams.

My resolve crumbles and gives way to my survival instincts.

I head for the bar.

2

JOSH

"What is this shit? I ordered a mojito. There should be mint and lime. You got that, boss?"

A dude in a baby-blue dress shirt flips his sunglasses onto his head, takes a long sip of the aforementioned mojito, and in turn pushes the half-drunk glass across the bar.

The bartender serving him is maybe twenty years old and has been working here at Devil's for less than a week. Nice enough guy, but definitely still learning the ropes. He takes the glass, dumps it into the sink, and starts to look in the fridge for the mint that we don't typically use, seeing as we are primarily a vodka soda type of establishment.

Sunglasses, annoyed that his drink is taking a moment, throws up his hands, muttering "Fucking idiot" loud enough to be heard above the thumping techno base. He catches my eye and holds out his hands as if saying, *Am I right? Or am I right?*

I grab a highball glass from the back of one of the high shelves. "Why don't I take this one?" I say to the new guy, who nods with a "Thanks, man" before turning to serve what is hopefully a far more amicable customer.

I place the glass on the bar, grab a few sprigs of mint from the back of the fridge, stir in the pre-prepped mint simple syrup he got served the first time, and stir. "You're right. This place seems to be full of idiots tonight." I scoop three cubes of ice into the glass. "They're letting anyone through the doors these days: real assholes, guys that never learned the life lesson that it's in your best interest to be kind to the person pouring your drink. Never know what can happen when you're not looking."

I smile, pulling out what is now his fully made drink from behind the bar and placing it in front of him. He glances down at it, suddenly uneasy.

"Enjoy." I push the glass toward him. "That will be eighteen-fifty."

He stares at me with a half-open mouth.

I take the credit card out of his hand and run it through the cash register before he can find a new reason to complain. I hand him the bill but not the pen, knowing full well I'm not getting tipped on this one.

The brunette beside him, who's been watching the entire exchange, smiles at me as he shoves the crumpled bill into his pocket, picks up the still-untouched drink, and storms off, letting a few choice F-bombs go in his wake.

She leans in, her long, dark hair spilling over her shoulder. "Bet he won't make that mistake again."

"Sadly, he probably will." I wipe the spot in front of her with my rag. "What can I get you?"

She places her credit card on the bar top. "One vodka shot." She pauses. "Actually, better make it three. I'm in the mood to make a few mistakes tonight."

I pull out three glasses and pour her order. She pulls two shots toward her and then pushes the third toward me. I smile and lift it to my lips. But as she tips her head back, I toss the cheap vodka over my shoulder, with her none the wiser.

She slams her empty glass onto the bar and picks up the last untouched shot.

"Maybe I'll see you around later?"

She's a beautiful woman. I have been at this job long enough to understand exactly what she's got in mind for later and learned long ago that my best response is a kind but firm "Enjoy your evening."

I basically grew up in a bar and have been pouring drinks since the tender and legal age of nineteen, which means I have been one of those favorite mistakes more times than I care to count.

It usually plays out the same way.

A woman comes in, she smiles and flirts. Sometimes she even buys me a shot. Then we go home together. Maybe we even go on a date or two. But when my work schedule has me unavailable most evenings and weekends, she suddenly wants a boyfriend who can take her to brunch or head up north on a Friday night for a cottage weekend with her friends. It fizzles out as fast as it started. Even without this job, I've never been a flowers-and-candlelight kind of guy. And although I tell women this up front, and they claim that's not what they want, they eventually show back up here on the arm of a new investment banker boyfriend who has a standing Friday-night reservation at some trendy place downtown. I'm nothing more than a memory of a night that got too wild.

The crowd in front of the bar shifts and a new body squeezes through. It's another beautiful face, but one that I'm used to see-ing fast asleep on the couch when I get home late or exhausted and hungry as she comes home from a long day at her agency job, passing me on the stairs as I head out to work.

"What's up, Brynn? How's your night going? I didn't expect to see you here."

I don't know Brynn all that well, but she does not strike me as a Devil's kind of woman. She's more the early-to-bed, early-to-rise, comfortable-sneakers type, though I will say she has no trouble pulling off the tight skirt and heels she's wearing tonight.

"Yeah, I'm very much regretting my life choices right now, which means I need to ask you a teeny tiny favor. I know we don't normally, um . . ." Her voice trails off as she breaks eye contact. "Any chance I could borrow five bucks?"

It's not the question I expected, but I turn to the tip jar next to the cash register, pull out a fiver, and hand it to her. "Yeah. No problem. Everything okay?"

She gestures to the group of women she came in with. "I just can't do that anymore, and my purse and phone are missing. If someone tries to open a tab on a Brynn Smothers Visa card, I don't know . . . maybe confiscate it or something?"

She looks tired. Not just the kind of tired that comes with a late night out. The kind of tired that settles into your soul, leaving your eyes just a little dimmer and knocking the bounce out of your walk.

"No worries," I say, then point at the five in her hands. "But how are you going to get home with that?"

We live in Leslieville. It's east of the parkway, a thirty-dollar ride home. Thirty-five with a tip.

She shoves the money into her skirt pocket. "I'm just going to take the streetcar. Although, now that I say it—how much is it for your cheapest tequila shot? I also need to borrow whatever that is. I was kidding myself when I bought these shoes."

Instead of reaching for more money, I grab a glass and pour a generous shot of the Casamigos Reposado we reserve for staff and the odd connoisseur who knows enough to ask. I slide it toward her. "For your feet. On the house."

She throws the tequila back and winces, then tips the empty glass toward me in a cheers. "You saved my feet, Joshua Bishop, and I'll pay you back. I promise."

With that declaration, she turns to head toward the door, but as she does, an uneasy feeling settles in my gut.

"Hey, Brynn," I call after her. "Can you wait, like, five minutes?"

She turns back around slowly, her eyebrows knit in confusion.

"I'll come home with you," I explain. "The streetcar is sketchy this time of night and I don't think they really need me for much longer."

She waves me off, hobbling a few more steps toward the door. "It's fine. It smells a little like Doritos, that's all. I'm not worried."

I nod at my manager, who's standing at the end of the bar, surveying the club. "Let me talk to my boss quickly. Two minutes tops."

She looks annoyed but nods. "Fine, but if they play the Beibs, I will self-destruct."

I can't help but smile. Although I love being a bartender, this place isn't exactly my hangout of choice either. I prefer some place more laid-back where the vibe is chilled out and unpretentious, where you might get up to dance if a great song comes on, but it's more about the company. And also the beer.

I glance at the single draft tap and the big-name Belgian brand.

It's a very real reminder that the whole point of working at Devil's is that it *isn't* my own place. No stakes. No expectations.

No reminders of all the things I've fucked up and lost. All that's expected of me is to pour drinks and run tabs, and as long as I show up for my shift on time, I'm pretty much a star employee.

Until now.

I approach my boss, rubbing the back of my neck in a lame attempt to look pained. "Hey, man. Not feeling so hot. Mind if I head home early?"

He checks his watch before eyeing the bar. "I guess the new kid is doing okay on his own. No tips if you leave mid-shift though. Company policy."

My tip-out is probably close to $400 tonight. Maybe even more. It sucks to lose out on the money. But the city's been doing road work on our street for the last two weeks. They've shut off power to the streetlights. It's a dark walk. On top of that, one of our female bartenders was mugged walking home the other night. The idea of Brynn alone on the streetcar, then walking, doesn't sit well with me.

"I'll come in early tomorrow and make it up to you."

He slaps me affectionately on the back as I head to the staff room to grab my phone from my locker. I don't plan on checking my messages, but there's a notification from my mom that has me quickly swiping open my voicemail and pressing my phone to my ear.

She doesn't usually call this late.

"Hi, sweet pea." She sounds normal. Soft voice. Tender and even. "So sorry to call so late, but I wanted to let you know that they set a date for the auction."

My heart double-beats at the word *auction*.

"I know you said before that you're not interested in trying again," her message continues, "but the bank is listing the place at a great price. Everyone would be delighted to see you come home. Now that things are settled with the estate, you should think about it. You have lots of time. The auction isn't until June twenty-first at seven. At least come up and check it out. You could stay the night, and we could have breakfast at Nana's in the morning. Call me if you want to talk about it. Okay?"

The voicemail ends with a soft click, but my heart stays lodged up in my throat.

My dad's old bar is up for sale again. Clearly, the new owners couldn't make it work any better than I could. I shove my phone deep into my pocket as if the action will also banish all the unwanted thoughts now swimming around in my head. For a brief second, I consider going up there. I haven't been back to Orillia since we sold the place. That bar has some of my best memories and a whole slew of my worst. But any plans I may have been making in my head stop when the door to the staff room swings open, bringing with it one of the barbacks and a chorus of female voices singing, "Baby, baby, baby, ohhh!"

Shit.

Brynn.

By the time I get back out to the main bar, she's barreling toward the coat check. I catch up just as she reaches the front door. Little Chuck gives me an approving fist bump as we exit onto the steps. I should probably explain that although I'm taking her home, I'm not actually *taking her home*. Instead, I watch the spectacle that is Brynn, gripping the railing with both hands, visibly wincing as she slowly makes her way down the steps.

"Why did you buy those shoes if they hurt your feet so much?"

She straightens at the question, as if trying to prove that she's not in that much pain. "I ordered them online. They were on sale. And I thought they looked cute, and then I was too lazy to take them back, and then my thirty-day return period was up, so I convinced myself that I could make them work." She stares down at her feet. "But I'm learning that mind over matter can only take you so far." She glances at the long length of the alley out to the street. "Don't worry about me. I'll be fine."

The way she winces as she shifts her weight says otherwise.

Without thinking, I snake my hand around her waist and scoop her into my arms. She stares up at me with wide eyes, blinking.

"Um, what are you doing?"

"I could not even tell you the last time I've been home before midnight," I explain. "I have my heart set on a solid eight hours of sleep, and at the pace you were walking, we wouldn't be home until dawn."

She relaxes a little, letting her cheek press against my shoulder.

"My inner feminist really wants to object to being carried like a paperback heroine right now, but after the day I've just had . . ." Her voice trails off.

"Rough one?"

She looks away, avoiding my eyes. "More like a rough year."

"Anything I can do?"

She shakes her head. "Not unless you have a magic wand. Or an excellent therapist?"

I laugh. "I could probably use both of those things myself."

She wraps her arms around my neck as I make my way out of the alley and down the three blocks to Queen Street. Her head bumps against my chest with every step. She doesn't say anything else until I come to a stop to wait for a traffic light.

"Is this something you do often or am I your first?"

I stare down at her, confused.

"Carrying women home in your arms?" she clarifies.

I hoist her up a little higher, adjusting my grip. "I can say with confidence that this is the first time and most likely the last."

She tips her head to the side. "So, Josh Bishop is not a romantic?"

"He is not. In fact . . ."

I set her down on her feet, then promptly take her hands and haul her up and over my shoulder, transforming her from—What did she call it? A paperback heroine?—to a sack of potatoes.

"This is more my style."

"What the—" she screams.

My arms tighten around her legs. Her body stills as she realizes she's not about to fly face-first into the pavement.

"You okay up there?"

Her arms dangle for a moment. "More of a warning would have been nice, but otherwise I'm good." She taps my back. "Giddy up, buttercup."

I carry her a few more blocks to the streetcar stop. When I finally set her down, she lingers momentarily with her hands on my chest, then leans in and sniffs the spot where my neck meets my collarbone.

"Why do you smell like a forest?" She tilts her head back and looks up at me. "It's like a mix of mint and pinecones and something else. I've been trying to figure it out for the last block and a half and it's driving me crazy."

I'm not entirely sure how I'm supposed to answer this question. "I'd like to claim that it's my natural man smell, but I think you might be referring to my deodorant. It's called Cedar Wood Lumberjack."

Her jaw drops. "Actually?"

"Swear to god. I saw it and bought it based on the name alone. Clearly, it did not disappoint."

She opens her mouth as if she's about to say something else but is interrupted by the arrival of the red-and-white streetcar, which opens its doors, flooding us with a wave of warm, body-scented air.

She holds up her hands as if she's proving a point. "I can say one thing. It's a definite upgrade from Doritos."

3

BRYNN

'm in a significantly better headspace as soon as I'm showered and dressed in my comfy cozies, with a bag of popcorn in the microwave and cold Pinot Grigio in my tumbler. When the popcorn is poured, I grab my fuzzy blue Snuggly from the end of my bed and head to my couch and the obscenely large big-screen TV purchased by my ex right before our relationship imploded.

My Netflix account has *Carson's Cove* ready and waiting in my favorites as if it too expected that I'd need a little comfort-binging tonight. But before I can pick up the remote and press play, the door to Josh's bedroom swings open and he wanders out wearing nothing but a pair of light-gray low-slung sweatpants.

This is not the first time he's wandered around my townhouse half-naked.

It started happening shortly after he moved in.

He emerged late one morning from his room in nothing but his gym shorts. To be fair, I was home sick from work. He likely didn't expect me to be there. But even when he spotted me lying on the couch, he didn't seem to care. I rationalized that I was just being a grouch. He was a new face moving into my personal space, and there was bound to be an adjustment period. Then one night, after a long cry caused by a SiriusXM bill that showed up at my house with Matt's name on it, I walked into the kitchen to find Josh making eggs in his boxers and this threadbare Anaheim T-shirt that he loves. It clings to all the right places and you can easily make out his nipples. It's almost as bad as being top-naked. He was talking to someone on the phone. His mom, I think. I could only make out bits of the conversation as he made his eggs, his forearms flexing as he flicked his wrist and flipped them from sunny-side up to over easy. I don't know if it was the arms, or maybe some culinary competency kink I never knew I had, but I felt the stirrings of attraction. I immediately knew it was a bad idea. He was my roommate. I had just reached the milestone of saying I was over Matt and actually being over Matt. The last thing I needed was Temptation Island in my kitchen making breakfast for dinner. I almost terminated our roommate agreement right there.

But I let him stay.

In this economy, beggars with variable-term mortgages cannot be choosers.

But in that moment, I made a choice to draw a firm boundary for our relationship, with Josh Bishop and his annoyingly sexy body on one side and me on the other. Up until now, it's been a hard line. That is, until my brief lapse in judgment when I borrowed money earlier tonight.

"So." He drops onto the couch beside me and heaves a single leg onto the coffee table. "What are we watching?"

I stare at him for a moment, just to make sure what I think is happening is happening.

"Well, *I* was about to watch *Carson's Cove.*"

He adds his second leg, stretching both of them out as he leans back into the cushions.

"And I guess you are watching it with me?" I ask.

He glances over, not looking the least bit fussed. "Is that all right?"

Is it?

"It's fine." My eyes dip for a moment to the golden bronzeness of his chest. "But you are going to need to put a shirt on first."

"What?"

"You've already witnessed enough of my humiliation this evening. Please don't ask me any more questions."

He eyes me as if debating if my request is legitimate. After a moment, he gets up, walks into his bedroom, and returns a moment later, pulling the threadbare Anaheim shirt over his head.

"No." I point at his door. "Different shirt."

He pauses with it half-on. Again, he waits to see if there's some punch line coming. When there isn't one, he repeats the earlier process and this time comes out wearing a newer-looking black crewneck.

Better.

"Anything else?" He sinks back down beside me, an amused dimple suddenly making an appearance on his left cheek.

"Yes. You need to promise not to talk."

His eyebrows rise a fraction of an inch. "But what if I have questions?"

"Then you need to ask them now." I click play and the opening credits begin to roll. "You have exactly thirty-six seconds."

"You've watched the entire series twice since I moved in, it's not like you don't know what's going to happen."

"That wasn't a question. It was an observation."

He reaches out and grabs a handful of my popcorn. "I wasn't finished. So, what's the deal with it?"

Unbeknownst to Josh, the question he's just asked is more intimate than anything Ford or Lainey or anyone else has asked me in a long time.

"This is going to take a lot longer than thirty-six seconds." I hit pause, mentally preparing the lecture he just unknowingly asked for. "*Carson's Cove* is basically the perfect television show. It's got everything: teenage angst and a small New England town where everyone and their mother is beautiful—and I mean that very literally. Then there's the banter—I live for the banter." I pick up a pillow and clutch it to my chest. "There's lots of drama but no out-of-the-blue twists. No red weddings. The home team always wins the big game, or the unassuming bookworm undergoes a makeover and becomes a beautiful prom queen. Even the super sad or tragic episodes work themselves out. The worst fight can always be fixed with a grand romantic gesture."

Josh raises an amused eyebrow. "I did not figure you for a cheesy romantic."

I shrug. "I'm not. In real life, I find public declarations of love absolutely mortifying, but in *Carson's Cove,* they work."

"Well, then," Josh says, grabbing another handful of popcorn, "I'm glad I'm finally checking it out." He settles farther into the couch cushions, making it clear he's invested, as I hit play again and the opening credits roll, panning over the quaint New England seaside town with its picturesque main street, then the famous white gazebo with its ocean views.

What I didn't fully explain to Josh was how the show became an anchor during my tumultuous teenage years. I'd have a fight with a friend, then come home and watch Sloan and Poppy—

best friends who always had each other's backs—and my faith in friendship would be restored. Or I'd find out my crush was into someone else, then spend hours watching *Spencer Woods*, who may date other people but always unwaveringly pines for the girl next door. *Carson's Cove* is comfort food in television form.

So when I came home one day at the age of twenty-six and found a note filled with every cliché I never wanted to hear— "We've grown apart . . . We got married before we knew who we really were as people . . . I love you, I'm just not in love with you anymore"—I started binging episodes again as if they were drugs. As my whole world shifted and my role changed from happy wife to divorcée, *Carson's Cove*'s predictable patterns were a balm. A steady presence as life as I knew it shattered around me.

"What do you think?" Josh nods at the television. "One more? Or are we calling it a night?"

I blink at the screen, only now aware that the episode has ended and Netflix has started loading the next one. Season five, episode twenty-three: the season finale, which unexpectedly became the series finale. America's favorite girl next door, Sloan Edwards, has a plan to finally tell her best friend, Spencer Woods, that she's in love with him after she wins the annual Ms. Lobsterfest pageant. But a missing dress messes up her plans, and she chickens out, leaving Spencer in the dark as he heads off to LA to become an actor.

It's the cliff-hanger of all cliff-hangers.

Will they return, or won't they?

Will Sloan ever get the chance to tell Spencer how she really feels?

It was the perfect textbook setup to keep viewers hooked until the following fall's season six premiere.

Except the show never came back.

It was the one and only time *Carson's Cove* fell short. Where it didn't deliver its satisfaction-guaranteed ending.

According to the fan blogs, ratings started to slip toward the end of season five. A few of the actors had started to cross over to movie careers and demand more money. Shortly after the season finale aired, the show was canceled.

I still remember the day they announced it. I sobbed so hard that I burst the capillaries in both of my eyeballs. My mother had to call my high school and tell them that my fictional dog died because she was too embarrassed to tell them the truth: Her daughter had sunk into a deep depression over the end of a teenage television show.

I glance over at Josh, who is still staring at me, awaiting my call to watch the next episode.

"No," I tell him as I kick back the last of my wine. "I think I'm going to head to bed."

The events of the day have drained me. The mental exhaustion has morphed into a full-blown body ache.

Josh stands and holds out his hand to help me up. I feel the urge to say something. A thank-you for the rescue and the talk. But as I open my mouth, I'm interrupted by a sharp knock on the front door.

Josh and I both freeze.

"Are you expecting someone?" I glance at my phone. It's 12:01 A.M. A little late for visitors, though maybe not unusual for Josh.

He shakes his head. "Not that I'm aware of, but maybe you should let me get it."

He moves to the door, but before I can object, he opens it a crack. Then, satisfied with whoever is on the other side, he flings it fully open.

Standing on my front step is a guy. He looks to be in his twenties, with bleached-blond hair that sticks up in every direction. He's wearing a pale-yellow T-shirt for a band whose name is covered by a large white paper box in his hands.

"Which one of you is Brynn Smothers?" he asks.

Josh turns to me and grins. "Looks like *you* were expecting someone."

The guy ignores Josh and holds out his box. "Uber Eats for—oh, hey—" He points to something behind me. "*Carson's Cove.* I love that show. I'm kind of embarrassed to say it, but I've watched the entire series at least twice."

This revelation instantly relaxes me. This man is one of my people.

"Don't feel bad," I tell him. "My number is more like six, and I've probably watched some episodes even more than that."

The stranger looks pleased. "Really? Which ones?"

I probably should be mildly mortified about my compulsive television viewing habits right now, but I want to answer his question. "Definitely the hurricane episode. I love how it's Spencer and Sloan alone in his house all night with nothing but looming danger and candlelight for practically the whole episode. I spent the majority of my teen years thinking that was the epitome of romance."

The stranger nods. "I like that episode too. But it drove me crazy that they never kissed."

My stomach flutters as I think about it.

"But you know it's not going to happen right at the beginning of the episode," I counter. "Right when the power goes out, Sloan makes some offhand comment about how they should probably turn off all the lights so they don't come blaring on in the middle of the night if the power comes back. But if you watch closely, they don't ever actually do it. It's the perfect setup to ruin an almost-kiss."

A slow smile spreads across the Uber driver's lips.

There's something about it that strikes me as familiar, as if we've met before, but I can't quite place it.

He holds out the white box. "Happy birthday, Brynn."

I take it from his hands, examining the dark-blue logo stamped on top, which reads Bake a Wish.

I flip open the lid and find a small white birthday cake covered with rainbow sprinkles. A single white candle is nested in its center.

"Oh, shit." Josh takes a step toward me. "Brynn. I didn't know it was your birthday." He peers into the box, his woodsy smell mingling with the delicate vanilla of the cake. "So, was that why you were out tonight? A birthday celebration?"

"Not exactly." I stare at the single white candle, once again reminded of the disappointments of the night, which leads to a new question: If my friends didn't remember my birthday, who did?

"Hey, who ordered this—" Before the sentence is out, it's interrupted by the sound of my front door closing.

I turn to Josh. "Where did he go?"

Josh looks from the cake to the closed door and shrugs. He takes the box from my hands. "Can I cut you a slice?"

Although the sweet vanilla scent still lingers in my nose, it's a little late for cake. . . . I shake my head. "I really shouldn't. We can just save it for tomorrow."

Josh lingers, giving me an *Are you sure?* look before nodding and then taking it into the kitchen. I fold my Snuggly over the back of the couch and search for the remote to shut off the TV. A picture of the cast sitting on the dock at the marina still lingers on the screen. I finally locate the remote under the coffee table. As I hit the power button, the room goes dark until I turn and see a tiny orange flame lingering near the kitchen.

It comes toward me like an eerie apparition until Josh's face appears behind it.

He's holding up a dinner plate with the cake with the single white birthday candle stuck in the middle.

"My nana always said that it's not a birthday until you make a wish. So you have to at least have a bite tonight." He hands me the plate. "Happy birthday, Brynn."

My usually cynical self—the one who would normally roll her eyes at something so sentimental—is quieted by the orange licks of flame twisting and dancing in the dark.

A wish.

What single thing do I want more than anything else in this world?

To get back together with Matt? Um, no. That ship has sailed.

To find love again? Maybe . . . but finding love wasn't my problem the first time. I want to keep it. I want my life to play out exactly as it's supposed to for once. No plot twists. No Bumble jerks with cinnamon roll profiles. Just friends who understand me and will forever have my back.

I want to finally get the perfect happily ever after.

So I close my eyes, hold on to that feeling, and blow.

4

BRYNN

'm in a beautiful dream.

The sun is on my face. A warm breeze ruffles my curls as I breathe in the smells of salty sea air and leftover campfire. Waves crash softly on the shore, and I feel at peace. Like I've finally come home.

The *beep beep beep* of my phone alarm even sounds like the sharp squawk of a seagull, but I squeeze my eyes shut, hoping to cling to the last few moments before I have to wake up and start my day—or, I guess, now that I'm officially thirty, the next decade of my life.

No, Brynn. Don't go there.

Even though it's just a metaphor, it feels too heavy.

As the fuzzy edges of my dream fall away and I become more coherent, I realize I must have forgotten to close my blinds last night because the sun is blaring so brightly through the window that it's painful to open my eyes. I lie with them closed for a few more moments and give props to the content creators on my meditation app because those ocean waves crooning through my phone sound very realistic.

I roll over to bury my face in my pillow but misjudge the distance to the edge of the bed. As I flip over onto my stomach, I start to free-fall.

"What the fudge—" My hands don't brace in time, and I hit the floor in a belly flop, knocking the wind from my lungs and smacking my chin so hard my teeth chatter.

Ow! My body retracts into the fetal position.

"What the H-E-double-hockey-sticks just happened?"

Wait.

I can't swear.

"Fudge. Shoot. What the ever-loving frick?"

Filthy profanities are being generated by my brain, but I cannot for the life of me make them come out of my mouth.

What is going on?

I roll onto my back, wondering if maybe I hit my head harder than I thought. But instead of the usual popcorn ceiling above, I'm staring at a puffy white cloud that looks like it came straight out of a picture book.

What is even happening?

I get to my feet, taking in my surroundings. I'm on a small wooden deck flanked by deep-green patches of beach grass, facing a shore. There's an ocean that definitely isn't from a meditation app. My bed isn't a bed at all, but a cushioned outdoor lounger covered in white fabric dotted with pale-yellow buttercups.

Am I dreaming? Or have I been kidnapped? I check my body for wounds but don't appear to have any notable injuries.

I'm still wearing the black lululemons I changed into last night.

The scrunchie I meant to put my hair up with has left deep red indents halfway up my forearm.

I must still be dreaming. It's the only logical explanation.

I turn to face the cottage behind me. It's a small Cape Cod–style beach house with pale-yellow shingles, white trim, and a large sliding glass door that opens to the deck I'm currently standing on.

Next door is an identical cottage with shingle siding in light blue.

A memory stirs, and my heart triple-beats, as if it knows something my brain doesn't quite yet comprehend.

I step toward the sliding door, pressing my face to the glass to peek inside. The walls of the cozy living room are a soft, buttery yellow. The furniture is all simple rustic wood save for the oversized sage-colored couch, which sits on top of a green-and-blue vintage rug in front of an old stone fireplace filled with white candles.

The living room opens to a kitchen with simple white shiplap walls and cupboards and rustic wood countertops. A glass shelf along the windowsill sports a neat row of pots with basil, rosemary, and mint. It's chic but inviting, like slipping into a pair of cashmere socks.

I have this desire to go inside, to run my fingers along the mantel and see if it smells like herbs and fresh linen.

I look down at the welcome mat below my feet, which is stamped with the words *Shut the front door,* and I know with every fiber of my being that there is a key underneath.

Now this is getting weird.

Sure enough, when I lift the corner and blow away a layer of dirt, it's there.

It slips into the lock easily, and as I push open the door, a thought occurs: *What if this isn't a dream?* What if there's some other explanation I've yet to deduce, and I'm breaking and entering right now?

"Hello?" I call out, not entirely convinced that no one will answer.

But the only sound is the crashing of the waves on the shore.

I step inside and instantly feel like I've come home. I have this urge to dive onto the couch, pull the fleecy white blanket over me, and wait for a thunderstorm to roll in.

But that nagging thought keeps surfacing. This feels too real to be a dream. I'm too coherent and my elbow is a little too achy from hitting the deck. I reach into my pocket for my phone to google, then remember that I lost my purse at the bar last night. I guess Dream Brynn lost hers too.

Okay.

No Google.

I just need to revert to good old-fashioned thinking. How do you tell if you're in a dream again?

I start with the obvious and pinch my forearm.

"Jesus H, that stings!"

And the crescent-shaped indents in my skin confirm what the fall to the deck already told me. I can, in fact, feel pain.

A mirror.

I think I once read that when you're in a dream, you're not supposed to be able to see your reflection.

There's a small mirror hanging next to the kitchen door. I look into it and find Regular Brynn staring back at me, a tiny patch of drool crusting the corner of my mouth. My dark curls are wild, as if I spent the night on a lawn chair.

Okay, maybe you *can* see your reflection in a dream, and I've mixed it up with vampires.

I glance again at my tired eyes and, in doing so, notice that beneath the mirror is a row of hooks. There's a single key ring with a silver key, a car key for a Mini Cooper, and a stamped metal lobster keychain painted bright red.

An alarm bell sounds from deep within the depths of my brain.

All of this is highly familiar, but in a bizarre way. It's like I've seen it all before, but I also swear on my life I've never been here.

Have I had this dream before?

I lift the keys from the hook and exit out the kitchen door to a small dirt pathway that connects to the blue cottage next door and leads out to the main road. Sitting in front of a small yellow one-car garage is a bright-red Mini Cooper, which chirps as I click the unlock button.

Although I'm aware that I'm possibly committing my second felony of the morning, I get into the driver's seat and start the car, rationalizing that if I'm not dreaming, then I've most likely been kidnapped, and the police will probably understand.

Backing out of the driveway, I instinctively turn right past another large patch of beach grass onto a paved road.

There's an outcrop of buildings in the distance that flank both sides of the road. It looks like the main street of a small town.

The closer I get to the buildings, the more uneasiness grows in my belly. Like the cottage, it all seems too familiar.

The cobblestone-lined sidewalks are littered with wooden flower boxes filled with bright purple and blue pansies, interspaced with welcoming stone benches gently shaded by tall red maples whose leaves are still a bright Kelly green.

At least my imagination is cute and quaint.

I creep slowly past the tiny shops. There's a dry cleaner, a pharmacy, and a barbershop with one of those red-and-blue swirling poles, but it's the bakery with its fluffy white cakes in the window that catches my eye.

Particularly the cake covered in bright-colored sprinkles with the single white birthday candle in its center.

I hit the brakes.

It's rather fortuitous because there are two men crossing the road ahead of me, carrying a ladder between them. They're followed by a woman whose bright-red hair is so familiar that I roll down my window and crane my neck to get a better look. I can't see her face. She's too busy yelling at the men as they lean the ladder against one of the lampposts. Instead, I watch as one man climbs and the other runs back across the street, returning a moment later with the end of a banner that is tied to an opposite lamppost. I stare as the banner pulls taut and the words 75TH ANNUAL MS. LOBSTERFEST PAGEANT—JUNE 21 7:00 P.M. are displayed in sparkly red paint.

Ms. Lobsterfest?

"No forking way."

All of a sudden, it all comes together. Like one of those 3D puzzles, the answer suddenly pops right out, as if it were right there in front of me all along.

I'm not in a dream at all.

My foot finds the gas. I'm sweating. A panicked feeling is climbing the walls of my throat.

It's not possible. It makes no logical sense.

I'm so preoccupied with my own panic that I don't see the guy as he steps off the sidewalk until it's too late.

My foot finds the brake pedal, but not before the Mini makes contact, and he crumples to the street below with an audible *thwack.*

5

JOSH

"Josh?

"Joshua?

"Joshua Brian Adam James . . . I don't actually know your middle name. But that's not really important right now. You have to wake up."

I crack one eye open, then the other. The outline of the wild-haired woman looming above me brings a needed rush of relief.

I did it.

I finally woke up.

That was possibly the weirdest and most vivid dream I've ever had. For a little while there, I was starting to worry it was something else entirely.

I try to pull myself into a seated position, but as my abs contract, a sharp pain shoots through my rib cage, and I have to lie back down to catch my breath.

"Oh, thank god you're alive." Brynn's arms squeeze my shoulders as she pins me down in a half hug, her dark hair falling onto my face.

"I didn't think I hit you that hard, but you crumpled like a leaf, and I did take that CPR class once, but the only part I remember is 'tongue, jaw lift, finger sweep,' but I'm pretty sure that's only for choking victims and—"

"Brynn!"

She pulls away, giving me enough space to take in my surroundings. The sky. The street. The giant hunk of bright-red metal pumping hot engine air out its front grille.

Any peace I may have been feeling a moment ago vanishes.

I'm not at home, passed out on the couch, and Brynn isn't trying to wake me up because I'm sleeping on top of the TV remote.

I'm still in the strange town, with no idea how I got here, and I've just been hit by a car.

"What the fudge is going on?"

Wait. What?

"What the fudge is going on?" I try again.

"Why the fudge do I keep saying *fudge*?"

Brynn throws up her arms. "You can't swear either. It's not just me. That's totally weird, right?"

It *is* weird.

Everything is weird.

"When did you get here?" I move my head tentatively, still unsure if I've actually injured anything.

"Just now. You jumped right out in front of my car," she says, almost accusatory. "What were you doing just walking into the street without looking, and more importantly, what are *you* doing here?"

I have no idea.

I remember getting home from the bar last night, then that weird guy at the door, and after that, everything becomes fuzzy.

"I woke up in this strange bedroom," I attempt to explain. "At first, I thought I might be dreaming, but it all seemed so real. It was in this old warehouse building. I walked down these steps, and there was a big room that looked like a bar underneath."

What I don't tell her is that, at that point, I was pretty sure I was in a nightmare.

I had them for months after my dad died. Panicked dreams where I was in his bar and I couldn't get the taps to pour beer, and people kept demanding more and more, but I couldn't make anything work.

This bar was different though.

"The place was empty. I actually wondered if maybe it was closed down. I was able to find the front door, and I started walking down the street. I was trying everything to wake myself up and . . ." I turn my head to the red Mini Cooper that hit me, its engine still running in the middle of the road. "Well, I guess I haven't succeeded yet."

Brynn reaches down her hand to help me up. I'm able to get to my feet this time. Nothing feels broken. I'm just a little dazed and bruised.

"I think I've figured out what's going on." She inclines her head toward the Mini's passenger-side door. "It might be easier to show you rather than tell you."

It takes a moment for my brain to catch up to what she's proposing. She waits patiently until I finally process that we're getting in the car, and I move to get in the passenger side. We both buckle up. I'm still uncertain of exactly what we're doing as Brynn pulls a U-turn and then slows the car to a crawl as we drive back down the main street.

"There." She points at a white brick building that reads PHAR-

MACY in etched gold letters on the front window. "That's Doc Martin's pharmacy. It's where Fletcher Scott bought his first pack of condoms when he decided it was time to lose his virginity, but then got caught by Spencer's dad. And that . . ." She points at what looks like a beauty parlor. "That's the salon where Poppy Bensen went from a homely nobody to a gorgeous redheaded bombshell and then won the role of captain of the cheer squad over her nemesis, Luce Cho. And that"—she points at a painted banner hanging above us—"is announcing the seventy-fifth Ms. Lobsterfest pageant. There is only one place that I have ever heard of that has an annual beauty pageant called the Ms. Lobsterfest."

I have so many questions, but Brynn doesn't allow me to ask them.

"Finally, there." She stops the car this time and rolls down her window so I have an unobstructed view of a white gazebo on a large patch of grass. "That's the spot where Spencer said goodbye to Sloan because he was leaving for LA. It's all here, Josh."

Brynn holds up her hands as if she's just presented an irrefutable case, but I'm still lost.

"So where are we?"

She pulls the car into a nearby parking spot and cuts the engine.

"We're in Carson's Cove."

I hear her. I compute her words but am as equally confused as I was a moment ago.

"Carson's Cove is a real place?"

She shakes her head. "No. I mean, it was supposed to be based on a coastal fishing town in Massachusetts, but it doesn't actually exist."

"Then how are we . . ." I can't even compose my thoughts enough to string together a complete sentence, but Brynn nods as if she gets it.

"That's the part I can't figure out."

We sit for a few moments in silence, watching a mailman make his way down the street. He waves to a woman in linen pants walking two goldendoodles, then to a bald-headed grocer spraying down the display of vegetables outside his shop.

"Josh."

I'm aware of Brynn calling my name, but I'm too preoccupied with finding a logical explanation.

"Josh." Her tone turns sharp enough to break through my thoughts.

She points at my thigh. "Will you stop it with the jiggly leg? It's starting to freak me out."

My leg is shaking like a jackhammer. I'm way past freaked-out and flat out of ideas.

"Could we have sleepwalked here?"

Her brow crinkles as she contemplates this. "Both of us?"

"Good point. Maybe we were kidnapped?"

She throws up her arms. "I thought that too, but who the hell would want to kidnap us? I need a roommate to pay off my mortgage. You work in a bar. I gotta think there are more profitable kidnappees out there."

"You're sure we didn't do drugs last night?" It's the only other explanation that makes sense.

She shrugs. "If we did, I don't remember it. You didn't eat any of that cake, did you?"

I shake my head. "No, did you?"

She thinks for a moment. "No. But I did—" She doesn't finish the thought. Instead, she gets out of the car, practically sprints across the street, and stands in front of a redbrick building with a large storefront window.

I follow, and when I cross the street, I find her with her hands cupped around her eyes and her face pressed so close to the glass that it fogs up with every exhale.

"What are you doing?"

She takes a step back, pointing at the window. "That cake last night. It looked an awful lot like the one on that stand, right?"

I glance at the display of cookies and sweets, as well as the cake in question. It does look almost identical to the one Brynn got last night, complete with the birthday candle.

"The name on the box seemed familiar," Brynn continues. "But I couldn't place it. The bakery wasn't really a big part of the show. The only episode where I think it's mentioned is the one where it's Sloan's sixteenth birthday. Everyone forgets because Poppy and Luce are campaigning against each other for who gets to be class president. Fletcher has been doing community service because he stole his aunt's car. Spencer is stressing out because the new drama teacher seems to have some sort of grudge against him. Then Sloan is all upset until she comes home late to a dark house, and it's all been a ruse for a surprise party." She looks like she's going to continue with her story but stops, her eyes searching my face.

"Sorry, you didn't need all of that background info. My point is that the name on the box from last night is the same as the one on this storefront." She points to the etching on the glass that reads BAKE A WISH. "I didn't make the connection at first, but I'm absolutely sure now that the bakery box was from Carson's Cove."

"But that doesn't make any sense."

I'm suddenly feeling a little weak in the knees, and I wonder if maybe the car hit me harder than I thought.

"Are you okay?" Brynn's fingers cup my elbow as she cranes her neck to peer up at me.

"I'm fine," I lie, but her brown eyes study my face as if she's not buying it.

"I've got an idea. . . . I wonder if . . ." Her eyes pan the street as if searching for something. "Actually. That's perfect. Come on." She grabs my wrist without further explanation.

We get back into the car and drive to the end of the main street. The last building before the road veers into the woods looks like an aluminum can flipped onto its side. Above it is a bright-pink neon sign that reads Pop's Old-Fashioned Diner.

"You want to eat?" I ask, not entirely sure of her plan.

"This is Pop's," she says, as if I'm supposed to know what that means. "It'll solve everything."

I follow Brynn out into the parking lot and watch as she skips up all three front steps of the diner and opens the front door.

But I don't follow.

This is too weird.

Even if Brynn is right and we are in Carson's Cove, how the hell did we get here? And, more importantly, how do we get home?

Brynn waits for me at the entrance.

"Are you coming?" she calls, as if she's about to walk into a Tim Hortons, not a fictional diner in a made-up town.

Maybe it's the tone of her voice.

Or the casual way she props the door open with her hip.

Either way, it snaps me back to reality.

"How is a fictional diner in a television show that we've some-how landed in supposed to solve everything? Are you hearing yourself?"

She narrows her eyes back at me. "I have a plan, Josh. You need to trust me."

"This is insane." I stand rooted to the spot, the weight of this morning finally hitting me. "You should be freaking out right now, but you're acting like this is totally normal. Like this is your secret fantasy come true."

"Okay." She draws out the word, walking slowly back down the steps until she comes to a stop in front of me. "You're right. And I was freaking out earlier. I woke up on a lawn chair in a strange place. I have gone through an entire gamut of emotions ever since. And, like you, I have a whole boatload of unanswered questions, but I'd also be lying if I didn't admit I'm a little curious. I have been obsessed with this place for years—at what is probably an unhealthy level. And now it's in front of me, and it's real." She takes my hand, cupping her fingers over mine.

"I promise you we will figure this out. That's why I brought you here." She nods at the diner. "If this really is Carson's Cove, we are at the place that will give us our answers. It's where all the characters go when they can't figure out what to do next. You tell your problems to Pop. He makes you a chocolate milkshake, and by the time you're done, you know exactly what needs to happen."

I only half believe her, but I follow her inside with no better idea of what to do instead.

The interior of Pop's looks exactly like I expected for a place that calls itself an old-fashioned diner. The floors are checkered black and white. There's a long white bar with red leather stools and rows of vinyl booths that look like they've been transported straight from the 1950s. Along the far wall sits an old-fashioned jukebox, although the music crooning out sounds more like late-

2000s emo than '50s rock. The whole diner smells like french fries and coffee.

There are no other customers. The place is empty save for a single guy standing behind the counter in a white apron and red-and-white-striped polo shirt.

When Brynn mentioned Pop, I pictured an old dude with gray hair and possibly a mustache. The guy behind the counter is in his twenties and has bleached-blond hair sticking up as if he went a little too heavy-handed on the gel.

"Is that Pop?" I ask Brynn, who is also staring at the guy.

Brynn turns to me, her eyes wide. "No. I have no idea who that guy is."

We both turn back to him as he looks up. "Oh, good! You guys made it."

6

BRYNN

"I have to say I'm a little offended."

The guy behind the counter places his hand over his heart as if my words have physically wounded him.

"I thought we shared something special last night."

With the mention of last night, I get a flashback.

The late-night visitor who looked so familiar.

The mystery cake.

"You're that Uber Eats guy," I say.

He smiles widely as he gives a slight bow. "Some days I am. But today, I'm *nondescript male, wiping down counter.*" He taps his Pop's uniform name tag. "But to make things easier, why don't you call me 'Sheldon.'"

He points at the two empty stools at the counter. "Have a seat. Take a load off. You must be tired. I was starting to get worried about you guys." He pulls a pad from his apron pocket. "Can I get you something to drink? A Coke? Or, I know! One of Pop's famous milkshakes? Cherry chip?"

I shake my head. Although I thought it was a good idea a few minutes ago, the thought of ice cream suddenly makes me queasy.

I do take up Sheldon's offer of a seat and sink down onto one of the counter stools, suddenly feeling the effects of a night spent on a lawn chair. Josh stays fixed in his spot next to the door. His eyebrows scrunch in a serious way as he stares intently at Sheldon.

"What did you mean when you said you were expecting us?" I ask Sheldon, leaning forward over the counter. "Do you know how we got here?"

Sheldon finishes wiping the spot in front of me, ignoring my questions and whistling a tune I can't quite place before tossing the rag into the sink. Then, in a single fluid motion, he hops over the counter and sits on the stool beside me. He slumps his shoulders, props his elbows on the counter, and rests his head in his palms, green eyes fixated on me.

"Haven't you always felt like that last *Carson's Cove* season left you unsatisfied?" he asks. "Like, there were all these storylines left half-baked: Spencer taking off to LA before Sloan had the chance to say those three little words and Sloan never winning the crown in the Ms. Lobsterfest pageant. Would you agree it lacked that gratifying, feel-good *Carson's Cove* ending we've all come to love?"

His words pluck at a sensitive spot in my chest. "Yes. Of course I would."

Sheldon leans forward so close that I can smell a faint hint of something sweet on his breath. "Well . . . I've brought you here to help me make it right." He holds out his arms. "This is our chance to fix everything. To bring to life the perfect ending that never happened."

A tiny ripple stirs in the bottom of my stomach. It works its way up to my lungs until I shiver involuntarily.

Sheldon's gaze holds mine, and I find myself almost willing him to go on.

"At first, I thought I'd just pluck everyone back into the lives they abandoned," he continues. "But then I realized that wouldn't work. It would be an absolute disaster to go through all of this effort to make *Carson's Cove* happen again, only to end up with the wrong ending a second time. Do you know what the definition of insanity is, Brynn?"

I open my mouth, but Sheldon doesn't wait for an answer.

"It is doing the same thing twice and expecting a different outcome."

With that, he leans back, giving me a moment to let his words sink in fully.

"So then I thought a little more and figured out the problem. I don't think Sloan was fully committed to the idea that she and Spencer should be together."

I open my mouth to protest, but Sheldon holds a finger to my lips. "Wait. Hear me out. She could have told him at the gazebo that she loved him. She could have gotten in her car to follow him to the airport. That's two examples right there, and I'm completely ignoring the countless other times she was alone with Spencer and never once even hinted at how she felt."

I want to argue back that her feelings were complex. There was history and hormones involved, not to mention over a decade of friendship to consider. But Sheldon has gotten to his feet and started to pace.

"If I don't have full commitment from Sloan, then my whole plan falls apart. So I thought, what do you do when you've got a damaged limb?"

I stare, not so certain I want to hear the answer.

He wheels around to face me. "You cut it off."

There is no expression on his face. No acknowledgment whatsoever that what he just said is downright creepy, if not morbid—especially if it's referencing bodies and not trees.

I almost ask him to clarify, but he resumes his pacing, this time shaking a single finger in the air.

"But then I had an epiphany. I couldn't just cut Sloan out. What I needed was a replacement. Obviously, you can't have a *Carson's Cove* revival without Sloan Edwards."

I find myself nodding. "I mean, there really wouldn't be a point."

Sheldon stops and slaps the counter so hard that the salt and pepper shakers clink. "Exactly! I needed someone who wanted this as badly as I did. Someone who watched five hundred and seventy-four hours of *Carson's Cove* reruns on Netflix. Someone who would wish from the deepest depths of their soul for things to work out right. Who could finally give Sloan the ending she deserves." He leers above me, making no effort to hide the way his gaze makes a slow assessment of my body from the top of my head to my toes.

I know that Josh and I are the only other people in the diner, but I still look over my shoulder to be sure he's talking to me. Sloan is sweet and kind and very blond. Aside from my dark, curly hair, I also lack that innocence, that glass-half-full, sunny-side-up attitude that makes Sloan so beloved.

"You want *me* to play Sloan Edwards," I clarify.

Sheldon picks up one of my curls, as if his thoughts are now following the path carved out by mine.

"No, Brynn." He shakes his head, smiling. "I want you to *be* Sloan Edwards."

Those tendrils of excitement that filled my lungs only moments ago now twist and contort into double knots.

I sneak a glance at Josh. His face is impossible to read, but he takes a step closer as if he too understands that something feels off here.

"What do you mean when you say *be*?" I turn back to Sheldon, who smiles as if he has fully anticipated this question.

"You, my friend, are no longer Brynn Smothers. From this point on, you are Sloan Edwards, Carson's Cove's beloved girl next door. I've got your story all worked out. It's been fifteen years since you left the island, never returning home after a summer abroad in Paris. Choosing busy and crowded Boston"—he spits out the word—"and your budding design career over your child-hood home." He frowns briefly, then shakes his head, the smile returning to his face. "Anyway, the point is, you've come back. Perhaps because you're feeling a little lost. Perhaps because the real world didn't live up to all its promises? Perhaps because your heart still belongs to the boy next door?"

All of a sudden, I'm struck by a very different thought. Spencer Woods. Certified teen dream. The object of my teenage fantasies. Does that mean he's here too?

"What about the boy next door?" I ask Sheldon. "Spencer is back too?"

Sheldon shoots a quick glance at Josh before returning his eyes to me, smiling. "You are going to love this one. Spencer Woods has just returned from LA to take a job as head of the drama department at Carson's Cove High School. Apparently, he too had some unfinished business on the island calling him home." He winks.

Josh, who has been notably silent until now, clears his throat. "I'm still not following. Are you making a new television show? Or is this just a reunion of all the cast members?"

Sheldon throws his head back and laughs. "You're really not

getting it, my friend?" He makes a show of wiping a nonexistent tear from his cheek. "I've brought the whole thing back to life—with a few minor adjustments. But overall, it's the *Carson's Cove* of its glory days. You wished it into existence, Brynn, and I made it happen."

His statement shifts the conversation. Up until now, I've been a passive participant. A victim, even, of whatever is going on. But claiming I caused this situation? No. That's not right.

I force myself to think about precisely what happened last night. My memories are a little jumbled. There was cake. I was sad. I was definitely working through some wine-fueled emotions.

"I think you're a bit mixed up," I tell him. "I did make a wish last night, but I did not wish for this."

Sheldon leans in again, so close that our faces are almost touching. He runs a finger down the ridge of my nose and bops the tip.

"Ahhhhh, but you did. You wished for a life free of plot twists. You wished for infallible friendships and a cinnamon roll next door. I believe you even used the term *happily ever after*. That's *Carson's Cove* in a nutshell, isn't it?"

I shake my head. "Yes, but—"

"But what?" Sheldon's jovial expression melts into something else. His mouth hardens into a firm line. "I worked very hard to make this happen. Why aren't you happy?" He stands. Spreading his arms wide, he turns in a slow, smooth circle. "I'm giving you the chance of a lifetime here. To see Spencer and Sloan together at last. To see Sloan with the Ms. Lobsterfest crown placed upon her deserving head. To have all of the loose ends wrapped up into a perfect bow. Isn't that what you wanted?"

"Yes, but—"

He holds a finger to my lips. "No buts. No excuses. I need you both to play your parts. Everything must go exactly according to my plans."

"Why does that sound like a threat?" Josh finally moves. Stepping forward, he seems to grow even taller than his usual six feet and two inches as he places himself between Sheldon and me, calling out the notable difference between Josh's broadness and Sheldon's lankier limbs.

Sheldon retreats, scrambling back over the counter and putting a barrier between them. "No threats here, my man. More like strong suggestions and a reminder that I am the one who brought you here and, therefore, the only one with the ability to send you home."

Josh grips the counter with both hands and leans across it. "Then prove it. Send us home."

"I will." Sheldon leans forward as well, suddenly bolder. "Just as soon as you give me the ending I want."

The shift in Sheldon's position brings him directly under an overhead light. Whether it's the new dark shadows under his eyes or something else, his features once again strike a familiar chord. "Who *are* you?"

My question garners Sheldon's attention. He takes a long side step away from Josh to stand across from me. "I'm just a guy, standing in front of a girl, asking her to give *Carson's Cove* the ending it deserves."

All of a sudden, it clicks. Sheldon's face. Why I know it. Why it took me so long to place him.

"No. You're not *just a guy.*"

It takes me a few more seconds to piece the final bit together.

"I knew you looked familiar," I say to Sheldon. "I've been racking my brain, trying to figure out why, but I couldn't place it until now. You're the *Extra Extra.*"

"The what?" Josh looks from me to Sheldon.

"He's in over fifty episodes," I explain.

"Fifty-four," Sheldon corrects.

"He's a legend in the fan forums," I continue. "'Extra' because he's a nameless character. The second 'Extra' because he always seems to stick out. The point is, he's played at least ten different characters. Most don't have any lines, and he's never named in the credits. It's like one of those internet mysteries. People are always watching reruns and spotting him in new scenes."

Josh shakes his head. "Okay, fine. He's part of the show." He turns back to Sheldon. "But how did you do this? And why am I here? I don't even watch the show."

Sheldon responds with an exaggerated shrug. "You were a bit of a glitch, if I'm being perfectly honest. My best guess is that Brynn's wish was so powerful that it sucked you in here along with her. It's a minor complication. One I'm willing to work with, especially since the original Fletcher was a handsome and clueless bartender, and you . . . Well, let's just say that with a big-enough sock, the shoe fits. What is important is that you are here. And we can finally make things turn out exactly as they were supposed to."

Josh moves as if he's going to jump over the counter. "You can't just uproot our lives. We have—"

There's a loud *ding* sound, followed by an "Order up!" from the kitchen.

"Excuse me." Sheldon holds up his finger. "Duty calls."

He disappears through a white swinging door before we can object. A minute later, the door opens again, but the man that walks through is much older. Although he's dressed in the same uniform, he has two puffs of white hair above his ears and the deepest brown eyes I've ever seen.

"Well, if it isn't Fletcher Scott and Sloan Edwards," he says in a Morgan Freeman–esque voice. "My gosh. It feels like it's been fifteen years."

The real Pop holds out his arms for a hug. I'm momentarily paralyzed at the sight of a face I've seen easily a hundred times before but never once in the flesh. He has a few more wrinkles around his eyes, and his arms are a little thinner than I remember. Still, I fold into them gladly, feeling like I am being reunited with an old friend.

"It's the darndest thing." His deep voice reverberates through my chest. "I had the urge to make a cherry chip milkshake this morning. Haven't made one in years. It's almost as if I knew you'd be back. Welcome home, Sloan."

The comfort of his arms melts away all of the uneasiness from before until I pull away and remember I still have so many more unanswered questions.

"Um, Pop." I choose my words carefully, still uncertain about how all of this works. "That guy who was out here before, Sheldon. Could you ask him to come back out?"

Pop's eyebrows knit together. "I'm not sure I know who you're talking about, honey. There's no one around here named Sheldon."

My stomach plummets.

"The young guy," I clarify, as if it will help, even though I suspect I already know Pop's answer. "Blond hair. Pop's uniform."

Pop shakes his head.

"I'm the only one working this morning, Sloan."

He doesn't seem weirded out at all.

"Hey, Pop?" I consider the best way to phrase my question. "What were you up to, uh . . . yesterday morning?"

He scratches his head. "To tell you the truth, I'm not really sure."

"What about the day before that? Or even the week before that? Can you tell me anything that happened between . . . uh, I don't know . . . May 2010 and today?"

He stares at me blankly. "I don't know what to tell you. I think I probably was just here."

Last question. "And what's the date? And the year, if you don't mind?"

He holds a palm up to my forehead. "It's the tenth of June, 2024. Are you feeling okay?"

I feel like I'm going to heave.

"I'm fine," I lie. "Just a little tired. Maybe we should save that shake for another time."

My eyes flick to Josh, who is staring right back at me. He doesn't say a word, but I know exactly what he's thinking.

What the H-E-double-hockey-sticks have we gotten ourselves into?

7

JOSH

"So what should we do now?"

The parking lot out in front of Pop's is empty, aside from the red Mini.

"I don't know." Brynn stares at the keys in her hand. "We could go back into town? Or maybe back to Sloan's house? Or I guess I can call it *my* house now—which makes me feel much better about breaking and entering this morning."

Up until now, I assumed that Brynn and I were still on the same page. The one where we both agreed that this whole situation was screwed up and that our objective was to get home, not to give in to some weirdo's fucked-up fantasy.

"Wait, you're saying you actually want to play along with this guy? Pretend that you're some fictional character?"

She holds up her hands. "Maybe? I don't know. I don't see you coming up with any other brilliant suggestions."

I don't have any brilliant suggestions. I'm still piecing together everything that happened back in that diner. All I know is that whatever this place is, I don't want to be stuck in it.

"What if we just leave?" It sounds so obvious now that I've said it. "You said we're in Massachusetts, right? Maybe we can drive home? We have a car. A full tank of gas. Do you know the way out of here?"

Brynn thinks about the idea for a moment. "I guess we could try. Carson's Cove is an island, but there is a bridge to the mainland at the other end of Main Street. We could go check it out and see if it's still there."

"Great. Give me the keys." I move to swipe the keys from her hand, but she pulls them to her chest before I can grab them.

"What? No. It's my car!"

"First of all, no, it's not. And second of all, you literally hit me twenty minutes ago. I'm driving."

She rolls her eyes but tosses me the keys with a disgruntled "Fine."

I slide in, start the car, and confirm that we do in fact have a full tank of gas before pulling out of the parking lot.

We drive back through town. Brynn doesn't say much, and I'm still a little shocked at the sight of this small town, which looks so stereotypically normal that it's hard to believe it isn't real.

There's a flower shop with yellow buckets outside filled with bright bouquets of flowers. A beauty parlor with women inside getting their hair done. And then, at the edge of town, that red-brick bar, the one with the apartment on top, where I woke up this morning.

Once we pass the buildings, the smooth pavement gives way to packed gravel and potholes.

"Right there." Brynn points to a bend up ahead, where the road disappears into a forest of Douglas firs. "That road should lead us to the bridge and take us off the island."

I rev the Mini Cooper's engine as if confirming that the car is up to the task.

We clip down the road at a solid eighty clicks, forest flying by on both sides until the ocean's blue waters appear ahead.

The bridge.

Proof that whatever is happening isn't quite as weird as we think.

As we clear the trees, the forest opens up to a rocky beach and a two-lane steel structure that looks old, but secure enough to travel across.

There's a rhythmic *thwack, thwack, thwack* as we leave the land behind and the ocean surrounds us on either side.

With every turn of the tires, the imaginary vise that's been squeezing my chest since I woke up this morning loosens just a little more.

But then I slam on the brakes. Brynn jolts forward as her seatbelt catches.

"What the heck is that?" Brynn says it before I can.

Ahead of us, on the bridge, is a thick white mist that was definitely not there a moment ago.

"I think it's just fog," I answer with far more certainty than I feel.

Brynn twists around in her seat to look out the rear window, then whips back around. "I think we should go back. That doesn't look like normal fog."

A quick glance in the rearview mirror tells me she's right. The road behind us is clear and sunny.

"Well, there's only one way to find out." I straighten my arms and hit the gas. The Mini jerks forward. Our windshield becomes an impenetrable wall of wispy white.

But as quickly as we are into it, we're out.

The thwacking gives way to the crunching of gravel, and we're once again surrounded by another tall forest.

I breathe a deep sigh of validated relief. "See. Regular old fog. We're not dealing with the paranormal here. There's an explanation. I don't know what the fudge it is, but—"

All at once, I get this strange sensation.

Like the blood in my veins has turned to solid ice.

"You can't swear." Brynn's voice is barely a whisper.

"Darn it."

"Jesus H. Christmas."

"Mother of pearl."

Fuuuuuuuuccccckkkk.

"I can swear in my head. It just comes out all wrong." I open my mouth to try again but stop as the forest clears and Pop's Old-Fashioned Diner comes into view.

Followed by the beauty shop.

The flower shop.

The redbrick building where I woke up this morning.

Then the most fucked-up sensation of déjà vu.

We're back in Carson's Cove.

But we can't be.

"I'm going to try again," I tell her.

I rev the engine, determined to prove that this is all some sort of misunderstanding.

The car speeds into the forest. . . .

Then over the bridge . . .

Then into the mist . . .

And we're spat right back out where we started.

My insides feel hollow. Like any hope I may have had was scooped out and left back there on the bridge.

"So . . ." Brynn side-eyes me as I slow the car to a much more reasonable speed. "I think we can officially cross driving home off the list?"

I pull the car into an empty parking spot in front of the bakery and cut the engine. My mind is still processing what just happened.

There's no way out of this place.

We're trapped.

"Okay." I undo my seatbelt so I can face Brynn. "Let's just say, for argument's sake, that we give Sheldon the happy ending he wants. What exactly would we need to do?"

Brynn undoes her seatbelt as well, then sucks her lower lip between her teeth before releasing it with a long breath. "Well, in the last episode, Sloan finally realizes she loves Spencer, but she knows that he still sees her as this sweet and innocent girl next door. So she enters the Ms. Lobsterfest pageant to try to win the crown and show Spencer and everyone else in town that she's a grown woman, worthy of love, which I fully acknowledge sounds horrifically cheesy and even borderline icky—but I promise you it was a really good episode."

She glances over at me as if expecting me to say something, but I don't.

"Anyway," Brynn continues, "the day of the pageant arrives, and Sloan has this whole plan to tell Spencer how she feels once she's a certified beauty queen, but her evening gown gets stolen, and Lois, the pageant director, won't let her on the stage, so she's disqualified and devastated. She runs to the gazebo to have a good cry, and Spencer follows her. It starts to rain. It's, like, the most romantic scene you can ever imagine. Spencer basically hints that he's got big feelings for Sloan, but for some unknown reason that I'm going to attribute to the writers wanting a dramatic season cliff-hanger, she chickens out and never ends up telling him that she's in love with him, and then he goes off to LA and she moves to Paris for the summer to be a fashion intern and that's how the show ended."

Brynn leans her head against the seat and studies me as if looking for a reaction. My thumbs drum against the wheel as I mentally dig through everything she just told me.

"Okay, so we need Spencer and Sloan to finally get together."

Brynn nods. "I think so."

"Can we just go to this Spencer guy's house? You can tell him how Sloan feels, make out a little, and then we're good to go?"

Brynn stares at me as if I suggested something stupid. "That's not how this show works. I can't just show up and make out with Spencer. There were five seasons of agonizing slow burn. *Carson's Cove* has a formula. Besides . . . we have a bigger problem."

"What?"

"Sheldon mentioned that Sloan had to win the pageant. If that humongous banner hanging above the main street is right, we're stuck here for at least a couple of weeks."

"So until then, we'd have to . . ."

She nods, following my thought. "Pretend to be Fletch and Sloan."

Damn. That's what I thought she was going to say.

I lean back, close my eyes, and let out a very frustrated groan.

"Hey." Brynn rubs the side of my arm with her knuckles. "How about this? We stick together and play along for a little while, just until we get a sense of how this place works. Or . . . until we can find Sheldon or another way out of here."

Stay here. Be them.

It's not what I want to do at all. Yet I don't see any better alternatives.

"Yeah, I guess."

Brynn rests her head against the window and stares out at the sidewalk. "I know it isn't ideal. But Carson's Cove is a great town. If we're going to get trapped in some nonexistent dimension, I feel like we could have done a lot worse. I think you'll change your tune when you finally get to try one of Pop's—"

She stops speaking suddenly.

I wave my hands in front of her face. "Brynn?"

My eyes follow hers to the sidewalk across the street, where there doesn't seem to be anything particularly notable going on.

"Huh?" Her eyes focus back on mine, as if she didn't hear my question.

"What's wrong?"

She shakes her head. "Nothing. Why?"

"You just stopped talking in the middle of a sentence."

"Oh." Brynn blinks. "Uh, right. I was thinking we should probably split up."

"What are you talking about? You literally just said that we would stick together."

She opens her door and steps out onto the sidewalk, and I scramble after her, once again utterly confused.

"I, uh . . . meant it metaphorically. But yeah, we should definitely split up. That way, we can cover more ground. It will be easier to find Sheldon this way. You can go back to the Bronze—that's the name of the bar where I'm pretty sure you woke up. And I will cover"—she gestures to the area across the street—"over there. And then we can meet up in a little bit and share what we've found out."

Something's up. My spidey senses are overloaded, seeing as this whole day has been weird, but I'd be an idiot not to notice that there's something she isn't telling me. Not to mention the fact that I have no desire to set foot in the place where I woke up this morning. What did she call it again? The Bronze?

"Yeah, I'm not going back to that bar."

Brynn throws up her arms. "Why? It's just a bar. If anything, it should feel like home to you."

It does. That's exactly the problem.

"Can't I just come with you?"

Brynn glances across the street again. "I really think it's better if I go off alone. Just for a little while. Sloan's the town sweetheart. It might throw them off to see her with your whole . . ." She makes an erratic gesture at my body as she starts to inch backward.

I shake my head. "But what if I run into someone? I don't know anything about this place."

She folds her arms across her chest. "How about I give you a crash course?"

She pulls me over to one of the benches under a giant maple tree. "I obviously can't catch you up on all five seasons, but the good news is that you're Fletcher Scott. You're broody and aloof, so if you don't recognize someone, you can make a smart-ass comment and no one will notice, but you do need to know your friends. First up is Sloan Edwards. She's Carson's Cove's sweetheart. Practically perfect in every way. She was orphaned at sixteen and then emancipated. A virgin . . . although it's been fifteen years, so who knows." Brynn shrugs. "Up next is Spencer Woods. Dreamboat. Golden retriever energy. Lives next door to Sloan. They've been BFFs since primary school."

This guy I do remember from last night. "He's the one with the hair, right?"

Brynn doesn't try to hide her smile. "Blond and beautiful. You're catching on."

"Yup. I think I got it."

Brynn holds up her hand. "We're not quite done yet. There's also Poppy Bensen. Sloan's other best friend. Fiery redhead. Her hair matches her personality. You'll understand what I mean when you meet her. Poppy's queen of everything. Cheer captain. Class president. Four-time Ms. Lobsterfest winner."

"Impressive," I say. "And not cliché at all."

Brynn gives me a flat look. "Then you're going to love this. Poppy has a nemesis: Luce Cho. Certified mean girl. If someone is in Poppy's way, it's usually Luce."

I think I got it. "So, Spencer, Sloan, Poppy, and Luce. Is that it?"

Brynn nods. "Only one you're missing is Fletcher Scott."

"That's me?"

Brynn smiles. "America's favorite bad boy. Beloved by fans, not so much by the citizens of the Cove. Fletch is the town's black sheep. He works part-time at his aunt Sherry's bar, the Bronze. It's a bit of a dive. Not really that busy from what I can remember."

A pit forms in my stomach. All of this is hitting a little too close to home.

"Don't worry." Brynn reaches up and squeezes my shoulder. "You are going to be fine. No one really expects too much from Fletch."

For whatever reason, that one stings a bit.

"So you want me to just hang around the bar all day?"

She nods. "Pretty much."

"What are you going to do?"

She eyes what looks to be a fudge shop across the street. "I'm going to look around as well. See if I can find any of the other main characters. They may know something we don't."

I don't love this plan. But I also don't have a better one.

"Fine. But how do I find you? I don't have my phone."

Brynn looks down at her pocketless lululemon leggings. "Neither do I. How about I come to find you later at the Bronze?"

Before I can tell her that I don't like the sound of any of this, she runs across the street and disappears into the fudge shop.

Okay, fine.

Pretend to be this Fletch guy.

He's a bartender. I'm a bartender.

He's the black sheep of his family. At least if I screw up, it's expected.

8

BRYNN

Ye Ole Fudge Shop reminds me of my Granny Smothers's house.

It smells like vanilla and baking cookies, and there's a disproportionate number of glass jars filled with hard candies placed atop paper doilies.

The little old lady behind the counter even looks like my granny when she glances up as I walk in and asks in the sweetest old-lady voice, "Is there anything in particular you're looking for, dear?"

I don't know the polite way to ask her if she's seen the first male to ever give me an orgasm—albeit with the help of his *Tiger Beat* centerfold poster and my electric toothbrush. Instead, I shake my head and smile back.

"No thanks. Just browsing."

Then I quickly duck behind a display of saltwater taffy.

There was a moment earlier when our escape plan failed for the second time and I was suddenly plagued with thoughts like: What if we are trapped here forever? And how will my mom know what happened to me? What about my job? Who will pay my mortgage? Thank god Matt and I never did go through with our plans to get a dog.

But then I saw him.

It was just a brief glimpse. A flash of summer blond as he crossed the street and opened the door of the fudge shop. It felt as if time stopped, and the only thing left moving was my beating heart, shouting *him, him, him.* It was then I knew, with every fiber of my being, that I was supposed to be in Carson's Cove, and Spencer Woods was the reason.

Now, as I push aside two boxes of gingersnaps to sneak a peek of the next aisle over, I've calmed down a little bit. Then he strolls into view, and my heart starts beating so hard that I wonder if he can hear it.

He's so close. I could easily reach out and stroke the flannel of his button-down.

Instead, I stalk him like a creep.

His back is half-turned. He's reaching for a bag of artisan pancake mix, and as he does, the hem of his T-shirt lifts just enough to expose a small strip of skin above his khakis. It's one shade away from paper white, with a small trail of dark-brown hair, and I have to grip the shelf in front of me to avoid melting into a puddle on the fudge shop floor.

"Who are we spying on?" The heat of breath in my ear makes me startle so badly that I knock the boxes of gingersnaps with my hand, causing them to crash into the neighboring aisle.

Luce Cho, my mystery whisperer, stands with her arms crossed over her cropped tee and an amused smile on her lips.

"Luce. You nearly gave me a heart attack," I whisper-yell.

She rolls her eyes. "I think you'll survive. And it's nice to see you too. It's been awhile."

I stare at her for what is probably a good three seconds past normal, still absorbing this brand-new idea that I am now Sloan Edwards, and so far, none of the characters seem to find that weird at all. Like Pop, Luce doesn't look fazed to have been plopped back into Carson's Cove life. If anything, she looks relaxed. Dressed in a pair of cutoff shorts and a simple white T-shirt, she has her black hair pulled back into a long, glossy ponytail, and her skin is a deep golden brown, as if she's spent some time in the sun recently. She's aged in the last fifteen years, for sure. Her body is a little curvier. There is a sharper cut to her cheekbones. If anything, she's even more beautiful than she was at eighteen.

"It's nice to see you too," I answer, unsure how to navigate things with Luce. She and Sloan weren't really friends. Luce was Poppy's rival at everything from class president to cheer captain, and with Poppy as Sloan's designated ride-or-die, it made Luce her adversary by default. There was a time during season three when the two characters got along. They both applied for a program director job at the Carson's Cove Sailing Club, and instead of making them compete for the job, the general manager decided the two should split it. Luce and Sloan bonded over their shared loathing of the rich jerks who treated them like second-rate citizens, but that camaraderie faded early in season four when Spencer formed a crush on Luce.

They only dated for a couple of episodes before they broke up because they had sex. The entire school found out when Spencer told Sloan, and then Sloan in turn wrote this deep, heartfelt poem about the whole ordeal, which Poppy accidentally lost, resulting in it being read by the halftime announcer at the school football game.

Sloan was rightfully devastated by the whole situation but had pretty much moved on with her life by the end of season four, when it was clear that Spencer and Luce were just friends again.

Sloan is sweet and forgiving.

I, however, can hold a grudge.

"I heard you were back in town." Luce makes a show of giving me a once-over. "Carson's Cove's favorite sweetheart has come home. It's been all anyone can talk about." She takes a step forward. "So, what's your plan? Is this a permanent thing or a stop until you move on to bigger and better?"

The tone of her voice is so breezily nonchalant that I can't tell if she's genuinely curious or making a backhanded comment. Either way, I don't know how to answer this question as Sloan. I can't even really answer it for myself.

"No definitive plans quite yet," I hedge. "I have some unfinished business I need to figure out. I guess it depends on how long that takes me."

Luce narrows her eyes, but there's a smile on her lips as if she's about to laugh. "Some unfinished business, huh? Well, I guess I better let you take care of it. Hey, Spence—" She nods at someone over my shoulder. "Look who I ran into."

She shifts her gaze back to me. "I've got to take care of some business of my own, so I'll leave you two to catch up."

She winks at me before heading out the door.

"Sloan? Sloan Edwards, is that you?"

His voice is so deep that it pierces my chest, sending waves reverberating through my entire body.

Closing my eyes, I turn to face him, not yet mentally prepared for what is about to happen.

When I open my eyes, he's there: glowing like an apparition. Blue eyes. Blond hair. An NBC demigod, so beautiful that I'm sure I'm imagining him.

"It *is* you," he says. "I can't believe it."

As I blink, I realize that the ethereal glow is coming from the ice-cream flavor display sign behind him. But the man is real.

He holds out his arms.

I crash into them. Real and solid, he holds me tight to his chest.

He smells of ocean breezes. Of sunshine and hope.

Spencer Woods.

We embrace for what arguably are the best four and a half seconds of my entire life until he pulls away and shoves his hands into his pockets.

"I can't believe I'm running into you like this," he says, completely oblivious to the fact that I just drooled on his shirt.

His hair is a little longer than it was on the show, and there are a few fine lines on his forehead, but he is so undeniably Spencer still that I feel like I'm going to cry.

"How are you?" he asks. "What have you been up to? My god, it's been, what? Fifteen years since we last saw each other?"

I swear to god, his eyes are the same shade as the ocean outside.

"Are you sure?" I play dumb. "It can't be that long."

He laughs, shaking his head. "I know, right? But I did the math as I was getting into town. It will be fifteen at the end of the summer. It was that day I left for LA. Time flies, doesn't it?"

Apparently. My smile wavers for a moment as I think about how that last episode was truly how Sloan and Spencer ended their relationship.

Sheldon was right. They both deserve better.

"Hey." Spencer rubs the side of my arm. "Are you feeling okay? You're looking a little pale."

"I think I'm just in shock," I answer honestly, then remember

I'm supposed to be Sloan. "You know, being back here. Seeing everyone. So what's new with you, then? I feel like I've missed out on a lot."

He nods as if agreeing. "Well, I just got back into town this afternoon. I got tired of the acting thing and really missed this place, so I decided to come home. It feels so surreal to be back again after all this time. It hasn't changed a bit though."

He glances at his wristwatch. "Listen, Sloan, I really hate to do this, but I'm expected at my parents' house in ten minutes. We're having a big family reunion brunch. My mom has it all planned." He holds up the pancake mix, corroborating his story.

"But we really need to hang out. We still have fourteen and a half years to catch up on." He pauses. "Actually, what are you doing tonight? Have you been out to the islands lately?"

The islands.

Spencer and Sloan's favorite place.

My heart flutters with the kind of nervous excitement that only comes with the possibility of something special.

It's a feeling I haven't had in years.

Not since Matt.

"No plans," I say in answer to his first question. "And no, I can't tell you the last time I've been out there."

He smiles. "Then you should join us. We're going to take the boat out later. Paddle around."

I find myself nodding enthusiastically until, once again, my brain catches up.

"Us?" My voice is half an octave higher than a moment ago.

Spencer nods, oblivious. "Yeah. Me and Luce. I ran into her just before I saw you. I told her it had been such a long time since I was on the water, and she suggested we go for a picnic tonight. I'm sure she won't mind if you tag along."

I'm sure she will.

If there was any doubt about my current relationship with Luce, it's obvious now.

Not friends.

Foes.

As I picture Luce and Spencer out there on the water, alone, something inside me snaps.

This isn't the way it's supposed to be.

Sheldon is right.

Carson's Cove didn't end the way it should have.

Sloan and Spencer were denied their happily ever after, and I can't let it happen again.

The beginnings of an idea start to form.

Something I'd never even think to attempt back home.

Except I'm not back home—I'm in Carson's Cove, and what may have worked here before might just work again.

For most of season four Poppy was casually dating the captain of the football team, Chad Michaels, until she got bored and dumped him. Chad then asked Luce to be his date to the watermelon festival. Poppy was not thrilled about Chad no longer pining after her, so she invited Spencer—the only person on the Carson Cougars basketball team with a higher points-per-game average than Chad—to be her date. The two guys spent the entire episode trying to one up each other until Luce got so pissed off that she left, and Poppy got Chad back. Could that same logic work here?

To pull off the same setup, I'd need a date.

"I'd love to come," I tell Spencer. "But is it cool if I bring someone?"

9

JOSH

The front door to the Bronze is locked.

It's a mystery as to whether it happened automatically when I came out of it this morning or if someone's been here since I left. Either way, I'm stuck out here on the sidewalk.

Great, just great.

I glance around the main street. The bald-headed grocer is still outside his shop, and there are a few people leisurely strolling along the sidewalks. I could probably ask one of them if they know where the bar's owner is, but I'm not like Brynn—ready and willing to jump into someone else's life. I need some time to process.

For a moment, I consider the half-broken brick at my feet. The place has enough cracked and broken windows. One more won't make much of a difference. But my conscience won't let me do it. So instead, I walk to the corner, find a three-foot gap between the Bronze and the building next to it, and follow that all the way to the back until it opens up to a single-lane alleyway.

As I step out onto the pavement, a flash of orange jumps from the blue metal dumpster beside me and lands at my feet.

"Hey there, little buddy." I bend down to pet the orange tabby, but he dodges my hand and skitters away, hopping up onto a black wrought-iron staircase. My gaze traces the path of the steps that seem to extend all the way up to the roof, with a brief stop at a tiny balcony right outside an open window.

"A fire escape, huh?" I say to the cat, who does nothing but blink back at me.

My memories from this morning are still a bit muddled from all the cross-dimensional travel, but the view from that window looks an awful lot like the one I woke up to. If I were a betting man, I'd bank that it leads straight into Fletcher's apartment.

"Well, that's rather serendipitous."

The cat hops off the step as I grab the handrails and start to climb. Sure enough, when I reach the top, the window is open a few inches and slides the rest of the way easily when I lift it.

As I climb inside, I hear the low groan of creaking wood somewhere from within the building and pause.

Shit.

I'm a strange guy climbing through an open window.

What if I have the wrong apartment?

I freeze half-in, half-out as my eyes adjust to the dim lighting.

There's not much to the place. A bed. A nightstand.

There's a narrow hall that acts as a walk-through closet, with bars of clothes on either side and a door that opens into a small bathroom with a sink, shower, and toilet.

Yup. It's definitely the same room I woke up in, right down to the crinkled sheets.

My heart settles back into an easier rhythm as I climb the rest of the way in and survey the place for the second time this morning.

I walk through the closet and find a few pairs of jeans and some T-shirts. Basics. "You are no fashionista, are ya, Fletch?" I say, picking up a simple gray hoodie that looks as if it would fit me perfectly. But I set it back on the shelf, not quite desperate enough yet to wear some other dude's clothes.

I stare at the bed for a few seconds, torn between the urge to make it and the stronger desire to dive back in, with the hope that I'll somehow wake up back in Toronto with one hell of a story. But there's another sound—this one coming from downstairs. Maybe Brynn has already given up on her search?

I take the same route as this morning, out of the apartment's door to a second set of stairs that leads directly down into an open warehouse with a large U-shaped bar right in the middle.

The place looks even more run-down now that I'm coherent enough to give it a second look. The lighting is dim, but there's just enough of it to tell that the floors are gray polished concrete and the walls are the same red brick as the outside. The windows are big and airy, but every third pane appears cracked. I can't see through them, and it's not evident if they're intentionally frosted or just in desperate need of washing.

Brynn is nowhere to be found.

"Hello. Anybody home?" I call as I descend the final step. My voice bounces off the brick walls.

Nobody answers.

When I woke up here this morning, this place reminded me so much of my dad's old bar that I couldn't stand to be here. But now, as I take a closer, more objective look, I realize that although it's a family-owned bar with an apartment above, it's really not like Buddy's at all.

Buddy's may also have been dimly lit, but it was a cozy kind of dark. It was tucked into an alleyway, and its dim corners felt homey. And although the decor might've been considered a little dated, its matching booths and high-top tables were made of quality oak wood, and the green leather cushions were cleaned and conditioned nightly. In this place, the furniture is a hodge-podge of mismatched tables and chairs strewn about in no discernible pattern whatsoever. There's a stage along the far wall, but the velvet curtains are faded from what I imagine was a bright red to what is now a washed-out pink, which is fine because the stage itself is too cluttered with old Christmas decorations to be useful.

Buddy's might have had its flaws, but you could see the love my dad had poured into the place, from the perfectly polished beer taps to the Polaroids of my dad and all his regular customers that hung behind the bar, next to the shelf of trophies given to him by all of the local kids' sports teams he sponsored. Buddy's had an old soul. This bar has no soul at all.

I take a seat on one of the stools and run my hands over the wooden bar. My hands come away dusty, and I have this urge to grab a rag and wipe it down. My dad was always and forever wiping his bar.

I miss him.

It has been almost five years since he passed suddenly and too soon. I never got the chance to say goodbye. Instead, I poured my heart and soul into Buddy's, his other baby, hoping I could keep it, just like he did, as a place in the community for everyone to gather. A shrine to my dad and the great guy he was.

Instead, I lasted six whole months.

Until 2020 happened.

All the community events and creative ideas I could come up

with to keep the place afloat were no match for a global pandemic. My mom even sold her and Dad's house with the hopes that it would bridge the gap to when my dad's life insurance payment would pay out, but everything was shut down. The money took a whole year to reach our accounts, and by that time, I'd already sold the place to a restaurateur from Toronto who had the cash flow to hold out for things to turn around.

It's my fuck-up.

My biggest regret, and now I'm stuck in this place, wondering if maybe it's some kind of penance. A reminder.

Like at any moment, my dad's going to appear behind me and say—

"You better not be drinking my good Scotch."

The strange voice startles me so badly that I actually jump.

A woman stands behind me, arms crossed, silver hair pulled into a tight knot on top of her head. She's rail thin and maybe five feet tall, but I get the distinct impression you'd never want to face her in a bar fight.

"You must be Aunt Sherry."

She tosses her purse on the bar, then ducks underneath, popping up on the other side. "Have you started drinking already, Fletch? I know you've been off gallivanting around the country these last few years, but the rules haven't changed. No drinking before noon. I'm telling you right now: If you're going to stay upstairs and not pay rent, you're sure as heck not spending the day lazing around like an asshole. This place was hanging on by a thread before you went off to find yourself and is still hanging by that same thread now that you're back. I need help, not a freeloading nephew."

I hold up my hands, showing her that I'm not hiding a drink, acutely aware of how this scene seems to be eerily similar to four years ago, back home. That makes me want to clarify something right off the bat. "If you're worried about this place going under, I'm definitely not the guy to save it."

She pauses for a moment, studying me. "Who said anything about saving it?" She hands me a rag and a spray bottle. "I'm just looking for a body to clean the bathrooms."

I almost reach for the spray bottle. This is mostly because, despite her stature, Sherry is a very intimidating woman, and also because bathrooms are at least something I know I can handle. But then there's another creaking sound, and this time it is Brynn, pushing open the front door of the Bronze and then stopping when she sees Sherry and me.

"Let me guess," Sherry says, addressing Brynn. "You're looking for Fletcher."

"Yes," Brynn says. "Do you mind if I steal him for a little while? I have something important I need him for." Her tone is unusually sweet.

"What else is new?" Sherry rolls her eyes and grabs the spray bottle from the bar.

"Hey," I call after her. "I can do that later."

She keeps walking but turns enough that I can hear her just before she disappears into the bathroom.

"If I wait for you, Fletcher, all I'll get is older."

10

BRYNN

"That's not a boat. That's a bird."

Josh stands, arms crossed, staring at what is technically a boat but more closely resembles a giant plastic swan.

When Spencer suggested a trip to the island, I pictured a quaint little wooden boat. Ideally with Spencer and me rowing side by side, our shoulders bumping with every gentle swell of the waves. When we arrived at the marina, I was as surprised as Josh to see two paddleboats tied to the dock. The unobtrusive blue one was quickly claimed by Luce for her and Spencer, leaving Swanzilla for Josh and me.

"Why do we have to do this again?" Josh takes the seat on the right and holds out his hand to help me in.

"We agreed to act like Sloan and Fletch." I ignore his hand and step into the swan, holding my arms out for balance. "This is what Sloan and Fletch do. Besides, we haven't seen even a glimpse of Sheldon all day. We might as well enjoy ourselves."

The moment I say it, a giant wave comes. It rocks the boat so badly that I have to reach for the swan's neck to steady myself, but my foot slips, and I instead plummet toward the water. At the last second, two hands find my hips and pull. I fly backward, my fall broken by Josh's body as I land in his lap.

"You okay?"

I blink up at Josh, who is studying me with a concerned ridge between his eyebrows.

"Your thighs are like rocks."

He stares down at me. "I generally refer to them as quads, and I'm going to take that as a compliment."

"You go to the gym?"

Josh shakes his head. "No, I run. Ten kilometers every morning."

Huh. I never knew that.

"Why do you look so confused?" Josh asks.

"I didn't know you did things in the mornings. I just assumed you were nocturnal and worked at night and slept all day."

He rolls his eyes. "I'm a bartender, Brynn, not an owl. I get up to many things while you're at work, most of which you don't know about."

Now I want to know. I open my mouth to ask what else he does, but Luce calls out from her boat, "You two okay over there?," reminding me that my ass is still in Josh's lap.

Again, he holds out his hand with a "Sure you don't need help?"

I do not go to the gym in the mornings, nor any other time of day. My below-average core strength leaves me with limited options, so I take him up on his offer and use his hand as leverage to lift my hips and hoist myself back into my seat.

Luce and Spencer are already waiting for us in the middle of the bay, making slow, lazy circles in their little blue paddleboat. I'm so preoccupied with watching them that when I reach to steer our boat toward them, I don't see Josh's hand doing the same.

I place my hand on top of his a fraction of a second after he touches the joystick. And as I jerk my hand away, I note that in fewer than two minutes, we've already had two romantic comedy moments. All the things I'd hoped for tonight are happening. They're just happening with the wrong guy.

"Why don't you drive?" I offer, tucking my hand under my thigh. Josh accepts and steers us out into the bay.

Our swan is propelled by two bicycle-like pedals and steered with a single joystick between the seats. We follow Luce and Spence as they weave between a dozen or so islands that litter the small bays and inlets along the coast. Some are just tiny piles of rocks. Others have thick cedar forests you could get lost in.

"See that?" I point to one of the larger forested islands ahead. "I'm pretty sure that's the spot where one of my favorite episodes of all time takes place."

Josh's gaze follows my finger. "Let me guess, the cast gets ship-wrecked and washes up on the shore and has to survive the entire episode on nothing but coconuts?"

I ignore the sarcastic tilt in his tone.

"You're actually not far off. Sloan and Spencer are heading out for a paddle in a very regular, boring rowboat when they notice some storm clouds in the distance. But they ignore them, claiming they're still far away, and decide they have lots of time to picnic and get home even if the storm does blow in. However, once they dock, they both assume the other has tied up the boat. While they're eating, they notice their boat has floated out to sea in a current. They're trapped. And, of course, the storm starts to build and get closer. It's all very suspenseful."

Josh slows his paddling. "But let me guess, they're rescued at the last possible moment."

I smile. "By Spencer's dad, who spotted the empty boat from shore."

Josh nods. "I'm starting to understand what you meant when you said that the show always works out."

I hold out my arms. "That's the beauty of *Carson's Cove*."

"But doesn't it get boring?" He stops paddling completely, letting our boat get carried by the waves. "Don't you ever wish they threw in something you didn't see coming, just to mix it up a little?"

I don't know how to explain to him that the worst moment of my life was something I didn't see coming. How to explain that I was so unprepared for Matt's sudden change of heart that I planned a trip to Cabo to surprise him for his thirtieth birthday. The trip was scheduled for precisely a week after Matt's lawyer served me the divorce papers. I'd completely forgotten about it; it was too late to cancel. I went alone. I arrived at the Hacienda Blanca Resort and Spa and had to sleep in a bed covered in rose petals because I never let the hotel know I was coming solo. They called me Mrs. Dabrowski the whole week. I died a little inside every time but was too mortified to correct them.

"Nope." I manage to keep my voice even. "I don't find it boring at all."

We follow Luce and Spencer, heading toward one of the larger islands, whose jagged, rocky shore does not look all that paddleboat-friendly until we turn the corner to a small bay with a yellow-sand beach nestled between two rock jetties.

"There's no dock." I point to the beach. "How exactly do we get this bad boy on land?"

As if answering my question, Luce and Spencer pick up speed.

They aim their paddleboat straight at the shoreline, and their momentum carries them onto the sand. Their laughter as they come to an abrupt stop carries across the water.

"Shall we see what our girl is capable of?" Josh gives the side of the swan an affectionate tap.

He doesn't wait for my answer but instead uses his turbo thighs to paddle harder. I join in, and our swan picks up speed.

Just as we're about to hit the beach, I see Luce tip her head toward Spencer's—as if they're sharing a secret—and it flips a switch in a dark little corner of my heart.

He's not supposed to be with Luce.

Spencer is Sloan's.

Just as we're about to hit the shore, I place my hand on Josh's and jerk the joystick left. We hit the beach directly behind Luce and Spencer, slamming into the blue boat like a bumper car.

The impact from the crash pitches us both forward. Josh throws out his arm in a soccer-mom save, but he's not fast enough.

My face hits the back of the swan's neck with an audible *smack*.

"Fuuuuddge!" My hands instinctively fly to my nose as my knees curl up against my chest.

"I'm sorry." My voice is muffled by my hands. "I didn't mean to do that. Well, I kind of did, but . . ." I peer at him between splayed fingers. "Are you okay?"

Josh appears to be unharmed. "When I said 'let's see what she's capable of,' you know I was referring to the swan, right?"

I did. I don't know what came over me. I want to blame the jet lag. Or whatever you call this feeling of being completely out of my element.

"Oh my god, Sloan, are you okay?" Luce appears on my left. "You're bleeding. What happened?"

Sure enough, when I remove my hands from my face, they're stained red.

"There was a bee," I lie. "It was big. I hate bees."

Luce nods along, as if bee-sting avoidance is a perfectly logical explanation. Spencer catches sight of the blood and starts to gag. "Oh, crap." His hand covers his mouth. "I don't do so well with blood. I'm going . . ." He doesn't finish the sentence. He just bee-lines back to his boat.

To be honest, I'm a little caught off guard by his reaction. I would have expected Spencer to swoop in and tend to my wounds, maybe even scoop me into his arms and carry me to safety, but he keeps his distance, his head turned in the opposite direction as Luce returns with a paper napkin.

"Here." She hands it to me. "A little pressure should do the trick, but if you're not feeling well, we should probably go back."

"No." Any goodwill she may have earned with that kind gesture vanishes.

I'm not leaving her alone with Spencer.

"It's just a flesh wound," I insist. "I'll be good in a second."

Luce waits a moment and, when she's satisfied that the bleeding is under control, leaves to help Spencer unpack their boat.

Once they're out of earshot, I look at Josh, knowing I owe him an explanation, if not an apology. "I'm so sorry. That was super dumb. And borderline homicidal. I don't know what I was thinking. It's just that he doesn't belong with Luce, and I hate how she always gets between them. I was aiming for a light bump. Just to startle them."

Josh raises an eyebrow, amused. "I didn't realize Sloan had such a dark side."

I shake my head. "Yeah, that wasn't Sloan. Sloan would have

ignored them, then angsted over it later with Poppy. That move was pure Brynn. Am I still bleeding?"

I remove the napkin. Josh cups my face gently in his hands and tilts it upward to get a better look.

"You might end up with a shiner tomorrow, but I think you can pull it off. But please give me a heads-up next time you feel the urge to maim someone."

"That was my first and last attempt," I promise, crumpling the bloodstained tissue into my fist.

By the time we exit the swan, Spencer and Luce have set up a small picnic on the other side of the rock jetty. There's a big blue blanket covered with baguettes, artisan cheeses, and what look like homemade jams.

The paddling and the adrenaline from the crash have left me famished, so I settle next to Josh, who tears one of the baguettes into two and hands me half, which I smother in what I think is goat cheese and strawberry jam.

"Oh my gosh." I moan involuntarily as I bite. "This is incredible. It tastes like summer."

"Thank you." Luce bows her head, her cheeks pinkening. "It's my third year doing the jam, but the cheese thing is new. I'm still finding my groove."

"You made this?" I ask, still not fully understanding.

"She's a woman of many talents," Spencer answers, smiling at Luce in a way that makes the goat cheese in my stomach curdle.

"Yeah." Luce shrugs off the compliment. "There's a weird little corner of the web called CheeseTok. It's amazing what you can learn online these days."

Beautiful. Cool. Cheesemonger. How do I even compete?

"So." I attempt to change the subject. "It's been so long since we've all been together like this, right?"

I've managed to time my question while Spencer and Luce are mid-bite. They both make mouth-full motions with their hands and look at Josh, as if assigning him the duty of answering.

"Yup," he deadpans. "I can't remember the last time I saw either of you—in person, at least."

I shoot him a warning look, which he shrugs off with an expression that seems to say, *Well, what else did you expect?*

Luce, now finished chewing, turns to me. "So I heard you sold your business. Everyone in town was talking about it. You made sundresses, right?"

I guess so. Sheldon mentioned some sort of business in Boston. Sloan wore many sundresses and dreamed of being a designer, so I guess it all makes sense. "Yeah, I sold it to, umm, Anthropologie," I lie. "I don't like to go into the details too much. It's all very hush-hush."

"Lots of espionage in the sundress industry," Josh pipes up. "You can never be too careful."

"Well, I think it's great that you went out and did it," Luce continues. "I kind of pegged you for two kids and a golden retriever by now. It's a surprise."

I don't know what Luce is doing. Whether intentional or not, she's said the worst possible thing. I have to grit my teeth and make another jam baguette to keep my chin from going wobbly.

I'm over Matt. It took thirteen months and signed divorce papers for me to stop wanting him back.

The part I've never gotten over, however, is the dream.

I had plans.

We had plans.

And when the imaginary kids and the imaginary golden retriever suddenly didn't exist anymore, I grieved them like a death, and you never completely get over a death.

"So, Luce." Josh hands me another hunk of cheese and bread as he speaks. "When was the last time you left the island, and how exactly did you do it?"

I shoot Josh a glare. He's being way too obvious. But Luce doesn't seem bothered by his blunt question.

"To be honest," she says, "I can't remember the last time. I'm a farmer now, and since it's just me out on my farm, it's really tough to get away."

I nearly choke on my bread. "Did you just say you're a farmer?"

She laughs. "I completely get that face you're making. Not exactly what I thought I'd be either. But I took an agriculture course randomly at State, and I got hooked. I own a farm on the south side of the island. Two horses, three goats, and a whole bunch of chickens." She holds up the cheese. "This is from my goats, Betty and Veronica. You should come to see the farm sometime."

Spencer holds up his bread. "It's really beautiful."

"You've been?" The goat-cheese taste in my mouth turns bitter.

"Yeah." Spencer nods, answering my question. "Luce picked me up early. She gave me a tour before we met you guys."

A lump of something forms at the back of my throat. It feels almost like a tiny piece of bread is stuck. But it lingers no matter how much I try to swallow it away.

Tonight is not going how I wanted it to—at all.

Spencer shouldn't be canoodling with Luce. He should be pining after Sloan, waiting for the perfect moment to tell her how he feels.

"Well, Fletch and I had a great day too." I lean my head on Josh's shoulder, trying a different tactic.

Josh, however, does not get the memo and shifts his body so that my head slides off.

"We're calling that great, huh?"

I smile as if he's joking. "Totally. We drove around a bit. Went to Pop's."

Josh snorts.

I attempt to whack him in the ribs with the back of my hand. However, he fully anticipates this move, catching my fingers in his before I make contact. He holds my hand for a moment and squeezes before setting it down on the blanket.

It's a move I fully interpret as a warning message. A firm but clear *Watch it, Brynn.*

Spencer, however, sees something else.

All of a sudden, he shifts from giving Luce admiring looks to staring daggers at Josh.

"So, Fletch." Spencer sits up from his elbows. "You still working at the bar?"

Josh shrugs. "Apparently."

"And Sherry's still running the show?"

Josh nods. "She appears to be."

"I'll bet you're hoping to get out of there soon."

Josh laughs a slow, low chuckle. "You have no idea, man."

This is good.

Exactly what I hoped would happen.

"Josh is a really great bartender." I give Josh the same look Spencer gave Luce about the cheese.

"Who's Josh?" Spencer looks understandably confused.

"I meant Fletch," I say, backtracking. "Josh is just the nickname I call him sometimes."

Spencer's eyes darken. "Are you guys . . . together?"

"No, no, no. We're just friends!" I answer, then realize I like how he's looking at me. "But who knows." I keep my tone light. "Now that we're all back in Carson's Cove, anything can happen."

"I guess. . . ." Spencer takes a long sip of his water, and as he does, Josh leans in, his voice low.

"What are you doing?" he growls in my ear.

"Nothing," I answer through clenched teeth. "Just making conversation."

He pauses for another breath, as if he's thinking about saying something else, but instead leans away.

"What about you, Spencer?" I ask. "Did you like living in LA?"

Spencer smiles, as if he's been waiting for me to ask this question.

"LA has such an iconic vibe. Iconic people. Iconic scene. It's really . . ."

"Iconic?" Josh deadpans.

Spencer nods, oblivious. "Yeah, but I missed this place. I missed the smell of ocean air." He closes his eyes and takes a deep breath.

"Isn't LA on the ocean?" Josh asks.

"Yeah." Spencer opens his eyes. "But it's different."

There's a question I'm longing to ask him. Has he pined for Sloan the way I know she has for him?

"Was there, um, anyone special in your life while you were out there?" I attempt to sound nonchalant. "Like a pet? Or a girl-friend?"

Spencer shakes his head. "I'm not the kind of guy that can be fulfilled by a superficial fling or a one-night stand. I think I've always been the kind of guy who believes that when you fall in love, there's no coming back from it. You fall hard. All in. And it either stands the test of time or it wrecks you."

My heart clenches.

Josh snorts.

Spencer glares at him. "I know it's been awhile, but I have a hard time believing you're suddenly an expert on true love."

Josh looks amused. "And why is that?"

Spencer crosses his arms. "Well . . . your track record, for one. You've always preferred quick and easy to anything lasting or meaningful. You started that band and then never played after your first gig. You ran that entire campaign to be prom king and never showed up to prom. Mandy? Tammy? What was that other one's name? Jolene? How many times have you quit the Bronze because something better suddenly came up? I'm not saying you're a bad guy, Fletch. You just tend to prioritize your impulses over long-term commitment."

"Come on, Spencer." Luce hits Spencer in the arm.

He ignores her. "What? You don't agree with me?"

"No, you're right," Josh says with a completely straight face. "Classic . . . Fletch. And you know what? I'm feeling the impulse right now to depart this picnic a little early." He gets to his feet, brushing the sand from his shorts. "Thanks for dinner," he says, mainly to Luce. "I'm going to go for a walk." He heads off in the direction of the woods.

Spencer seems to shrug off Josh's sudden departure as Fletch being Fletch, but Luce watches him leave. When he's out of sight, her focus shifts to the sky and the sun that is now no more than a hazy hue of orange on the horizon.

"I'm thinking we should probably head back soon," she says, more to me than to Spencer. "It's getting kind of late, and the wind coming in from the east makes me think there's some weather coming."

Her eyes flick to the woods and then back to me.

"I guess I'll go get Josh," I offer, then realize my mistake. "Fletch. I'll go get Fletch."

She narrows her eyes but nods. "Thanks. I'll pack up the boat."

I get to my feet and follow the path Josh took earlier.

I find him at the very edge of the forest, sitting on a rock, ripping the bark from a stick he must have picked up along the way.

"What is wrong with you?"

He looks up at the sound of my voice.

"What is wrong with me?" He gets to his feet, throwing the stick to the ground.

"Yes. What was that? You just stormed off."

He crosses his arms. "What are you doing, Brynn?"

I hold up my hands, wondering why it isn't obvious. "I'm checking to see if you're okay."

He shakes his head. "No. I mean, what are you doing tonight? What was that weird game you were playing?"

"I'm not playing anything."

He takes a step forward, his eyes pinning me. "I'm not stupid. You were using me to make him jealous."

"I was not . . . I didn't . . ."

"That is what you actually want, isn't it?" He takes a step closer. "To date Mr. Dreamy Blue Eyes? Fall in love?"

My gut wants to brush him off with some noncommittal comment, like *They're more of a seafoam color,* but I can't get that out, nor can I get out the actual reason.

Josh shakes his head as if he knows an answer isn't coming and starts to walk off again.

"Okay, okay," I call after him. "Fine. I got to thinking about it more, and maybe we should give Sloan the ending she deserves."

"Unbelievable." Josh scoffs and keeps walking, but he doesn't get it. He doesn't understand.

"Please, Josh." My voice cracks, and this time he does stop. "It's really important."

I can see the rise and fall of his back as he breathes, but he doesn't turn around. "Why?" he finally says.

"Why what?"

"Why is it so important?"

I don't know what else he wants to hear.

I have many reasons, most of which I've barely admitted to feeling, let alone said out loud.

That Sloan deserved better. That she gave everything to Spencer, and he just walked away without a second thought. Without ever looking back.

Josh grows impatient and starts to walk away again.

"It's for me too," I call after him. "I need this, Josh."

I don't know why that came out. But as I turn the words over again in my head for a second time, I realize how true they are.

"This will probably come as a shock," I continue, "but my life hasn't exactly been going how I wanted it to." My voice wavers, and I consider leaving it there for a moment, but the rest rushes out before I can stop it. "I thought I found my person. But we never made it to the happily-ever-after part. Which means either that he wasn't the person I was meant to be with in the first place or that everything we've been told about love is complete and total crap. Because if that's the case, you can find your soulmate, your perfect other half, and he can wake up one day and decide, *Sorry. I changed my mind. This just isn't for me anymore.*"

Josh turns slowly back around, but as his eyes find mine, I chicken out and drop my gaze to the hollowed log at his feet. "And although I'm still a little jaded when it comes to love," I continue, "I'm not quite ready to start believing that it's all hopeless." I finally look over at him again. "And that's where Sloan comes in. Spencer is her guy. He always has been. If love doesn't work out for them, in a place like this, where everything works out exactly as it's meant to, well, then the rest of us are doomed."

I finally find the courage to meet Josh's eyes, but now his face is so unreadable that I immediately regret telling him all of this.

"Wow. That became much more of a monologue than I intended." I make a lame attempt at making my voice light. "Sorry for the rant. I'm being stupid, I know."

He takes a step toward me. "You're not being stupid at all."

His voice is low and soft, and his eyes are so kind as he reaches out his hand, as if he's going to pull me into a hug, but then stops, letting his hand fall to his side.

"Thank you," I tell him.

He shakes his head, confused. "For what?"

"For not making fun of me."

He folds his arms across his chest. "I don't exactly know what you or Sloan see in Spencer, but I'll help you if I can. I'll even act like this Fletch guy—the handsome and charming bartender everyone secretly adores—if that's what it takes."

I snort, and he smiles, as if that was the reaction he wanted.

"I don't know if I used the words *handsome and charming*." I walk toward him, closing the remaining gap between us. "But thank you, I appreciate it."

He holds out his fist. It takes me a second to realize he's looking for a bump.

As our fists connect, a cool breeze blows through the woods, sending out an echo of soft cracks of breaking branches.

"It's getting pretty late. I think Spencer and Luce want to head out pretty soon. You ready?"

He nods. "As ready as I'll ever be."

We walk silently out of the woods.

When we get back to the beach, the picnic is gone, and Luce and Spencer are nowhere to be found.

"Where'd they go?" I ask Josh as I notice that the blue paddle-boat is also missing.

"Maybe they decided to take a paddle around the island while they were waiting for us," Josh offers.

His words make logical sense.

I, however, know better.

We take a seat on the rock jetty and wait for five minutes, just to make sure, but there is no blue paddleboat coming around the bend.

Luce.

I knew it.

This was probably her plan all along. Wait for the perfect moment and then make a move to get Spencer alone.

"We better get going." I rise to my feet. "I don't think they're coming back."

Josh looks up at me, his eyes wide. "Um, Brynn. Did you remember to tie up our boat?"

Panic floods my chest. "Oh my god. Oh my god."

My eyes flick to the sky, searching for storm clouds as I start to run to the spot on the beach where we last left our boat.

"Hey, Brynn," Josh calls after me.

I slow just enough to turn my head back to him.

He's wearing an almost manic shit-eating grin.

"I'm just fudging with you."

11

JOSH

"This is so typical Luce," Brynn grumbles for the third time as we push the swan back into the water and climb in.

"She was probably planning it all night," Brynn continues. "Waiting for her perfect opportunity to get Spencer alone."

I'm tempted to point out that she already had Spencer alone when he went to pick her up, but I don't think Brynn wants to hear it.

"She's always in the way," Brynn goes on. "Always messing things up, and I'm sick of it. She hates Sloan."

This is where Brynn and the events of tonight don't jibe. I get that Brynn's watched this show a lot, but the Luce I met tonight and the Luce she's describing are not one and the same.

"She seemed pretty nice to me. It may have been something else," I offer. "A family emergency or something."

Brynn shakes her head. "You'll see soon enough, Josh, trust me."

I drop it. This is an argument I know I can't win.

We weave in and out of the islands in our best attempt to retrace our path from earlier. It's gotten dark since we left, and although the water is relatively calm, the warm breeze from earlier in the evening has cooled to a slight chill. I look over at Brynn. The smooth skin of her arms prickles with a rush of tiny goosebumps. She shivers.

"You warm enough?"

Brynn rubs the exposed skin of her arms with her palms. "Sloan's sundress designs may be fashionable, but they are not all that functional."

It occurs to me for the first time that she's not wearing the same clothes from this morning. "Where'd you get the dress?"

She pulls the hem down in an attempt to cover her knees, which is futile, as it rides back up with every turn of the pedals. "Sloan's closet. It's full of them. She's lacking in the hoodie department though. Believe me, I looked."

"Here." I take off my sweatshirt. "Fair warning, I have been wearing that thing since last night, but it will keep you warm."

She shakes her head, refusing to take it from my hand. "I'm fine. I don't need it."

"You're shivering." I place it in her hands. "Just take it."

Her eyes momentarily drop to my arms before she grabs the sweatshirt. "Fine. You win. And thank you."

She puts my sweatshirt on. We paddle for a few more minutes, and I start to feel tired. Not because of the exercise, but from the feeling that the adrenaline of the day has finally worked its way through my system, leaving me spent.

"It has been a day," I say, more to the universe than to Brynn, but she snorts as if in agreement.

"Is it weird that I keep thinking it's a dream?" I ask her. "Like I'm going to wake up at any moment?"

Brynn tilts her head toward mine. "At one point this afternoon, I convinced myself that I must be in a coma. That my lifeless body was hooked up to one of those breathing machines, and I was going to open my eyes and find myself in a bed at St. Mike's Hospital."

I let my hand skim the surface of the water. As I lift it back into the boat, it drips tiny droplets onto my lap. Very real droplets. "Is it what you thought it would be?"

Brynn's eyebrows knit together. "What do you mean?"

"This place," I clarify. "You've watched the show a lot. I assumed you had a preformed idea of what it would be like to live here. Is it everything you thought it would be?"

She leans her head back against the seat and stares up at the sky for a moment. "I guess so. It looks the same. Everyone is a little bit older, obviously, but yeah, it's Carson's Cove."

We paddle in silence for a few minutes. The night is quiet, and if you ignore that we're trapped in an alternate reality, it's kind of peaceful.

"I know this is a bit of a random question," Brynn says, breaking the silence. "But what is Fletch's room like?"

It's so far from the question that I was expecting that I don't know how to answer. "What do you mean?"

She shrugs, and I'm not sure if it's that my sweatshirt is so large on her or that she's intentionally shrinking down, but she almost looks embarrassed. "It's just that they never showed it on the show. Every other character had all sorts of scenes in their room, but Fletch never did. I've always been . . . I don't know . . . curious?"

I think about Fletch's room. "I wish I had more exciting details to tell you, but it's fairly basic. Bed. Nightstand. Closet and bathroom. It's actually eerily similar to my old apartment. Straight down to the stairs that go into the bar."

"You lived above a bar?" Brynn raises one brow, as if she doesn't quite believe me.

"I did."

"Actually?"

I gave Brynn my previous addresses and employment when I first moved in, but I was never sure how deeply she looked into it.

"My dad owned a bar," I explain. "I worked there and lived above it until he passed away a few years ago."

Brynn's face clouds with that familiar look of pity. "I'm sorry. Were the two of you close?"

"Very," I tell her honestly. "That whole thing with Spence and the Bronze earlier . . . It triggered some stuff that I thought I'd dealt with. . . ."

She reaches out and touches my shoulder. It's just a light press of her fingers, but I can feel their warmth beneath my shirtsleeve.

"This is going to sound completely clichéd, but someone once told me that grief is love with no place to go. Sometimes it bubbles up at the oddest of moments." She holds my gaze as she says it. "If you want to hear about an overreaction—my ex, Matt, used to have this bright-blue polo shirt that he loved. After we divorced, I automatically hated any man wearing a bright-blue polo. Didn't matter how nice the guy or the shirt was, the reaction from me was visceral." She pulls her hand away from my shoulder. "Now I can't even set foot inside a Best Buy."

She laughs, and I find myself laughing too until a thought occurs. "Hey. I used to have a bright-blue polo, but it went missing from the dryer shortly after I moved in."

Brynn turns her head, but not before I catch her smiling.

"Yeah, sorry about that. I'll replace it if we get back."

"*When* we get back," I correct her.

She shakes her head and closes her eyes, but when she opens

them again, her gaze shifts to something up ahead. "We're not home yet, but at least we can say we made it back to the marina." She points to a smattering of yellow lights in the distance.

Sure enough, as we get closer, I start to make out the outline of the boathouse, then the dock with a bright-blue paddleboat tied up next to it.

I follow Brynn's gaze to the person sitting on the end of the dock, khakis rolled up to mid-shin. Spencer waves as we approach.

"Hey! You guys made it. I was starting to get worried."

His open shirt catches in the breeze.

"You're sure about him?" I ask.

Brynn's smile falters for a second. Or maybe I just imagine it. "Of course I am. Why wouldn't I be? He's Spencer Woods. He's the dream guy. When he and Sloan finally get together, it's going to be . . . don't judge me for using this douchey frat-boy word . . . it's going to be epic."

This is what she wants.

I can't say I understand it.

But I recognize that look she had in her eye earlier when she said, *I need this.* It's the same look I saw in the mirror right after my dad died. When I was so determined to continue with his bar and not let his legacy die too.

I couldn't make that work.

But maybe I can help Brynn with this.

I make one last push to get us to the dock.

"You can't argue with epic."

12

BRYNN

Spencer reaches out his hand to help me from the boat and pulls me onto the dock, where my legs wobble like Jell-O, although it's unclear if the cause is his sudden proximity or the fact that my legs are still recovering from all the pedaling.

"So glad you guys made it back. It was wild." He nods at the blue boat tied up to the dock at a weird angle. "We started to take on water as soon as we left the beach. It was a slow leak, but we didn't want to chance it and thought it was safer to get back to the marina quickly. My guess is the damage happened with our little accident earlier."

My stomach sinks, and my eyes accidentally find Josh's as he steps from the swan to the dock. I half expect him to give me an *I told you so* look, or at the very least a shake of the head to remind me that not only did my boat rage cause the issue, but that I also blamed Luce.

But all he does is nod, as if agreeing with Spencer's assessment. "Glad you guys are all right."

I look around the empty marina, which appears dark and closed up for the night. "Where is Luce?"

Spencer points to something out at sea. "She thought a storm might be blowing in and wanted to check on her animals. Her horse, Westley, gets spooked if there's thunder. But I wanted to wait for you to get back. I was thinking we could walk home together, since we're neighbors." He glances at Josh. "Unless you have other plans."

My blood rushes with that heightened buzz I haven't felt in years. "Plans? Why would I have—"

Josh.

"Why don't you two go ahead?" Josh answers, as if sensing my dilemma. "I'm going to head back. I could use a solid night's sleep."

"Are you sure?"

Josh holds my gaze. "All good. I'm gonna take off. I'm really anxious to get home."

The double meaning isn't missed. He's not just helping me here. He's helping *us*.

We watch as Josh heads through the parking lot to the road that leads into town. He's a tiny dot in the distance when Spencer holds his arm out with a "Shall we?"

I take it, loving the fact that we're finally alone as we start off on a slow stroll down the dock and past the marina to the road.

Unlike the pristine pavement of Main Street, this road is made of rustic gravel. The streetlamps are spaced too far apart, leaving unlit gaps in between. We hit a patch of darkness, and my foot slips into a sizable divot, twisting my ankle and lurching me forward. But just before I hit the road, two strong hands grab hold of me.

"Whoa. Whoa." Spencer lifts me back onto my feet. "I almost lost you there."

The streetlamp hits his eyes at an angle that makes them sparkle, and I catch the faintest whiff of cedar forest.

"I wouldn't want that to happen again. I've really missed you, Sloan." He tucks a strand of hair behind my ear, and his hand lingers on my cheek.

"I've really missed you too, Spencer."

I'm not even playing the part now. I *have* missed him and the way I feel right now. Comfortable in these familiar surroundings. Safe.

His finger traces the hem of my sweatshirt. "I meant to tell you earlier; you looked so pretty in that dress."

I look down at my sweatshirt.

No.

Not my sweatshirt.

Josh's.

I want to be her. That sweet, agreeable girl that Spencer and the rest of this town adores.

My fingertips find the hem and pull. As the sweatshirt slips over my head, I realize it wasn't Spencer who smelled like the forest at all.

It was the sweatshirt.

"Ah." Spencer takes it from my hands. "There's my girl."

He reaches for my hand.

I expect warm fingers, a zing, or a tingle. What I get is a palm, cold and clammy. And as we walk on, the feeling travels up my arm and down my chest until it settles in my core.

I'm cold.

And I kind of want the sweatshirt back.

We continue to walk. The night gets a little darker as the trees thicken, forming a canopy until there's a break in the woods and the sky opens up again as the beach comes into view.

However, with no trees to shelter us, the breeze from the water picks up.

Goosebumps prickle up my arms, setting off an inner battle of Brynn versus Sloan. Warmth-seeking practicality versus the desire to be exactly what Spencer wants.

I hold out at first, telling myself it's just a breeze.

Mind over matter.

But then my teeth begin to chatter, clattering so loudly that I'm shocked Spencer doesn't say anything.

"So . . ." I attempt to distract myself from the cold. "Tell me more about LA. Was it everything you hoped it would be?"

Spencer smiles. "LA was LA, but it wasn't Carson's Cove." He slows his walk. "There's something really special about this place. There's nowhere in the world quite like it, and I'm just really glad to be back. Especially with you."

My heart swells with unabashed hope.

Our cottages come into view.

"Looks like we're home." Spencer nods at his own house, then Sloan's house next door, which is all dark save for the yellow porch light.

"It was great to see you again." He pulls me into a hug. My cheek crunches against his collarbone, and I get a whiff of something. It's definitely not cedar. But before I can place it, he pulls away. "We should do this again soon."

He doesn't move. Not closer. Not even farther away. He just stands there.

I do the same, rooted in my spot on the road.

This is the point where it happens. Where the scales tip in one direction or the other. Where we decide to take this a step further or call it a night.

Everything is perfect. The moonlight. The sound of the waves. All I need to do is reach out my arms. But for some reason, I don't.

He steps away first.

"Well, I'm beat. I'm going to head in. I'll see you tomorrow though?" He asks it like a question, and I find myself nodding along.

"Sure, yeah, me too. You know, all of that pedaling."

He starts to walk toward his cottage but stops halfway, turning slowly back to face me, and I think, *Here it is. Right now. It's the moment I've been waiting for.*

"Hey, Sloan."

He pauses, and my mind completes the sentence in a hundred different ways:

I've always loved you.

I've finally realized we are soulmates.

I regret leaving fifteen years ago without ever telling you how I felt.

He takes a deep breath, and I know whatever he's going to say next is going to change my life.

"I forgot to give you back your sweatshirt."

He tosses me Josh's hoodie, then waves and heads inside the house next door to Sloan's.

Fifteen years and still oblivious.

13

BRYNN

I wake to the sound of repeated knocking, growing louder and more agitated by the second.

With the grace of a newborn calf, I roll out of bed, then stumble down the hall and stairs, bleary-eyed and bushy-haired. I pass through the kitchen to the back door, where I pause with my fingers on the lock, my city-girl instincts forgetting for a moment where I am.

"Who is it?"

There's the sound of a deep sigh on the other side of the door.

"Only the best thing that's ever happened to you."

It's a female voice.

A voice that I'd know anywhere.

I fling open the door.

"Poppy?"

She stands poised with her hands on her hips. "The one and only."

Again I get that now-familiar thrill at seeing in the flesh a face I stared at on TV for years. Poppy was—and apparently still is—

Sloan Edwards's best friend. They met in the ninth grade when Poppy's dad got a promotion and moved Poppy and her twin brother, Peter, to the island from Minnesota. She knows all of Sloan's secrets and is Sloan's unwavering ride-or-die (with the exception of the first half of season two, where she had a brief relationship with Spencer).

"It's so good to see you." I take in the sight of her. "You look—"

She holds up a finger. "Choose your words wisely, woman. There is only one correct way to finish that sentence."

"Exactly the same."

She does. Poppy Bensen looks as iconic as she did at sixteen. Her hair is cut to shoulder length now, but it's still her signature cherry red, as is her lipstick, expertly applied and as meticulous as the quiet luxury look of her Chanel jacket.

She crosses her arms and sighs again, but there is a satisfied smile on her lips. "I was thinking *absolutely fabulous,* but I'll take it."

"Seriously." My eyes roam over her still-perfect complexion. "You haven't aged a bit."

Poppy breezes past me into Sloan's kitchen with a laugh. "Well, if you're talking to Chad, the reason is Pilates and the fact that sixty percent of my diet is bone broth, but between us girls, Doc Martin is doing Botox out of the back of his shop. You should stop by." She cups my chin with her hand, the pad of her thumb smoothing the spot between my eyebrows. "He's really quite excellent."

I ignore what might have just been an insult, too caught off guard by the diamond ring I just noticed on her finger.

"Oh, so you and Chad are still . . ."

Poppy holds out her hand, wiggling her fingers. "Sixteen years of wedded bliss, or whatever."

"Wow!" I attempt to school my shock. "That's really great."

Poppy and Chad were a huge controversy both on and off the show. After the Watermelon Festival incident with Luce and Spencer, Poppy started to lose interest again and dumped Chad a second time. Instead of just confessing his feelings like a normal jilted ex, Chad proposed. Two episodes later, they were married in a very elaborate beach ceremony at the tender age of seventeen. NBC got so many angry calls from disgruntled parents that they sort of avoided any storylines that directly referenced their marriage and pretended it never happened the entire last season.

I and a majority of the *Carson's Cove* fan forum assumed they would have broken up immediately after high school. Apparently, we were all wrong.

"So." Poppy takes a seat on one of the kitchen barstools. "I wasn't going to say anything, but you know me, no filter whatsoever." She leans forward, fixing me with her stare. "You've been back in the Cove for twenty-four hours now and have yet to call, text, visit, or send a carrier pigeon. I am starting to feel like you're avoiding me. Are you avoiding me?"

"No. Not at all. I was going to—"

"Good," she interrupts before I can finish. "Because Chad said I was acting like a psychopath and that you were probably still getting settled, but I needed to come right over and clear that up. Because Poppy and Sloan are back! And not a moment too soon. You would not believe some of the things I've been putting up with around here lately." She holds up a perfectly manicured hand and examines it.

"Like what?"

Poppy continues to study her nails. "Oh, you know. People being annoying and not knowing their place. But I can sleep with one less Ambien tonight because I have my sidekick back." She holds out her arms. "I missed us, boo."

I walk around the counter and wrap my arms around her. "I missed us too."

She pulls away, holding my shoulders. "There are, like, a million things we need to do now that you're back. You don't have plans today, right?"

My eyes subconsciously shift to the window and the blue cottage next door.

"Oh, sweetie." Poppy follows my gaze. "Don't tell me you're still pining?" She reaches up and cups my cheek. "Aw, you are. I don't get it. I mean, I get it; you were always the romantic type, but I kind of thought you'd have grown out of it by now."

I get a flashback of last night. Of how everything was so perfect until it wasn't.

"Maybe I should? It might be easier."

Poppy tsks. "Still got his head up his butt, huh? That doesn't surprise me. I guess you've talked to him, then?"

I nod. "Yes, we went out to the islands last night."

"A date?"

I shake my head. "No. Just hanging out."

She tilts her head to the side and studies me. "But did it seem like he could be into you?"

My insides twist into a familiar knot.

"I don't know. There weren't exactly sparks. He didn't seem interested in me at first, and then I got a little bit of an inkling on the walk home, but nothing happened. I'm kind of getting the impression he just wants to be friends."

She crosses her arms over her chest. "You and I both know that Sloan Edwards and Spencer Woods are meant to be so much more than friends. As much as I hate to admit it, you two are soulmates. When we were growing up, there was always something holding one of you back, but now that you're both back in town, it feels serendipitous. Like it's your time."

"Maybe."

"Oh, honey." She rubs my back in slow, soothing circles. "He might just need a little nudge. You two have been friends for so long. He still sees you as that girl next door that he's always known. That's always been your problem. We need to show him you're a woman now." She snakes her arm around my neck, pulling my head to hers. "And I know exactly how we're going to do it."

"The salon?"

Poppy holds out her arms in a way where the proper accompanying expression should be *ta-da*.

"Where else would we go?" She takes me by the hand. "If you want Spencer to finally realize he's in love with you, you've got to address the most obvious problem." She pets my head, but her fingers get caught in my curls.

"My hair?"

She nods. "And a few other minor things. Just trust me." .

Curl Power is Carson's Cove's one and only beauty salon. It was a regular set on a show that tended to have a disproportional number of formal events, from seasonal proms to dancing telethons, fashion shows, and pageants.

Poppy throws open the front door, having presumed my trust is secured, and waves to Lois, the salon owner and head stylist, who stands behind a maroon leather spinning chair as if she has been expecting us.

"This is 911, Lois." Poppy flings her purse into an empty chair. "Sloan is in need of some hair therapy. She's desperate."

I take a seat and try not to take offense at the use of the word *desperate* or the way that Lois frowns as she picks up one of my dark curls between her fingers and then promptly drops it.

"I'm thinking the works," Poppy says as Lois covers me with a vinyl apron. "Blonder, straighter, maybe even some extensions, and could you do something about the . . ." Poppy points to the space between my eyebrows, to which Lois responds with a knowing "Of course."

Lois promptly pulls over a wheeled cart filled with blow-dryers, styling tools, and containers filled with bright-blue liquid. She reaches down to the bottom shelf and pulls out a piece of cardboard with tiny swatches of hair in varying shades of blond. She hands it to Poppy, who points to a swatch that I swear reads Malibu Sunrise, but I can't confirm, as Lois swiftly takes the card and tucks it away.

"I've cleared my whole morning," Lois says to Poppy, leaving me to wonder why I have yet to be included in this conversation. "It may take a few attempts to strip all of this out," Lois says. She pulls a lock of hair straight and then lets it bounce back into a curl. "I'm thinking a relaxer. Definitely bleach. I'll also heat up the wax."

She moves to leave, but I hold up my hand. "Hold on." My heart is beating rapidly. "Bleach feels a little bit drastic, don't you think? I was thinking more along the lines of a trim. Maybe a few highlights?"

I watch in the mirror as Lois and Poppy exchange a look behind me.

"Sweetie." Poppy leans forward to level her head with mine. "You know I think you're beautiful, right?"

She nods and holds my gaze until I nod too.

"Good. All I'm suggesting is that we make your outer beauty match your inner beauty so that everyone in town can see how gorgeous you really are." She leans in closer, her lips right at my ear. "Especially Spencer."

Whether she meant to or not, she has said the magic words.

And just like magic, I'm closing my eyes, nodding, and even convincing myself I actually want this extreme makeover as Lois begins to paint my head.

An hour later, I have a head covered in tinfoil.

"Smile." Lois pokes at my frowning lips. "You'll be beautiful before you know it." She adjusts the final foil, then wheels the dryer over and places the bowl over my head. "Isn't it every girl's dream to walk into the salon and then come out of it as a whole new woman, ready to turn heads?"

Her question remains rhetorical as she flips the dryer's switch, and all conversation is drowned out by the low whirring.

She isn't exactly wrong.

An ugly duck turning into a beautiful swan is a tale as old as time.

Especially in a place like this, where Lois's makeovers always seemed to be at the center of any girl-must-reinvent-herself storyline. Even Poppy's.

When she first moved to Carson's Cove, Poppy was a homely nobody with big ambitions, but her dirty-blond hair made it hard to stick out in a town where everyone was a ten. Until the day she walked into Lois's salon, where Lois dyed her hair to its signature fiery red. From there, everyone began to notice her. Her make-over made her confident. It was the catalyst for a high school career of overachievements: cheer captain, prom queen, and Chad Michaels's girlfriend.

Maybe Poppy is right, and it's exactly what Sloan needs.

Three hours later, my resolve begins to wear thin. I'm still in Lois's chair. I've been stripped, cut, straightened, bleached, and glued and have grown a new appreciation for why makeovers in movies are always shown as montages. I'm exhausted, and I've completely lost feeling in my right butt cheek, so when Lois asks, "Are you ready to see?," my breathy "Yes" is said more out of desperation to get out of this chair than excitement. But as she turns me toward the mirror, I hear a gasp and realize that the sound is coming from my own mouth—because the woman staring back from the mirror is undeniably beautiful.

It takes three more blinks to fully comprehend that the reflection is, in fact, me.

Gone are my dark curls, replaced with silky smooth waves the color of honey.

My eyebrows are pristine.

My lashes are long and dark.

I look stunning.

I look like Sloan.

As Lois said, it should be a dream come true, and yet . . .

"Do you love it?" Poppy throws her arms around me and squeezes. "Oh my god, Lois, you made her cry."

Poppy pulls back and places a hand on her heart. My fingers swipe my cheeks and, sure enough, come away wet—yet I wouldn't say I'm filled with joy.

"You look absolutely lovely," Lois says, wiping away her own tear. "Oh, gosh, just like a princess."

"No," Poppy says, shaking her head. "Like a queen."

There's a notable pause as Poppy and Lois exchange another look in the mirror. It's just a brief glance this time, the slightest dip of the chin in a knowing nod, but I get prickles up my arm.

"So, Sloan, babe." Poppy sits on the arm of my chair, her tone unusually high. "I'm not sure if I mentioned it earlier, but Lois and I are co-chairing the pageant this year. As you probably already know, it's the seventy-fifth anniversary—a really important year. So, as you can imagine, it's crucial that our contestants hold up a certain image. Now, I know the last time you entered . . ." She exchanges another look with Lois. "Well, it didn't turn out how you hoped, but Lois and I are both thinking that with your new hair and look, maybe this year is your year. . . ."

She continues to talk, but her words blend into an indecipherable *womp womp womp* as I unpack what I think she is suggesting.

The Ms. Lobsterfest pageant was the climax of the last *Carson's Cove* season finale. It was supposed to be Sloan's chance to show Spencer and the rest of the town that she was no longer the quiet, innocent girl they once knew. She had grown up, become a force to be reckoned with, and was now ready and willing to take on the world—starting with the boy next door.

Her whole plan started off so perfectly. She transformed herself from an unassuming girl next door to a full-blown beauty queen using YouTube makeup tutorials and a well-executed chignon. She even found her dead mother's evening gown from twenty years earlier when she was crowned, and it fit like an absolute dream.

During the pageant, Sloan wowed the judges in the question round. Her years of studying and love of books culminated in thoughtful answers that poked just enough at the important issues of the day without actually offending anyone. By the evening gown round, the crown was in sight.

The competition had been whittled down to Sloan and three other girls: Poppy, Luce, and some random cheerleader who never had an official name. But when Sloan went to change into her dress, it was nowhere to be found. Then, when she tried to go out on the stage in her casual wear, Lois disqualified her.

From there, everything fell apart.

Sloan lost her confidence. She didn't tell Spencer how she felt, and he left for LA without ever knowing her true feelings.

"So." Poppy nudges my arm, reminding me that we're still in the middle of a conversation. "What do you think?" she asks. "Are you in?"

That pageant was Sloan's darkest moment and, I imagine, her biggest regret. Yet the thought of actually participating in one gives my feminist heart the creeps.

"I don't know." I look up, intending to catch Poppy's eyes in the mirror—but there is someone else staring back at me.

He's wearing a hot-pink Curl Power T-shirt that's a size too small, and it strains against his chest as he washes a woman's hair at the sink. His own normally wild hair is combed into a smooth pompadour with a streak of shirt-matching pink running through it that was definitely not there yesterday. I may not have even recognized him if not for his eyes: light green and piercing.

"Sheldon?"

He doesn't say anything; he keeps on washing, but his eyes remain on me.

As if he's waiting . . .

The pageant.

I'd almost forgotten.

He wants Sloan to win.

It's the linchpin in his meticulously laid plan. Win pageant. Win Spencer. Brynn and Josh get to go home.

"So, what do you think?" Poppy draws my attention away from Sheldon for a moment.

"Think of what?" I ask her, having missed half of the conversation.

"The pageant," she says. "Are you in?"

I ignore her and look back to the sink again, but this time, Sheldon is gone.

My eyes scan the sinks and the rest of the chairs. The door. There is no sign of Sheldon anywhere.

"I need to go."

I move to stand, but Poppy pushes me back down. For such a tiny person, she's freakishly strong.

"Sloan, come on."

"Can we talk about this later?" I make a second, far more successful attempt to get to my feet, but as I move to the door, Lois and Poppy block my path.

"No. This is important."

I need to find Sheldon.

"Whatever you want, Poppy. Just tell me, and I'll do it."

Her smile is immediate. Her hands find mine, and she squeals. "Oh my god, this is going to be so much fun. Just like old times."

I tear the vinyl cape from my neck and power walk toward the front door. As I push it open, I hear her yell, "Sloan Edwards, Carson's Cove's next Lobsterfest queen."

I look down at my arms, and I have goosebumps.

14

JOSH

Sherry may preach a no-drinking-before-noon rule, but she definitely doesn't practice it. It's either that or the raccoons around here have excellent taste in Scotch.

I find an eighteen-year-old bottle of Dalmore open on top of the bar, along with two glass tumblers that look like they've been filled and then emptied of their contents. There are no other signs of Sherry—or anyone else—in the bar this morning, but I can hear low voices that grow louder as one of the doors to what I think is a storage closet opens and two people emerge. The first is Sherry, with her hair pulled back like yesterday, dressed in jeans and a light-blue T-shirt with the Bronze's logo embroidered over her heart. I recognize it only because it matches the T-shirt I stole from Fletch's closet this morning. She spots me, and we make brief eye contact, but she otherwise ignores me as she holds the door open for a middle-aged man with a beer gut and an impressively thick beard. He's carrying a large aluminum ladder. His shirt says *Larry's Lighting* in thick black letters, which I read as he sets the ladder down next to the bar and helps himself to a second, very generous glass of Scotch. I presume Sherry didn't offer this one, which I have deduced solely from the low growl coming from Sherry's throat that's aimed in Larry's direction.

"I'm glad you're fixing the lighting." I attempt to make pleasant conversation. "It was getting tough to see in here."

Her growl, which is now very much aimed at me, grows louder. "You'll have to learn to live with the lights we have, seeing as I just sold Larry our ladder."

As if illustrating Sherry's point, Larry sets his now-empty glass down with a clink, picks up the ladder in question, and throws us a friendly wave before carrying it out the front door.

"Dickhead," Sherry mutters under her breath.

"Why'd you sell him the ladder, then?" I ask, and immediately regret my question as Sherry shoots me a glare that I swear I feel all the way through to the back of my rib cage.

"Because he paid fifty dollars for it." She ducks under the bar and reaches for the open Scotch bottle to screw the lid back on.

I shake my head, still confused.

"Lights are useless when you can't pay the electric bill, Fletch." Sherry rolls her eyes, as if disappointed that she has to explain further. "You know how I feel about useless things." She makes no point of hiding the fact that this time she means me. And although I know she's trying to make light of the situation, I can't ignore the familiar churning in my gut.

I'd bet that if you asked her right now, Sherry would insist that the two of us have nothing in common. But I've stood in her metaphorical shoes. The ones where you make the choice between paying your water bill or your waitstaff. There's never an easy option.

Sherry comes out from behind the bar, weaving the same path to the front door that Larry took only moments ago.

"Where are you going now?" I call after her.

She stops but doesn't turn around. Instead, she sighs. "If the Lord spent a little less time on your looks and a little more on your brains, my life may have turned out differently. I'm going to pay the electric bill. God knows why though. This place might actually make some money if you can't see your hand in front of your face."

"Is there anything you want me to do while you're gone?" I offer. "We've probably ruled out anything involving a ladder, but otherwise, I'm pretty decent with my hands."

Sherry turns around. Her left eyebrow is making an impressive arc. "I think it's probably better for everyone if you keep your hands to yourself. Just don't burn the place down while I'm gone, okay?"

She's gone before I can promise I won't.

I stand for a few moments, just staring at the empty bar.

The place has its flaws. It's dirty and dimly lit. There is actual graffiti on some of the walls, and it's not the intentional *this place is edgy* kind.

Anyone walking in would say it is a lost cause, and yet . . .

The giant U-shaped bar in the center is crafted with the type of precise woodworking you just don't see anymore. There's a great mix of beers on tap—a few local crafts alongside the big brand names that everyone loves. The liquor selection isn't too bad either. Some top-shelf bottles. A few others that will get you drunk for cheap. All of them are mixed together on the same shelf, just hanging out.

This place could be so much more with a few small adjustments.

Before I fully realize what I'm doing, I find myself ducking behind the bar to find a rag. I rationalize it by telling myself that

I owe Sherry for room and board, and I'm making up for it with hard labor.

The dust and watermarks are easy enough to tackle. It takes half a bottle of Bar Keepers Friend and some serious elbow grease, but whatever genetic trait my dad had that made him compulsively wipe down his bar has clearly been passed to me because two hours later, it's gleaming so beautifully that my dad would be proud.

I find a storeroom under the stairs with some cleaning supplies, a few extra kegs, and a big sink, where I rinse the rags and clean my hands. When I get back into the main area of the bar, there's a blond woman sitting at one of the barstools, waiting.

"Sorry, but we're closed," I call to her.

She turns her head. "I'm tight with the bartender. We crossed a space-time continuum together. It's bonded us in weird and wonderful ways."

Her words and her voice crash together inside my brain in a too-familiar way. "Brynn?"

She swivels the rest of her body around to face me.

It's Brynn, for sure, but she looks different. Her dark, wild hair is gone. She's wearing makeup, I think. Everything about her is perfectly polished.

"You're blond."

She rolls her eyes as she reaches down to adjust one of her high-heeled shoes. "And you need to work on your compliments."

I shake my head, all the right words currently escaping me. "Sorry, I didn't expect . . . What happened? What did you do to your hair?"

She fingers the strands, the smile from before slipping from her lips, and once again, I regret my word choice.

"It's called a makeover, Josh. Or you might be more familiar

with the more colloquial term *glow-up*. You know? A radical transformation to highlight what was hidden in there all along?" She
slides off the barstool and begins to walk toward the door. Halfway there, she spins back around and holds up a single finger.
"Actually, that's not even why I'm here. I came to tell you that I
saw Sheldon this morning."

My pulse spikes.

"What did he say? Did he tell you anything important?"

Color rises in her cheeks. "I was getting my hair done. I
couldn't get to him in time. He was there in the salon one minute,
and then he took off before I could talk to him."

"Where is he now?"

She glances at the door. "That's the million-dollar question. I
looked in every single shop on my way over here, but the dude
has vanished. He's a sneaky little fu . . . uhhhh." She groans.

We need to find him. "We should keep looking. Come on."

I grab her hand.

We walk back out onto Main Street. It's another beautiful
blue-sky day. The grocer is watering his vegetables again. The
woman is walking her goldendoodles.

The picturesqueness is almost irritating.

My eyes scan the street. The pharmacy. The fudge shop. Even
the ladder where a pair of town workers are adding giant plastic
crustaceans to the lamppost with the Ms. Lobsterfest banner.

No sign of Sheldon at all.

Until I spot a blond busker outside the general store.

"Over there," I tell Brynn and run toward him.

"I'll catch up," she yells. When I turn around to see why she's
not following, she holds up one of her high-heeled feet. "It's like
walking on two toothpicks. The best you're going to get from me
is a brisk walk."

I abandon her and sprint across the street, but just as I reach the spot where I saw Sheldon, I realize that in the brief moment I shifted my gaze to Brynn's footwear, he somehow managed to disappear.

"Where did he go?" Brynn reaches me a moment later, her breathing shallow and labored.

"I don't know." I scan the street one last time. "He couldn't have gotten far. Maybe he ducked inside?"

The bell above the door to the general store chimes as I open it. There is a man with a mustache behind the counter, ringing up the items of a tall female. Neither of them look up as we walk in, so we head to the back, walking the length of the frozen-food section, checking each of the aisles.

There's no one down the first two, and when I check the third and fourth, they're also empty.

"We could ask Mr. Wilder." She nods toward the front. "He's the guy behind the counter."

We start to move down the aisle toward the front, where the man with the mustache is now bagging the woman's groceries. Their heads are bent low in conversation. But as she leans across the counter, I catch a very clear "It's about time that place was dealt with," and something about the tone of the woman's voice makes the hair on the back of my neck prickle.

I stop. Brynn does as well, tilting her head toward me with a curious glance as I crane my neck to hear them better.

"That place has been an eyesore for years," the woman continues. "I, for one, will be happy to see it go."

Mr. Wilder shakes his head. "Yeah, but that Sherry Scott is a good woman. She just never seemed to be able to get people in there after the accident. It's sad. I can't remember the last time a business went under in this town."

Sherry.

They are talking about the Bronze.

I get that sickening feeling of acid crawling up the back of my throat.

I know the Bronze is not Buddy's.

It's not even a real bar.

But it still feels like the past is repeating, and once again, I can't stop it.

Brynn places her hand softly on my forearm, almost as if she can sense the turmoil going on in my head.

"Do you know what they're talking about?" I whisper, suddenly needing to know more. "The accident he mentioned. What happened?"

She nods slowly. "I think they're talking about season five." Brynn's eyebrows draw together to the point where they almost touch. "Every season, *Carson's Cove* always seemed to have this one tragic episode. It was usually a veiled PSA about the dangers of underage drinking or drug experimentation. The setting was usually at some wild, out-of-control party. Some minor character would wrap their car around a tree or drive off a cliff, and the rest of the cast, who were usually drinking as well, would all learn a valuable lesson about the dangers of alcohol or drugs. In season five, the cast went to the Bronze with fake IDs, and even though Fletch knew they were underage, he served them alcohol. This one guy . . . I can't even remember his name, but he got into his car, even though Spencer told him not to drive, and he killed an innocent extra on his way home."

My stomach twists. "What happened after that?"

Brynn pauses as if thinking. "To be honest, nothing, really. Everyone was understandably upset for the rest of the episode, but then it ended, and everyone was over it by the next one.

Fletch was given some community service. There was a scene with him in a jumpsuit collecting trash, but that was it. But now that I think about it, there really weren't any more episodes set at the Bronze after that."

And now the place is going under.

Rationally, I know it's not my fault. I wasn't there. I'm not really Fletch. It happened on a fictional television show. But this place is messing with my head. And for some reason, I feel this sense of responsibility.

"Are you okay?" Brynn's fingers lightly brush the inside of my wrist.

"Yeah." I shake my head. "I just wish there was something I could do."

"I wouldn't stress too much." Brynn glances at the counter. "Mr. Wilder is a bit of a gossip, and even before the accident, the bar was pretty run-down. It's one of those things that's unfortunate but probably inevitable."

That doesn't sound like much of a happily ever after.

"We should probably go." Brynn inclines her head toward the front door.

I nod, suddenly needing air.

We walk toward the exit, but as Brynn reaches for the handle, the door swings open before she touches it.

"Spencer, hey!" Brynn freezes in place as Spencer steps inside.

"Hey, Sloan. Wow!" His eyes comb the length of her body. "You look beautiful. Is that a new dress?"

Brynn spins around, the bottom of her skirt billowing out around her in a circle.

"It is. And thank you for noticing." She throws me a look, as if saying *See? That is how you're supposed to compliment a woman.* Whether she intended it or not, it brings Spencer's focus to me.

"Oh, hey, Fletch. Didn't see you there. Are you two going somewhere?"

Brynn shoots a panicked look in my direction. "No . . . I mean, yes . . . I mean, no, I'm not going anywhere with Fletcher specifically, and yes, I was shopping for . . ." She picks up a package of double-A batteries. "These."

"Batteries?" His brows knit together in confusion.

Brynn looks down at the package in her hands. "Yes. I was changing out all of the batteries in my flashlights. You never know when a storm is going to blow in."

Spencer nods as if he agrees. "You really don't."

He starts to take the batteries from her hands but pauses. "Did you do something different with your hair? Whatever it is, I like it."

Brynn twists a loose lock around her finger. "Yeah, I went and saw Lois at the salon. I was in the mood for a change."

He smiles at her. "It suits you."

He shoots a glance in my direction before returning his attention to her. "Hey, do you remember the old observatory up on the hill?"

Brynn's breath catches. "Yes, of course."

"Well, I was thinking of heading up there to check it out. Would you maybe want to come with me? Just the two of us."

I can't see Brynn's face, but I notice her voice shifts up an octave as she says, "Um, yeah. I would love that."

Again, he looks in my direction. "How about tonight? I can pick you up at seven."

I watch the back of Brynn's head as she nods. "Seven is great."

He holds the front door open for her. "Great. It's a date."

She walks through, abandoning both me and her batteries. "It's a date."

I stand for a moment, alone in the aisle, until the guy behind the counter clears his throat. "Fletcher. Don't usually see you in here. Is there anything you need help with?"

My eyes scan the shelves. For a moment, I consider picking up Brynn's batteries, but there's a box of industrial string lights beside them that are marked down on clearance.

They give me an idea.

What did Brynn call it? A glow-up? A radical transformation to highlight what was there all along. I don't know if I can manage *radical,* but then again, I have nothing but time right now.

I hold up the box. "Just these."

When I get back to the Bronze, I head straight to the storeroom, where I find the cleaning supplies.

By one o'clock, I have the floors swept and washed. By three, all the windows are clean. By five, my arms are killing me and I definitely do not smell like Cedar Lumberjack, but I have managed to clear out almost all of the stage, leaving enough space for a band.

It's far from a miracle makeover, but the place looks exponentially better. I get to work next on the string lights I picked up from the general store, stringing them back and forth from the rafters until there's a full canopy of tiny lights.

It looks like a blanket of stars, casting a soft orange glow over the bar that makes the whole place look warm and inviting. I'm so engrossed in my project that I don't hear Sherry come back until she's standing right behind me.

"What the heck happened in here?"

I jump, yet again, at the sound of her voice.

"Do you sneak up like that on everyone? Or is it just me?"

She ignores my question and instead does a slow 360-degree survey of the bar.

"I had nothing I needed to do today," I attempt to explain. "So I started to clean the bar, and then I just kept on going, I guess."

She draws a long, deep breath in through her nose. I've yet to determine if she's angry or pleased.

"Are you on drugs?" she finally asks.

Great question. "Definitely still a possibility, but I don't think so."

I get a slow nod and another full turn. "Well . . . it looks good in here. Who knows? Maybe a few more will wander in now that you can actually see what you're drinking. I guess we will find out on Friday."

Friday. Right. I noticed when I was cleaning the windows that the posted hours are only Friday and Saturday nights.

Maybe it's seeing how far I've come today, or maybe it's the comfort of being in someone else's life, but I have this sudden urge to see what this place is capable of.

"Is there a reason you're only open on the weekends?"

She turns to the bar, grabs the Scotch from earlier, and pours herself a shot. "I only have the energy to wrangle you into working Friday and Saturday, Fletch. By Sunday, I'm too old and too tired." She downs the shot in a single gulp.

"I know it's Sunday, but what if I opened up tonight? Just to see if anyone does show?"

She looks around the bar and then shrugs. "Fill your boots. Just don't expect too much."

15

BRYNN

There's a soft *tap tap tap* on the kitchen door at exactly seven o'clock.

I peek out the window and see Spencer outside my kitchen door, ready for our date to the observatory, wearing a freshly pressed pair of khakis and a soft linen dress shirt with the sleeves rolled up his arms, and I have to grip the kitchen countertop as my heart beats so damn hard that for a moment I think I'm actually going to swoon—that is, until I notice the bicycle behind him.

I assumed when he said "Pick you up at seven" earlier that he meant in his car. Now, as I stare out the window, I notice that Spencer is holding his bike, and my swooning shifts to panicking because I do not bike.

Or at least I haven't since I was in middle school, and even then, my skills were questionable.

My brain immediately seeks out an excuse. Injury? Weather? Strong belief that it's next to impossible to look cute while riding?

But by the time I get outside, Spencer is already inside Sloan's shed, pulling out her mint-green cruiser.

"It's such a beautiful night." He wheels the bike toward me. "I thought we'd go for a spin. I know how much you like to ride."

I stare down at my sundress. Today it's a two-piece matching set made of pale-pink fabric with yellow flowers. It has a smocked-waist top and a full skirt that falls to the knee. No one in their right mind would look at it and think it's cycling attire.

Except for Sloan.

That was her thing.

Zipping around town in her cute dresses, hair flowing in the breeze.

And now her thing is my thing. So I smile my best Sloan Edwards smile and grab the handlebars.

"Sounds like fun."

Fun is maybe a bit too ambitious of a word.

I almost crash three times before we even get to the end of Sloan's street.

Then I do crash.

While I'm making a sharp left, my sandal slips off the pedal, and my fall is broken by an overgrown hydrangea bush.

When Spencer comes to pull me out, I blame a nonexistent pothole.

Post-bush, things do take a slight upturn.

By the time we're out of the main area of town, I'm starting to get the hang of things. I'm even thinking dangerous thoughts like *Maybe they weren't so wrong when they coined the phrase "It's like riding a bike."*

Then we hit the hill.

Here's the thing about observatories. They work best with an unobstructed view of the sky. Which means the tops of hills are prime real estate. Which means two-point-five miles straight up on yet another questionably maintained road.

"Stupid forking pothole," I swear as I narrowly avoid another hydrangea incident.

Spencer cruises up beside me and flashes an easy smile. He's not sweating or swearing or struggling for oxygen. "What did you say?"

"Just admiring the view," I gasp out between labored breaths, nodding at a field of horses.

There are two brown mares grazing in the grass next to the fence.

"Are you feeling okay?" He leans forward to get a better view of my face. "You're kind of turning purple."

I'm also starting to see little black specks at the edge of my vision. I was not cut out for this much cardio.

"Just peachy." I wheeze in a deep breath of much-needed oxygen.

"Great." He pops up off his seat, picking up speed. "I'll race you the rest of the way, then."

He takes off before I can tell him that's easily the worst idea I've ever heard. A few moments later, I hear a loud "Wahoo" from up ahead and silently pray it's him claiming victory.

By the time I reach the top, he's already parked his bike and is pulling his backpack off.

I stop at the edge of the parking lot. It's mainly because I'm out of breath and need to catch it before I attempt conversation again, but it's also to take in the scenery.

The observatory is on a stretch of flat rock surrounded by grass and low-lying shrubbery. There's an unobstructed view of the whole island and ocean as far as the eye can see. The observatory itself is a large cylinder made of gray stone, with dark ivy running up the side and a big white globe protruding from the roof.

It was the setting for one of the most iconic and swoony episodes of *Carson's Cove*—*ever*. That episode contained the kind of moment that makes you wish you could self-inflict some sort of temporary, targeted amnesia so that you can live it for the first time over and over and over again.

Funnily enough, this heart-clenching moment wasn't even between Spencer and Sloan; it was between Fletch and Maya Colletti.

For most of the third season, Fletch had a bit of a drug problem. He ran track at Carson's Cove High and hoped to get a scholarship—until he failed his biology midterm. He started buying Adderall to study. Over the course of the season, he became more and more addicted to it. The climax came when he punched a wall at Poppy Bensen's after-prom party and tried to cover it up with Mr. Bensen's painting of *The Last Supper*. No one spoke to him for weeks.

Enter the new girl: Maya Colletti. Very beautiful. Very opinionated. A little bit pregnant. Her soon-to-be-teen-mom status made her an instant outcast, so she and Fletch became fast friends. She helped him get clean through tough love and an epic monologue in the middle of a thunderstorm. So when her parents found out about the soon-to-be baby and tried to ship her off to a home for unwed mothers, Fletch proposed.

He wasn't the father. But he took Maya to the observatory, filled it with candles, got down on one knee, and promised that if she took a chance on a screw-up like him, he'd take care of her and her baby forever.

America swooned and fell in love.

Maya said no.

Her refusal left Fletch moody and devastated for most of season three, while Maya left the show (possibly because the actress who played her got a role in an action movie franchise).

As much as I know that it's completely unrealistic to expect candlelight and soul-baring declarations of eternal love, I have high expectations for my date with Spencer.

What I get is the same blue blanket from last night spread out on the floor and a playlist of John Mayer hits played from Spencer's iPhone.

"I packed us a picnic." Spencer pulls several containers from his backpack. Unlike last night's picnic of Luce's homemade bougie cheeses and bread, this feast includes a few brown glass bottles, some tiny jars, and a box of something that appears to be carbohydrate in nature.

"Here, let me help you." I sit down beside him, chastising myself for being silly. He's obviously put a lot of thought into the evening. I should learn to manage my expectations.

"What's this?" I open a plastic container and take a sniff. The stench makes me gag, which I cover with a cough, snapping the lid and tossing the container off the blanket. "I think that may have gone bad."

Spencer retrieves it with a laugh. "It's called kefir. Everyone in LA eats it. It's great for digestion."

I digest just fine on my own. And I stand by my earlier assessment that something has gone seriously wrong inside that container, but I ignore it and instead turn my attention to the silver flask Spencer is handing to me.

"Here. Try this. I brought an entire case of it with me when I came back from LA. It's impossible to get outside of California. I think you're really going to enjoy it."

I take a swig. I think there's a part of me that was fooled by the flask and expected booze. So when the taste of rotten apples hits the back of my mouth, it's twice as bad.

"What do you think of the kombucha?" he asks.

It tastes like sadness.

I don't tell him this, of course. Mostly because my mouth is still full and both unable and unwilling to swallow.

Instead, I draw a deep breath through my nose, telling myself that on the count of three, I'll force it down.

One . . .

Two . . .

I'm too late.

My gag reflex overpowers my sheer will. Instead of swallowing, I spray. Like a Saturday-morning cartoon. All over the picnic blanket.

"I'm so sorry!" I pound my chest with my fist. "That must have gone down the wrong way."

Spencer reaches up and tucks a kombucha-soaked strand of hair behind my ear. "It takes a little while to truly enjoy kombucha, but don't worry, I've got lots of other stuff for you to try."

I watch as he unloads several more containers from his backpack, each with a painstakingly long explanation of how hip/healthy/hard to find the item is. The entire time, all I can think about is how slimy and wet my hair is behind my ear and how desperately I want to untuck it. I honestly think this date cannot get any worse.

Then it gets worse.

"Try this." Spencer holds up one of the containers, then watches with genuine enthusiasm as I try his homemade kale chips, followed by these brown disks that he claims are crackers but are more like patties of birdseed that stick so badly to the inside of my throat that I almost, almost consider taking another swig of kombucha just to get them down.

"Are you enjoying the picnic?" Spencer asks as I force down the final bite of birdseed.

"Mmmmm hmmm" is all I can think to answer, because even though I've wanted Spencer and Sloan to finally go on a date for years, I cannot deal with this food. I just can't.

I'm searching for my next excuse. I'm full. Allergic. Feeling the onset of a stomachache. But before I can come up with something plausible, Spencer reaches into his backpack and pulls out yet another container. This one is a brown paper bag with the logo for the Carson's Cove general store on the side.

"I got you something." He holds out the bag.

I hesitate, terrified that there's more food inside. But Spencer continues to hold it out until I relent and take it from his hands.

"Earlier, when I saw you at the store, you said you were there to buy batteries for your flashlights, but then you forgot to buy them," he explains. "I figured I'd pick a couple up. I know how much you used to hate the dark."

Sure enough, when I peer into the bag, there's no food inside. Only two small flashlights. They're plain and silver, and yet they make my insides gooey. This is the Spencer that I have been waiting for. The guy who knows his best friend down to her core. Who remembers that the night Sloan's parents died, the power was out, and she had an irrational fear of the dark for years.

"Spencer, this is really so sweet. I'm touched. Thank you."

Spencer dips his head to hide the faint blush on his cheeks. He reaches over and pulls one of the lights from the bag, flicks it on to prove that it works, and then places it back inside. "I know it doesn't bother you as much as it used to, but I figured I'd have these handy just in case. Be right back."

He gets to his feet and disappears behind a door, and a moment later, there's a loud machinelike whirring. All of a sudden, the roof opens up, and the sky above is filled with a million twinkling lights. It's spectacular. He settles onto the blanket beside me. Neither of us says a word. We just stare. Exist. Bask in the reminder of how insignificant we are. As I gaze up at the soft shimmer of the Milky Way, I feel it. That catch in my chest. That assurance that somehow Spencer knew me and how much I'd love this moment. That knowledge that all of this is somehow meant to be.

When I finally tear my eyes away, I find him staring at me with an unreadable look on his face.

"Thank you for this." My eyes drift back toward the sky. "It's really beautiful, and I love it."

Spencer shifts his weight, moving him another inch closer so that our hands are almost touching.

"I need to ask you something." His voice is so deep that I can practically feel it in my core.

"Anything."

"Are you and Fletch . . ." He leaves it there. It takes a full breath before I realize that he's asking if Fletch and I are together.

"No. Absolutely not."

He lets out a relieved breath. "Good. I thought I noticed something between you last night, and when I saw you two together today . . . well, I wanted to make sure."

"We're just . . ." Friends? Roommates? Co-victims in Sheldon's deranged plot? "We're not like that."

His eyes soften at my answer. "Well, I'm relieved to hear that."

He drops his head, and a lock of blond hair falls across his forehead. I reach out, on instinct, to brush it away. He looks up, catching my hand in his.

He tugs me toward him. And somehow, I know exactly what's about to happen. I've seen that look in his eyes before. Watched it on repeat when my own life was falling apart. "That's very good. Because if you were, I couldn't do this."

I brace for stars. Firecrackers. The feeling that I'm falling. That I'm coming home.

His lips press hard into mine, clanking our teeth together.

His tongue parts my lips.

It's wet. And swirling. And tastes like kombucha.

And still swirling.

My stomach doesn't bottom out. My head doesn't swoon. If anything, I'm acutely aware of the rough texture of his sandpaper tongue.

And then it's done.

He pulls away. "Wow, Sloan. That was . . ."

Bad.

Really, really bad.

I want to tell him that it must have been a fluke. That we weren't yet properly calibrated. We were too long apart. We weren't quite back in the Sloan-and-Spencer groove.

He reaches out and grabs my hand. "That was incredible."

I stare back at him, dumbfounded, searching his face for something to explain why the kiss I just experienced and the kiss he just described do not match. But his eyes are all big and blue and absolutely sincere.

"I hate to say this, but we should probably head back." He holds out his hand to help me to my feet. "It's getting really late."

I help him pack up the picnic, dissecting the kiss in my head.

Is he lying?

Or is he too polite to admit the kiss was terrible?

Because it *was* terrible.

It definitely wasn't the epic culmination of five long seasons of sexual tension.

So what was the problem?

Was it him? It can't be him. He's Spencer Woods.

It must be me and the fact that I am not Sloan.

Or worse, that underneath it all, I'm no longer capable of a toe-curling kiss.

I've suspected, long before arriving in Carson's Cove, that my relationship with my ex broke me more than I thought. That maybe there's something wrong with me. That all of my failed dates were my doing and this bitter taste in my mouth that I can never seem to swallow is because I am no longer capable of feeling that spark. That I had my shot at love and I blew it and this is just how I exist now, stuck in that sad place where I know what love feels like, but it's on top of a big hill, and my pedaling legs no longer have the stamina to reach it.

I'm so lost in my own thoughts on the ride back into town that I actually ride my bike with zero issues down the terrifyingly dark hill. I'm so in my own head, figuring out where exactly I went wrong tonight, that I have to swerve when Spencer stops unexpectedly at the edge of town.

"What is going on there?"

He points at the Bronze, which is all lit up. People are milling outside the door, and from what I can see, there are more inside as well.

Spencer rolls his bike up closer. I can hear the sound of classic rock every time someone opens the door.

"I thought that place was essentially shut down. I wonder what happened?" he asks, meeting my eyes for the first time since the kissing incident.

A funny feeling settles in my stomach.

I have a very good idea.

16

JOSH

"Hey, buddy, can I get a . . . ummm . . . uhhhhh . . ."

A short guy with thick black glasses squints at the row of liquor bottles behind me.

"Need some help?" I offer, stepping aside to give him a better view.

He looks up and blinks at me twice. "Actually, yes. I don't know what to order. I haven't been in too many bars."

"Well, then, we're gonna start with your ID."

I wait while the guy fishes his wallet from his back pocket and slides a Massachusetts license across the bar top. The picture matches his face. Danny Strong. Born in 1994.

"What is in a cement mixer?" he asks, staring at something on his phone. "I'm not much of a drinker."

I grab a pint glass. "Why don't we start you off with a beer, then? A nice, easy-drinking lager, and we'll see how that goes?"

He nods, and I feel a swell of pride as I pull the tap.

The place is decently busy. Exceptionally busy if you compare it to what I estimate it pulls in on a regular night.

The string lights make a huge difference. There's a cool, laid-back ambiance to the place now. Everybody who has walked in here tonight has been a little apprehensive at first. But once I get a drink in their hands, they become one of the many relaxed, happy faces.

That is, all but one.

Brynn plunks down onto a barstool in front of me just as I hand Danny his beer.

"What. Did. You. Do?"

She's scowling, arms crossed over her chest. And although I fully interpret her meaning, I play dumb.

"Do? Not sure I get what you mean."

She holds out her hands. "There are people in here. Drinking. Dancing."

"It's a bar." I shrug. "You told me I needed to act like Fletch, so I am. I'm bartending."

She scoffs. "I did not— I didn't mean—" She lets out a de-feated huff, leaning back in her seat. "How did you do it? I don't think I remember it ever being this busy."

The place is even fuller than it was the last time I looked around, with more pouring in through the front door.

I point to the guy on stage with a guitar singing acoustic ver-sions of old pop songs. "I found him busking outside the hard-ware store. I chased him down, thinking it was Sheldon again. Things got awkward until he said he was a one-man band with-out a stage. I told him I was a guy with a stage that needed a one-man band. Things just escalated from there." I pull a flyer from a stack on the bar. "Then I made a bunch of these and handed them out around town."

She takes the paper from my hands. "Who are Seth and the Hungry Dingos?"

I nod at my busker. "Well, that's Seth. There are no actual Dingos. I added that part because *Just Seth* felt a little plain."

She watches him play for a moment. "He's not bad."

"He's not good either, but no one seems to care."

It's true. The moment I say it, two women get up and push their table to the side to form a dance floor. They dance to Seth's best attempt at an old Carly Rae Jepsen song. Out of the corner of my eye, I catch Danny downing the last of his beer. He slams the empty glass on his table, takes a deep breath, and dances over to the women. There's a moment where I'm not sure how his bold move is going to play out, but then they widen their circle, and their dance party of two becomes a threesome.

Brynn, who has seemingly been watching the same scene, drops her head into her hands and groans.

"You okay there?" I grab another beer glass, fill it with a hoppy IPA, and set it down in front of her.

She looks up. "I'm fine. It's just that everything is backward." She takes a long drink. "That guy dancing is Danny Strong. He was captain of the math decathlon team in this one episode where Fletch joined to avoid detention and discovered he was secretly gifted at math. Danny isn't supposed to be dancing with cheerleaders." She looks at Danny, then back at me, but then does a double take, her attention shifting to a table on the other side of the dance floor. "Wait, is that Mrs. Chuang the librarian and Doc Martin the pharmacist?" She pushes up high in her seat, leaning across the bar to get a better look. "They're not sup- posed to be together either. And you!" She turns to me and glares.

"What did I do?"

"Fletch isn't supposed to be the sexy, popular bartender get- ting eyed by his former English teacher."

"Who's my former English teacher?"

Brynn points across the room. I spot an older blond woman looking at me from the corner. When our eyes meet, she winks.

I snap my focus away from her. "Wait, did you just call me sexy?"

"No." Brynn rolls her eyes. "Well, technically, yes, but you know what I mean."

I try to hide my smile. "I don't. You'll have to enlighten me."

She growls. "Forget it. All I'm saying is that the Bronze isn't supposed to be the happening spot in town, and Spencer and Sloan aren't supposed to be . . ."

The rest of her thought is cut off as she sighs deeply into her glass.

"I'm going to go out on a limb and guess it wasn't a dream date with Malibu Ken?"

She looks up. "No, not exactly. I don't know." She slumps to the side, resting her chin in her palm. "Maybe I set my expectations too high? Or maybe things are going exactly as planned, and I need to be patient and let our story build a little more. I guess I was just expecting our first real date to be magical. Instant sparks, you know?"

She drains what is left in her glass and sets it down on the counter. I reach for it at the same time she pushes it toward me, causing our hands to touch. There's a sharp jolt of electricity between us.

"What was that?" She pulls her hand away, cradling it to her chest.

I shake mine. "Maybe that was the spark you've been looking for?"

Brynn rolls her eyes.

"You said you wanted magic." I scuff my feet and then give her another zap on the arm.

"Magic? Or science?" She gets to her feet and mimics my own scuffing motion from a moment before. "Bibbity, bobbity—"

Bang.

The moment Brynn's finger connects with my forearm, there's a loud pop from somewhere in the bar.

Then complete blackness.

"Ahhhhh!"

The bar is filled with screams, including Brynn's. But as our eyes adjust to the new dark and the noise begins to die down, I catch Brynn whispering, "Please tell me I didn't do that."

"No," I answer, knowing exactly what has happened. The all-too-familiar feeling of failure rises up my throat.

This is insane.

It's like my own personal *Groundhog Day.*

A living nightmare I keep recalling over and over.

The electric bill.

Sherry implied she was behind on paying it, but I had hoped it was a joke. Her cutting sense of humor. But now I know the bills aren't getting paid, and if they are cutting the electricity, the water is next. Then the bank comes calling—if they haven't already. There's nothing I can do here. I was stupid for even thinking a couple of good nights could turn things around. This place is too far gone to save. It's—

"Hey." Brynn's hand reaches across the bar and pokes me in between my ribs. "Do you know where the fuse box is?"

The fuse box?

"It's in the storeroom, I think. But that's not the issue, Brynn, it's way worse—"

A beam of light flashes up from beneath Brynn's chin. It illuminates her face from underneath, giving it an eerie orange glow.

"Take this." She flips the flashlight around and hands it to me.

"I have another one in my purse." As if to back up her point, she reaches into her bag and pulls out a second light. "The storeroom is beside the bathroom, right?"

I open my mouth to tell her I'm probably going to have to shut down for the night. This place is beyond help. But she's already gone, weaving her way through the crowd toward the storeroom. I have no choice but to follow her bobbing light all the way to the back of the bar.

"In there?" she asks, cutting the beam of her light to the closed storeroom door.

"Yeah, but . . ." I tell her as she pulls the door open, ignoring me. Her flashlight beam scans the walls until it lands on a small gray box. I follow her over to it and watch as she opens the cover. There are a dozen or so black switches inside. Only one is set in the wrong direction. Brynn reaches out and flicks it with a loud click.

There's a collective cheer from the bar, followed by the sound of a strumming guitar and Seth's voice, amplified by the microphone. "I think this calls for a cover of 'Dancing in the Dark,' don't you?"

There's another cheer as Seth plays the opening notes.

Unlike the bar outside, the storeroom remains dark.

"Crisis averted." Brynn tucks her light between her arm and rib cage as she uses both her hands to snap the door of the fuse box shut. It closes with a soft click, which is followed by a soft "Oh, sugar" as her light slips out from under her arm, hits the floor with a metallic clunk, and then rolls underneath an aluminum shelving unit filled with cleaning supplies.

I flash my light beam to the spot where we last saw her light. "Here." I try to hand her my light. "Let me get it."

"No, I'm good." She drops to her knees and reaches under the bottom shelf, then retracts her hand quickly, bringing the lost light to her chest.

I reach my hand down to help her up. "Do you always carry multiple flashlights in your purse?"

She takes it and lets me pull her to her feet. Suddenly it feels like there's a lot less air in here. "I think maybe I should start. Carson's Cove does seem to love its power outages. . . ."

Her voice trails off, but her hand still lingers in my palm.

The heat of it mingles with the strawberry scent of her shampoo.

She's so close that I can hear her soft puff of breath as she exhales.

And although we're standing in the dark, it's as if a light comes on inside my head and suddenly I'm seeing everything differently.

Brynn visibly shivers and pulls her hand away. "I think I got another shock, just there. You should really do something about the floors."

I don't think the floors are the problem.

I shake my head, clearing away the semblance of a thought still rolling around in my mind.

When we get back out to the bar, there is a steady stream of thirsty customers looking to placate their dramatic blackout experience with more beer.

Where earlier in the night I could afford to stop to chat or make a beer recommendation, now I'm pouring drink after drink with no time to pause in between.

Seth keeps playing one hit after another.

The dance floor is so full that I can't even see the base of the stage.

And the more people dance, the thirstier they seem to get.

And as fast as I'm pouring, I can't seem to keep up.

I'm at the point where I'm seriously considering finding a way to track down Sherry to come and help me because the happy faces are getting increasingly annoyed as they need to wait for their next rounds. I don't even realize I've run out of glasses until I reach for a pint and my hand comes back empty.

"Here." Brynn lifts a tray of clean glassware onto the counter beside me.

"Where did that come from?"

She points at the dishwasher. "I ran a load while you were pouring whiskey shots. You were running low."

I want to thank her, but the bar is crowding up again, and people are starting to get pushy.

"Fletcher, a refill on my Diet Coke when you get a second?"

"Do you know how to make a dry martini?"

"I liked that beer you recommended earlier. What was it called again?"

"Two Buds, would ya, Fletch?" a tall football-player type calls.

Before I can reach for them, Brynn has the beer fridge open and the caps off.

"What are you doing now?"

Her response is to grab a pint glass and pull the beer tap for a local IPA. "I'm helping you." She glances at the packed bar. "This town likes beer way more than I imagined. I'm a little afraid to see what happens if they don't get it."

She serves the beer in her hand to the waiting customer, then picks up a bottle of cheap rum. "Besides"—she flips the bottle in a complete 360-degree turn and catches it—"not to brag or anything, but I spent two whole summers working behind the bar at

Applebee's." She tosses the rum bottle again and attempts to catch it on the back of her hand. Her aim is off, and the bottle hits her knuckle and then falls to the floor, where it catches the edge of the mat and rolls—still intact—toward the dishwasher.

"Reflexes of a cat," she says as she bends to pick it up, then goes back to pouring the rum.

Fortunately, the next two hours are free of major disasters. No power outages. Ample glassware. Brynn is a blur in my peripheral vision, serving beer, talking to customers, and smiling.

I could have used her back home at my dad's place. Not that an insanely busy night was ever my problem, but I like this feeling that she's got my back. That we have this ability to communicate without actually saying anything.

I hand her the vodka she's about to ask for. She slides me the malty stout my next customer doesn't even know he's going to order yet.

She tosses me a bar rag to wipe the spot where my last customer sloshed his beer. "Hey, we're running low on—"

"Moosehead. I know. I got it."

By the time I have the keg out of the storeroom and hooked up, it's two A.M. The place has cleared out some, but there are twenty-odd bodies still finishing their drinks or slow-dancing to the playlist Seth left running after his last set.

I ring the old brass bell hanging from the corner of the bar.

"That's all for tonight, folks. Get home to bed and then come back tomorrow and spend your money. If you need a safe way home, come and talk to me. Otherwise, good night."

Twenty minutes later, the place is basically empty.

The only other person left inside is slumped over next to the taps, one arm extended toward an empty glass. She's pulled her hair up into a sweaty bun, but she missed a piece that is stuck to her neck. The blond is fine, but she looks better like this. Less hair, more of her face.

"I don't know how you do this every night." She lifts her head up just enough so that she can look at me. "It's exhausting. My cheeks hurt from smiling. My legs hurt from squatting, and my emotions hurt from being so nice to everyone."

"Thank you," I tell her, swallowing down the sudden swell of emotion that catches in my throat.

She looks up, a little surprised, as if she's picked up on it. "I've got your back, Josh Bishop." She smiles. "You can repay me with undying devotion and a free beer."

"Done."

I loved everything that happened tonight. If I could copy this night a thousand times and repeat it day after day, I probably would.

I pull open the fridge, grab two chilled bottles, and hold out my other hand to her. "If you can stay on your feet for another two minutes, I'll show you something cool. It will be worth it. I promise."

Brynn groans but takes my hand. I pull her to her feet and lead her up the stairs to Fletch's room.

She stalls in the doorway, "Uh, Josh . . . That cool thing you were going to show me, it isn't . . ." Her eyes drift to the bed.

I cross the room to the window. "No, it's out here."

I lift the window and step out onto the fire escape. But instead of climbing down to street level, I head up, waiting for her at the top, watching her face as she climbs onto the roof and discovers what I found earlier this afternoon.

"Holy smokes. Look at this place."

Her reaction is the same one I had when I found it. It's a run-of-the-mill roof for the most part. It has a simple concrete floor and a three-foot-high brick railing that runs around the perimeter. There are a few air vents and what looks like an HVAC system. But the view is incredible. You can see the entire length of Main Street and the twinkling lights of the beach houses in the distance. Then, if you look up, there's a sky full of stars above.

"So, was this my discovery?" I ask her. "Or are you about to tell me about some episode of *Carson's Cove* that happened up here?"

She shakes her head. "I've never seen this place before. Wow, you can see the entire town." She braces her arms on the ledge and leans forward. "And right into Doc Martin's apartment. Wow . . . I guess he and Mrs. Chuang are definitely together, and nope—" She takes a quick step back. "Definitely didn't want to see that." She whips around to face me, not realizing I'd followed her to the edge. Our sudden proximity makes her teeter, and her arms brace against my chest.

She doesn't step away or remove her hands, and I swear that I can feel the beat of her heart through her fingertips.

"So tonight was good?" Her voice is unusually high.

"It was."

"We work well together."

"We do."

I feel a jolt of something: a crackling between my ribs.

Brynn's mouth falls open in surprise, like she's felt it too, and it's as if something changes. Like the air shifts between us.

I can't read her.

I can't tell if what I'm feeling is entirely in my head or if she's right there with me.

To be honest, I don't even know exactly what I want to happen.

Her eyes meet mine, and she inhales as if she's about to say something. And I find myself also holding my breath.

"I kissed Spencer." Her confession comes out in a rush.

Okay, that was definitely not what I wanted to happen.

"Earlier, at the observatory," she continues. "We were looking at the stars, and I kissed him. Or maybe he kissed me. Either way, kissing definitely happened."

Any confusion from a moment ago becomes painstakingly clear. She's here for Spencer. Her leading man. I am just the bartender, making everything complicated.

"Well, that's good, right? That's what you wanted?"

She finally steps away, removing her hands and leaving the place where she touched me suddenly cold.

She walks over to an air vent and sits down on its concrete ledge. "It *is* what I wanted, but—" She looks up, but her eyes seem to focus on something off in the distance. "It wasn't exactly a great kiss."

My blood rushes. It feels a little like relief. And although I hate that Brynn is upset, I'm glad their kiss sucked, and I think that says a lot about me as a person.

"I know I have this tendency to build things up in my head." Brynn's eyes meet mine again. "I overanalyze a lot. But I don't think I'm doing that now. Josh, it was really bad."

I join her on the air vent. "First kisses can suck. There's a lot at stake. I'm sure it was just a fluke."

She shakes her head. "But what if it's not?" She turns toward me so that her knee is pressing against my thigh. "When my ex, Matt, left me, I'm worried it . . . it broke me. And I don't mean it in that overused metaphorical way people usually reference when doing hard things. I changed, Josh. I decided at that moment that

I'd never again let someone hurt me the way he did, and now I'm wondering . . ." She looks up at the stars for so long that I'm not sure if she's going to complete her sentence.

"I'm wondering if I've done something permanent. Like my heart got confused, and while it was protecting itself from ever breaking again, it also severed the part that lets me feel at all."

She closes her eyes and takes a deep breath. "Sorry . . . You brought me up here to hang out and have a beer, and I turned it into therapy. I didn't mean to unload on you like that." She shakes her head.

"It's okay. I know exactly how you feel."

She looks up, her eyes big and round. "You do?"

I don't want to get into this now. I prefer to forget about it completely. If a drug existed to strike an entire year from my life, I'd probably take it. That time right after my dad died fucked me up in ways I'll never be able to really explain. But she's shared something really personal with me tonight, and I don't want her to think I don't understand how hard that is to do.

"I told you my dad had a bar. It was a place that was really important to him, and I inherited it after he died and wasn't able to make it work."

"That really sucks, Josh, I'm sorry."

It may be the alcohol, but I like the simplicity of her answer. When it happened, it seemed like everyone had an excuse. The pandemic. The insurance company. No one just came out and said, "Fuck, that sucks," and it's really the only thing that I needed to hear.

She closes her eyes and shakes her head.

"What?" I ask, wondering what she's thinking.

"I just had a very different idea of you in my head . . . until tonight." She opens her eyes and looks at me. "You give off this air like nothing fazes you. You're always smiling and so confident. I've been jealous of how . . . easy it all seems for you."

"Nah. I'm just practiced at hiding it. Putting on my hospitality face. The bartender is not the one who is supposed to have the problems. He's supposed to listen to yours."

"You're really good at it." She reaches out and places her hand on top of mine.

"At looking happy?"

"At being a bartender. I mean, looking happy as well, but I was talking about downstairs. You ran that show tonight. People were loving it."

She could have said a thousand different things just now, but that is somehow the perfect compliment.

"Tonight felt really good. It was actually the best I've felt in a long time. I owe you one. I wouldn't have been able to pull it off without you."

She starts to remove her hand from mine but stills suddenly. "Hey, Josh." She turns her whole body to face me. "This is going to sound weird, but I need you to do something for me."

"Sure," I answer automatically. "What do you need?"

Her attention drops to my lips. "Would you . . . kiss me?"

I freeze, certain I've misinterpreted something.

"You'll be honest with me," she continues. "I don't know if it was the kiss that was wrong or me, and I need someone who will tell me straight up." She turns her head away again. I can't see her face, just the profile of her eyelashes blinking rapidly. It gives me a moment for my head to catch up with what just happened.

"Hey, Brynn, I don't think it's such a good idea."

"Please, Josh."

There's pleading in her voice, and as she turns to face me, I can tell by the way the moonlight hits her eyes that those were tears she was blinking away a moment ago.

Fuck. It's hard to say no to a crying woman. It's impossible to say no to a crying Brynn.

"Fine." My mouth makes the decision without my brain. "One kiss."

What the hell am I doing?

I have kissed a lot of women, yet I find myself struggling to start.

My fingers graze her cheek and cup her jaw. Her skin is so damn soft. I bring her face to mine until I catch the faint scent of her strawberry shampoo again.

I used it once by accident.

One day, when I was showering, I reached for the wrong bottle. Now every time I eat a strawberry, I subconsciously think about her, and now I wonder what else she'll ruin for me once I taste her.

I bring my mouth to meet hers. Just a simple press of the lips.

Chocolate.

For some reason, she tastes like chocolate.

And beer. Damn. My two favorite things.

Her lips part, and even though I planned on a quick, chaste kiss, I slide my tongue inside. She makes the softest moan, and any resolve I may have had a moment before is completely gone.

I press closer, cupping the back of her head with my hand, tipping her face back so I can kiss her even more deeply.

Before I realize it, the single kiss turns into two. Then three. Then something else entirely.

I've forgotten why this was a bad idea.

Until she pulls away, her eyes wide, as if she's also processing everything that just happened.

"Whoa."

"Yeah." I'm still catching my breath.

She blinks at me. Those fucking lips are all swollen and plump and kissable.

I almost go back.

But then she scoots away, putting space between us. "So, what's your verdict?"

I have many thoughts.

"No worries there, Brynn. It's definitely not you."

17

BRYNN

wake sometime in the night.

Sloan's bedroom is dark, but I can hear the sound of the ocean waves and feel the soft breeze coming through the window.

The room is quiet, but I get this inkling. This prickling that crawls up my spine and alerts me that someone else is here.

Josh?

No. It can't be Josh.

We said good night hours ago.

And if it were Josh here, I wouldn't feel this panic in my stomach, this clenching in my chest that makes my heart beat so fast that I feel like there's a strong possibility that I am about to have a heart attack.

"Who's there?" I whisper.

No one answers. Not that I really expected them to. My hand reaches for the bedside light, but just as my fingers find the chain, a hand clamps down on my mouth.

I scream.

The sound is muffled.

But I also yank on the light chain hard, and the room fills with soft yellow light.

My attacker is all in black. With a balaclava over their head. But there is a lock of hair peeking out of the eyehole. It's an unmistakable shade of red, and I know exactly who is hovering above me.

I rip the hand from my mouth.

"Poppy?"

She laughs and pulls the mask off her head.

"You should have seen your face a moment ago. Classic."

"What are you doing here?"

She stands back up, folding her arms across her chest. "Get dressed. I need your help."

I blink a few times just to be sure that she is real and that this isn't some bizarro dream. But Poppy is very much Poppy as she heads for my closet and pulls it open.

I watch as she sifts through the racks of clothing and pulls out a pair of black cargo pants and a black long-sleeved bodysuit that I'm pretty sure was from the Halloween episode where both Sloan and Poppy dressed like sexy cats.

"This will have to do, I guess." She tosses the clothing onto the bed. "Hurry up. We need to get up there before the sun comes up and I have to be back at town hall by noon."

I reach for the clothes and pull them on, still completely in the dark about what it is we're doing.

When I get downstairs, Poppy is holding open the back door with her foot. She taps her toe as I pull on Sloan's one and only pair of non-heeled shoes. As I stand, she presses a black ski cap into my hands.

"You can wait until we get there to put this on."

I tuck it into my back pocket. "Are you going to tell me where we're going?"

Poppy smiles wickedly. "This is a DFA."

A *DFA* was Poppy and Sloan's code phrase for *I need you, but don't ask what for.* I had always assumed the *F* between *don't* and *ask* stood for *fucking.* Now that I'm here, I'm not so sure. Either way, DFA was a phrase that could be uttered during dire times of need. Sloan used it once when she needed Poppy's help to steal the biology midterm from Mr. Nguyen's classroom when she had to work double shifts all weekend to bail her estranged delinquent half brother out of jail. Poppy used it when she needed help stealing the mascot costume from Carson's Cove's rival football team—a bold move that ultimately secured her spot as cheer captain junior year.

It was a blood pact.

You don't ask questions and you show up.

I'm still not fully awake as I get into her silver BMW. Poppy offers no further clues on where we're going or what we're doing as we drive along the dark and twisty back roads away from town. At least a full fifteen minutes of driving pass before we turn down a dirt road and a small farm comes into view. As she pulls the car behind a large bush at the very end of the driveway, I get a sinking feeling in the pit of my stomach.

"I need you to be my lookout." Poppy puts the car into park and cuts the engine. "I figure I have at least thirty minutes."

Even in the dark, I can tell that this place wasn't a set on the show. Yet, despite its unfamiliarity, I get a sneaking suspicion that I know where we are.

"Whose farm is this?"

Poppy seems unfazed by my question. "Luce's, obviously."

Shit.

"And why exactly are we here?"

Poppy reaches into her backseat and grabs a white plastic bag.

"Luce has been walking around town all week telling people she's entering my pageant. I am simply going to remind her that the crown is meant for another head. Mainly yours."

She bops me on the nose before reaching into her bag and pulling out two cans of spray paint.

"What are you going to do?" I ask, already suspecting the answer.

Poppy shakes the cans, the little balls clinking against the aluminum.

"Relax. I'm just going to send her a little message. Nothing we haven't done before."

Right. Poppy and Sloan were notorious for their own brand of vigilante justice. Toilet-papering Chad Michaels's house when he took Luce to prom instead of Poppy. Egging Mrs. Garret's car when Sloan failed her chemistry midterm, dealing a crushing blow to her GPA.

These pranks may have been funny back on the show, when Sloan and Poppy were in high school, but this is one of those *Carson's Cove* quirks that hasn't aged well.

"Poppy, I don't think this is a great idea."

She ignores me and gets out of the car. I follow her down the darkened driveway toward the barn.

"All you have to do is stand over there." She points to a small shed between the barn and the white farmhouse. "Give me a signal if you see Luce coming. That's all."

"A signal?"

"Yes. A warning. Just hoot like an owl or something."

I don't like this.

It's wrong.

But Poppy is also Sloan's best friend. She's been there for Sloan through everything. It doesn't leave me with much of a choice.

Besides, it's just a little spray paint.

"Fine, but hurry up."

I creep over to the shed and peek around the corner at the house. It's a small two-story white building with vertical shiplap and wooden porch beams. It's cute. I can envision Luce living there.

I watch the darkened windows for a few minutes, listening for any sign from Poppy that she's done and we can leave. But then a light flicks on, illuminating a small white kitchen and a person who is definitely Luce yawning in front of her coffee maker with a mug in her hand.

My heart hammers hard against my ribs as a silent alarm in my head screams *Abort, abort, abort.*

I cup my hand around my mouth. "Oooooooo-ooooo, oooooo-oooooo!" My best attempt at an owl call carries through the yard.

My eyes scan the stretch of farm surrounding the barn. Poppy isn't where I left her. Nor is she in the driveway or near the shed.

There's no sign of her at all.

My eyes flick back to the house.

I can no longer see Luce in the kitchen.

My already pattering heart kicks up another notch as I get that sinking feeling that things are about to go very wrong.

I hear twigs snapping behind me.

And just like I knew there was someone in my bedroom this morning, I know that when I turn around, I won't be alone.

I twist.

It's an eerily slow 180-degree turn as my brain chants over and over, *Please be Poppy. Please be Poppy. Please be Poppy.*

It's not Poppy.

The creature snorts.

It's not Luce either.

I have always thought horses to be docile creatures. But this one flares its nostrils as if it knows why I'm here and it doesn't like it.

Beside it are a second black-and-white-spotted horse, two goats, and a chicken.

"Hey there, friendly creatures of the barn." I make my best attempt to sound gentle, but these are not the sweet and fluffy farm animals that used to frolic through scenes of *Carson's Cove*. I'm looking at an angry farm animal gang, and they're all staring at me with the same expression: *Intruder.*

"So . . . I'm just gonna sneak past you guys, if you don't mind." I attempt to move around them.

But they do mind.

They mind a lot.

As soon as I take a step, the chicken squawks and flaps its wings. It startles the goat, which then rams into the side of the first horse, which snorts so loudly it irritates the other horse, which rears up onto its hind legs, letting out a loud *nehhhhh.*

My heart lurches, letting out a stream of adrenaline that pumps through my entire body.

I sprint full-speed away from the barn and the horses and the chicken and the goats, back down the driveway toward the spot where we left the car.

The sound of galloping hooves behind me only fuels me to run farther and faster. As if my life depends on it.

The black-and-white horse overtakes me as soon as I make the final turn at the end of the driveway back onto the road.

But only because I stop dead in my tracks as I realize that Poppy's car is gone.

"Come back!" I yell, not entirely sure if I'm talking to Poppy or the horse that is now barreling down the road toward town.

Neither return, and I'm left alone in the middle of the road, attempting to piece together what just happened.

Luce's animals are freely roaming the countryside.

Poppy is definitely gone.

Whether those two events are directly connected is not completely clear. Neither is whether Poppy intentionally abandoned me or fled in fear.

"Okay, no need to panic," I say to no one but the birds.

The sun has risen enough that I can see now without a flashlight, which is great because I seem to have dropped mine.

I start to walk, following the same road taken by the fleeing horse.

It's a long, flat stretch of country road serving as a visible reminder that I have a very, very long walk ahead of me.

I spend the first thirty minutes straining my ears for the sound of tires on gravel, sure that Poppy is looping back to pick me up at any moment.

I spend the next thirty minutes cursing her name because *who the fuck does she think she is,* dragging me out of bed and leaving me like that?

The last thirty minutes are a blur.

I'm hot.

I'm dehydrated.

I'm exhausted, and my stomach is grumbling because our morning crime schedule didn't include time for breakfast.

My god, I'd give my left arm for an Egg McMuffin right now.

My footsteps start to stagger.

There's even a point where I swear I do smell eggs and bacon.

But the road ahead seems to grow even longer with every step.

The heat makes the horizon a blur.

When a man comes into my line of vision, I'm sure he's a mirage.

His body glistens in the morning sun as his arms and legs pump rhythmically with my beating heart.

Lub-dub. Lub-dub.

He's shirtless.

He's running.

My body floods with a feeling of euphoria.

Spencer.

Our date last night may have fallen a little flat, but maybe I was getting too ahead of myself. Expecting too much.

Maybe this, here, is the storyline we were meant for. I'll collapse into his arms from sheer exhaustion. He'll tell me that Poppy came to his beach house, frantic because she lost me, and that he, sick with worry, didn't even have time to put on a shirt before he tore out the front door to come to my rescue.

The sun behind him is casting a hazy glow that forms an angelic halo next to his sun-kissed skin.

He looks like a god.

A bronzed god.

Except Spencer would never be described as bronzed.

He's an SPF 50 kind of guy.

A soft cream color on a summer day.

The runner gets closer, and I realize that it's not Spencer coming to rescue me.

It's not Spencer at all.

"Josh?"

He removes an earbud from his ear as he slows his run to a walk.

"Brynn. What are you doing way out here?"

I don't want to answer that question.

"I was about to ask you the same thing."

He pulls a water bottle from a pack around his waist and squirts it into his open mouth. It spills down the front of his chest, and I have to restrain myself from pouncing on him and licking up the droplets.

Because dehydration.

"Ten K. Every morning. Remember?" He wipes his forehead with the back of his hand.

"Me too," I lie. "I thought that since we're trapped here, I should take advantage of the opportunity to work some more cardio into my life."

Josh nods, either not picking up on the lie or too polite to call me out on it.

"I was just about to turn around." He points at the road behind him. "Do you want to run back with me?"

Dear god, no.

"I would, but . . ." I clutch the side of my waist. "I got a cramp in my side. I can't seem to get rid of it."

He steps toward me. "Here, let me help."

Before I can think of another excuse, his hand is sliding up my waist. His palm is warm and I swear his voice is unusually husky as he says, "Lift your right arm above your head."

I obey. There's no hesitation.

He grabs my upheld hand by the wrist and pulls it just hard enough that my side becomes taut, allowing him to really lean in and work his thumb in firm circles, kneading the muscles that were perfectly fine to begin with.

A picture floats into my vision.

Josh, holding both my hands above my head.

Firm but gentle as his golden body looms above me.

The euphoria returns in a rush, followed by a feeling of light-headedness.

"That feels so good," I moan. And I swear Josh's hand stills for just a moment before he clears his throat.

"Breathe. Just keep breathing through it."

I'm not sure if he's talking to himself or me.

My knees give out from underneath me. I mentally blame my morning of unplanned exercise as I lean into him. My hand is braced on his shoulder, and my breast presses against his biceps.

"Does that feel better?" he asks.

I can't find words, so instead, I nod. My magical state is only broken when he releases me and steps away.

"We should probably take it easy and just walk back. Is that okay with you?" He points at the road.

Again, all I manage is a nod. "You can keep running if you want. I'm fine to get back on my own."

Josh shakes his head. "Naw, it's fine. I'll probably have time for another one later."

I applaud his stamina.

We start to walk toward town.

Our hands accidentally bump every few steps, and I realize I'm not walking in a straight line and try to correct myself. But a few more steps later, I find my way back to him again.

I blame Sloan's fashionable but not-so-functional sneakers.

Josh doesn't say anything about it at first. But after a third hand bump, he looks over.

"You haven't said a word in fifteen minutes. It's starting to creep me out a little."

"Really?" I shake my head to clear some of the fog. "Sorry. Just thinking, I guess."

Josh nods. "Anything you want to talk about?"

I don't think he wants to hear that I'm craving the feeling of his hand on my waist again. Or that my concocted fantasy of him looming above me has been burned into my eyelids. Or that every time I bump into him, I think a part of me is secretly hoping I'll trip and have to brace against his chest again. Or that I like his sweaty smell.

I lock my eyes on the road and try to clear away the thoughts I should not be having about Josh and his glistening body. Part of me is thrilled that I'm once again feeling that stir of desire, which confirms that I'm not, in fact, broken. But there's a very real problem in that those feelings are aimed at Josh and not Spencer, and as enjoyable as it is to lust after Josh, doing so isn't going to get us home.

The monotonous stretch of dust and gravel is a welcome distraction until a speck appears up ahead, then, as it gets closer, grows into the form of a bike.

Its rider's familiar pale arms are almost reflective in the sunlight.

"Spencer?"

Josh, who hasn't yet noticed the biker, shakes his head. "You want to talk about Spencer?"

"No. Spencer." I point to the bicycle, panic rising in my throat. "He's coming. Quick! We need to hide."

I search the roadside for any sort of cover. There's a large flowery bush. But when I attempt to dive into it, Josh blocks my way.

"Wait. Why are we hiding?"

He doesn't understand.

I told Spencer last night that there was nothing going on with Fletcher and me, and if he sees us together out here, early and alone, with Josh all sweaty and looking like Josh, he's going to think I lied to him.

"He keeps finding us together. He's going to think something is going on."

"I'm sure it's fine—"

"No!" I get my second adrenaline rush of the morning. This one is exponentially more powerful. I mean to push Josh out of my way, but I'm hopped up like the Hulk and make firm contact with his shoulders. He takes a step backward, but the road gives way to a slight slope and it's enough to keep the momentum going. I swear I hear a hard and true "Shit" as he lands in the middle of a bush, flowery branches engulfing him.

It was not what I intended, but it's the outcome I was looking for. As Spencer cruises up, it's as if I'm completely alone.

"Sloan, hey. I thought that was you."

Spencer takes off his red bike helmet. It matches his red-and-black spandex biking onesie perfectly. He pulls his mirrored wraparound sunglasses from his face and hangs them in the deep V created by his half-zipped zipper. I can't help but compare the sickly white of his clammy skin to Josh a few moments ago in all his bronzed glory.

Spencer sees me checking out his chest and puffs out like a preening peacock. He leans over the handlebars of his bike so that we're perfectly at eye level and gives me the Spencer Woods half smile he's famous for.

"I really shouldn't be stopping." His voice seems intentionally low. "I like to get to ninety percent of my optimal heart rate for at least six miles to really get into my pinnacle fitness zone, but I had to tell you that I haven't stopped thinking about you or our kiss since last night."

This declaration surprises me in a way that I can't explain. "Really?"

The bush starts to move. Spencer turns his head to investigate, but I jump in front, blocking his view. "There's a raccoon in there." I attempt to contort my body into a shape to achieve maximum bush coverage. "I saw it earlier. Pretty sure it's hibernating. Possibly rabid. Definitely doesn't want to be disturbed. We should ignore it. You were saying something about our kiss?"

Spencer blushes. "I'll be honest. I thought it might be weird. We've been friends so long. I didn't expect it to be so, so, so . . ."

I brace, expecting the worst. That he slept on it and came to the same realization that I did last night. It was terrible.

"It was epic!" Spencer says. "I think it may have been the best kiss of my life."

I ignore the *epic* and let his sweet words run over me. This moment is exactly what I've been waiting for.

My stomach should be swooping right now. My heart should be hammering hard against my rib cage. I should be feeling things. Picturing our future children. Or our matching rockers on our wraparound porch. But the moment Spencer said *kiss*, I pictured the roof last night. And kissing Josh.

"Ahhhhh." Spencer reaches up and cups my cheek. "Are you picturing it too? Well, I'd suggest we try again right now just to make sure it wasn't a fluke, but I've got numbers to hit." He points at an elaborate fitness watch. "And you," he says, reaching out a finger and bopping me lightly on the nose, "have a pageant meeting to attend."

"I do?"

Spencer eyes me as if he's uncertain if I'm joking. "Yeah, the Lobsterfest pageant meeting for all the contestants. I saw Poppy at your place as I was leaving. She said she was there to pick you up." He rechecks his watch. "She mentioned the meeting starting at noon sharp. You might want to get going."

This new information about Poppy only adds to my confusion, but all thoughts about her are temporarily put on hold as Spencer leans in, and for a terrifying moment, I think he's going to kiss me.

To my relief, he instead reaches out and squeezes my shoulder. "I will catch up with you later." He lowers his head so his eyes are level with mine. "I've got plans for us, Sloan. Big plans." He winks before remounting his bike. I watch him ride off down the road, trying to will myself to feel something for him.

As soon as Spencer is out of sight, I run to the side of the road and pry back the branches of the bush.

Josh is lying on his back, hands folded behind his head. I ignore how my eyes are drawn to his lips and the stupid smirk on his face and the way his laid-back pose flexes his biceps and instead direct my attention to the fact that he's staring up at me, making no effort to move.

"You pushed me into a bush." His tone isn't mad, but more matter-of-fact.

I hold out my hand. "Technically, I pushed you, and then you fell into a bush."

He raises his brows, ignoring my hand.

"I'm sorry," I tell him, fully meaning it. "I panicked. I honestly didn't mean to shove you that hard."

He nods as if accepting my apology and takes my hand, but instead of letting me pull him to his feet, he tugs hard and quick, and I pitch forward, the branches of the bush only slowing my fall as I topple directly onto him.

He's grinning at me as if inviting a reaction and although my instinct is to roll off immediately, I find myself studying the tiny flecks of green in his eyes.

"Now it's you who pushed me into the bush."

He grins. "Technically, I pulled you. It's quite nice in here. I thought you should experience it firsthand."

He's so close, and his cedary scent is mixing with the delicate sweetness of the flowery blossoms, lulling me into a trance where I almost consider burying my face in that place between his chin and his collarbone and just hanging here for a while.

Instead, I find the will to heave myself into the mound of dirt beside him. Sprigs of scented purple flowers spring up around both of us.

"You were right," I tell Josh. "For a bush, it's surprisingly comfortable. I'm almost tempted to stay here for a little while."

Josh reaches up, picks a flower blossom from its stem, and inhales slowly before offering it to me. "So why don't we? I have nowhere I need to be."

I do. If Spencer was right, I'm expected to be at some pageant meeting, and we're still some ways out of town.

I take the flower from Josh's fingers and smell it like he did a moment ago. Its fragrance is so sweet and summery that I don't even realize I've closed my eyes until I open them again and find Josh watching me.

I feel his gaze all the way to my toes. It zips through me like an electric shock.

"Here." I shove the flower back into his hand, the feeling in my chest shifting from whatever it was just doing to more of a panic.

"We should get going." I sit up a little too quickly, my vision clouding with the sudden head rush. "I have a Lobsterfest meeting to get to."

Josh moves at a fraction of my speed, pushing up to his elbows. "Remind me again what you're doing with the lobsters?"

"It's a pageant. Sloan needs to win it, remember? Spencer was saying there's a big meeting that I'm supposed to be at."

"Sounds serious." Josh eyes me momentarily, then gets to his feet in a single smooth rock and roll. He holds out his hand. "Shall we?"

He pulls me out of the bush and continues to hold my hand as we climb out of the ditch and back onto the road. When he finally does let go, my fingers tingle, filling me with this urge to touch him again.

"Hey, Brynn." Josh steps toward me. His hand reaches for my face, his thumb skimming the line of my jaw as if he too was suddenly missing that contact. For a moment, I think he will cup my cheek and kiss me again.

I still.

But his hand finds my hair and pulls something from it. A tiny hydrangea blossom. He holds it up and twirls it between his fingers.

"A souvenir of our time in the bush." He tucks the blossom behind my ear, but before I can reply with the appropriate response, he turns and takes off.

"Hey! You're not going to wait for me?" I call after him.

He turns and starts walking backward, smiling. "I figured I'd stay ten paces ahead. Don't want someone to see us together and get the wrong idea." He winks. "I've got Sloan's reputation to protect. She's got a crown to win, and we look like . . . well, we look like we've been rolling around in a bush."

18

JOSH

The Bronze looks like it has been ransacked.

Or at least hosted one hell of a party.

After a long shower, I change into another set of Fletcher's clothes and start cleaning up last night's mess. The familiar rhythm of righting chairs and wiping tables is so automatic that it takes me a good three attempts to realize someone is calling my name.

"Fletch.

"Fletch.

"Fletcher."

The sound is coming from the front door.

I abandon my current project—doubling the size of The Bronze's existing dance floor—and wipe my hands on my jeans, wondering when I'll ever automatically respond when someone calls me Fletch—I hope never.

"One sec. I'm coming," I call to whoever is on the other side as I flip the lock and pull.

But as the door swings open, there isn't a whoever on the other side.

It's more like a whatever.

"Hey there . . . horse."

The animal stares back at me, its brown ears twitching.

I stick my head out just enough to see onto Main Street, but no one else is around. It's just a horse, with no saddle or owner, standing in the middle of the street.

"Were you the one calling me?"

I fully acknowledge that I'm talking to an animal but I'm also not entirely sure it won't answer back.

It has been one fucked-up week.

"What the heck are you doing, Fletcher?"

This voice is not from the horse.

I turn in the complete opposite direction to see Sherry at the back door of the bar, propping it open with a keg on a dolly, staring at me like . . . well, like I'm talking to a horse.

"I'm talking to this big guy." I step aside to show her the beast, but the doorway is empty and the horse is now nowhere to be found.

Sherry eyes me, rightfully suspicious. "Well, if you're done with whatever you think you're doing there, I could really use your help."

I let the front door swing shut as I walk-jog to the back of the bar to take the keg off Sherry's hands. As I wheel it in the rest of the way, Sherry disappears and then reappears a few minutes later with a large cardboard box clanking with what I presume to be liquor bottles.

"You had quite the night last night." She sets the box down on the bar, pulling out a full bottle of Jim Beam, replacing the one I ran out of halfway through last evening.

"It appears this town likes to dance." I nod at the new and improved dance floor.

Sherry unloads the rest of the box and then breaks down the empty container, folding it flat. "And apparently they work up quite the thirst doing it." She hitches her head in the direction of the keg she brought in. "Make yourself useful and hook up the new one, would ya?"

I grab the dolly and wheel the new keg to the end of the bar, next to the old one. I turn off the CO_2, release the pressure in the lines, and then grab a wrench to disconnect them. It's a process I've done easily a hundred times. My dad made me do it as soon as I was strong enough to lift a keg. Definitely before I was legally allowed to. The practiced movements of cleaning and rinsing the lines are oddly soothing. I think I'd even go as far as to say that I missed them, or at least missed the way they give me a few moments to clear my head and think. Today, I find myself thinking about Brynn. About that kiss and about how I've been thinking about it far more than I should.

"Hey, Sherry. What's the deal with the whole lobster queen thing?"

Brynn wasn't super clear on what exactly she had to do.

Sherry's response to my question is a loud snort. "When you say 'deal' do you mean: Why are they still running the thing, seeing as it's an antiquated, fabricated farce?" She holds up her hands. "Who the hell knows? Who the hell knows why the town does half the things it does? Your friend Red, she's the one calling all the shots now."

My brain files through Brynn's flash-card explanations. "Do you mean Poppy?"

Sherry shrugs as if she couldn't care less. "That sounds right. The whole deal is happening next weekend. As you may have deduced, I will not be in attendance. But if you care to go, we can probably shut this place down for the night. Even if last night wasn't a fluke, no one is showing up here the night of the pageant, even if it's a Friday."

Friday. That's right. If time presses on back home, the way it does here, which presumably it does, next Friday is also the night of my dad's auction.

I don't know what's going on in my head—if I'm still running on the adrenaline high of last night's success or what—but I'm getting this itch to try and see what else I can do with this place.

My thoughts break enough to notice Sherry staring at me. Her mouth is pressed into its usual unimpressed line, but there's a slight lift to her left eyebrow, as if she finds something about me slightly amusing.

"Think you'll be back at it tonight?" she asks.

I knew the answer to that question the moment the first customer walked in here yesterday. "Yes. Definitely." She gives a curt nod and taps the bar twice before turning toward the door. "I just hope the power holds out this time."

Sherry turns back around, the lines between her eyebrows deepening. "What do you mean 'holds out'? I've never once had issues with the electricity. And we had some wild parties here back in the day." She squints, her expression turning momentarily dreamy. "Good ole Axle. I wonder what he's up to these days?"

I let that question remain rhetorical. "Yeah, it's the weirdest thing, then. We blew a fuse last night. The whole place went out."

Sherry squints like she's not fully believing my story. "You can't trip the whole place at once. It's all on multiple breakers. You might blow one, but never all of them at the same time. It must have been something you did?"

I open my mouth to argue but instead pause, a funny feeling swelling below my ribs.

What if it was something I did?

"Weird. I'll keep an eye on it. And maybe I'll start locking the storeroom."

19

BRYNN

"Sloan, babe." Poppy waves at me from the other side of the town hall's auditorium. "Where have you been? I was starting to freak out."

She moves at a considerable speed despite her four-inch heels, which clack loudly on the wooden floors as she crosses the auditorium to meet me. She's shed her black clothing from this morning and is wearing an emerald-green sundress. Her hair appears to be freshly curled and her classic red lip is perfectly intact. When she reaches me, she grabs me by the arm and pulls me over to a quiet corner of the room. A tall whiteboard on wheels shields us from the curious gazes of the other contestants.

"Why haven't you changed?" she whispers in a tone that feels unnecessarily sharp.

"Uh, I didn't exactly have time." I draw a deep, cleansing breath through my nose. "You forgot to mention there was a pageant meeting today. The only reason I knew to come here was because I ran into Spencer while I was out on my very long walk home from Luce's place, where you abandoned me." The last two words come out sharp and irritated.

Poppy, seemingly unperturbed, reaches up and smooths my hair with the palm of her hand. "What are you even talking about? First off, I absolutely told you about the meeting. I said we had to be back by noon sharp, and second, I didn't abandon you. You made the owl call. That was the signal to abort. I had no idea which way you went, but I figured you could take care of yourself."

Again, I'm lost on how to respond.

"What were you even doing this morning at Luce's?"

Poppy holds her palms up as if the answer is obvious. "Helping you win this pageant."

When I shake my head, she rolls her eyes. "It's pageant sign-up day, right?"

I nod, having gleaned that piece of information from the giant sign outside.

"Well, if Luce doesn't have her name on that sign-up sheet by the end of the meeting today, she can't enter the pageant. I just created a small problem that would require her immediate attention. And I doubt anyone will sign her up on her behalf." She brushes her hands together. "Problem solved."

She reaches out and plucks the purple blossom from behind my ear, crushing it in her fist before letting the petals fall to the floor. "I do wish you'd found some time to change though." She sighs loudly. "Oh well, there isn't much we can do about it now, is there?"

She steps out from behind the whiteboard before I have a chance to respond, leaving me on my own to find a seat in one of the many rows of aluminum chairs.

The town hall is packed. It feels like every unmarried woman in Carson's Cove is in attendance.

Everyone but Luce.

"Okay, ladies, let's get this show on the road."

In the brief minutes since I left her, Poppy has found a megaphone. The natural shrillness of her voice, amplified by fifty watts, is enough to have everyone scrambling into their seats.

"We have a lot to cover today."

A PowerPoint presentation appears on the screen behind Poppy. It features a picture of her in her Ms. Lobsterfest crown and sash. It's from her very first win at the age of sixteen. I recognize the midnight-blue sequined dress.

"Ladies." Poppy has dropped the megaphone, and her natural speaking voice carries easily through the now-quiet hall. "This is the seventy-fifth anniversary of the Ms. Lobsterfest pageant. And you know what that means? It means that this pageant needs to be everything this town stands for: beauty, perfection, meticulous attention to detail. Everything must be executed absolutely flawlessly. There can be no mistakes."

Poppy continues to talk.

My stomach starts to churn, as if I've swallowed something bad.

I look at the women on my left and right. They are laser-focused on Poppy and every word that's coming out of her mouth, nodding along as she lays out what she expects of each and every one of us.

I remember loving the pageant episodes. The gowns. The drama. Seeing the characters transformed from their regular everyday selves into glamorous beauty queens. But as I sit here, listening to it all, it suddenly feels different. Maybe I'm older or wiser. Maybe the outside world has evolved so much that now this pageant feels dated and icky. Or maybe it always was, and I never really noticed.

"I will be passing around the sign-up sheets now." Poppy nods to Lois, who hands a clipboard out to each side of the room.

"If your name is not on this list by the end of this meeting, you will not be able to participate in the pageant. No exceptions." Poppy's eyes shoot to something at the back of the room.

I follow her gaze. She's looking at the door. No one is there.

The churning in my stomach starts to bubble up. Higher and higher it climbs, burning my lungs and crawling its way up to my throat.

I think I'm going to be sick.

"Here you go, Sloan." The woman to my left, a younger brunette I don't recognize, passes me a clipboard just as the woman to my right does the same. I have two lists of names in my hands.

I scrawl Sloan's signature on one of them, sealing my own fate.

I will win this pageant.

Spencer will see me as more than just the girl next door.

Things will turn out exactly as they're supposed to.

This will be my ticket home. Josh's too.

However, just as I'm about to pass the clipboards back to the front, I notice a blank space on the other list.

It's stark and it's white. A reminder of something missing.

Some*one* missing.

My pen lingers above the page.

Poppy may never forgive Sloan for what I'm about to do.

But I may never forgive myself if I don't do it.

I scrawl down Luce's name on the other sheet, doing my best to disguise my handwriting because although I'm having a crisis of conscience, I'm still slightly terrified of Poppy.

My stomach instantly settles.

The meeting goes on for another hour.

Sixty full minutes on the appropriate way to wear our hair and select our evening wear. There's even a suggested meal plan for the coming week. It pretty much cuts out all carbs, sugar, and joy.

Rehearsal attendance is mandatory.

Listening to all of it is twice as exhausting as my unplanned hike this morning, so when Poppy picks up her megaphone and proclaims in what I've come to realize is an unnaturally grating voice, "You are dismissed," I bolt from the town hall before she has the chance to find me.

I decide to walk the beach home.

Mostly to avoid Poppy tracking me down, but also because it's another banner day.

The rest of Carson's Cove may be showing its flaws, but the sun is warm, and the sound of the waves is soothing. I find myself stopping to close my eyes and turn my face to the sun, enjoying the warmth and this sense of serenity.

Until I open my eyes and find a pair of familiar brown ones staring back at me.

"Ahhhhh," I yell as I recognize the horse from this morning.

It doesn't rear this time.

Or run away.

It just stares back at me, ears twitching, nostrils flaring until it lets out a horse-sized snort, covering me in horse boogers.

I wipe my face on my sleeve. "Okay. I get it. I probably deserved that."

The horse turns its head, and I see Luce riding up the beach on the black-and-white-spotted horse. "Sorry about Buttercup there," Luce calls to me. "She's a curious girl with no sense of personal space." Luce sidles up next to Buttercup, whispers a soft

"Whoa, boy" to her own horse, then reaches down to retrieve Buttercup's reins.

"Need a ride?"

"On the horse?"

Luce rolls her eyes. "No, I'm offering you a piggyback. Of course, the horse. I'm headed right past your house."

This is not a good idea. Not only do I have a spotty history with this horse, but I'm still not sure if Luce knows I was at her farm this morning.

"It's okay, I'm good. I was really looking forward to the walk."

Luce looks down the beach, off in the direction of Sloan's house. "You sure? Your place is a good six miles."

She's right. And I can feel the blisters already forming on my feet.

I eye the horse. "How do you feel about this?"

I don't know how I expect the horse to answer, but I am surprised when she nudges my hand with her nose. I'm equally surprised with myself as I stroke her coat with the palm of my hand and find that I'm definitely not hating the way Buttercup's ears flick, as if she's also okay with this new corner we've turned.

"You know what? Why not?" I tell both the horse and Luce. "A ride home would be great."

It takes several attempts to get into the saddle. Luce is surprisingly kind, showing me where to place my feet and how to hold the reins. Once I'm set, we start to move slowly down the beach.

"You've never struck me as much of a horse girl," Luce says as Buttercup starts to pick up speed. "But look at you go. You're a natural."

I don't need to be; Buttercup is a horse with an opinion. She ignores my heel clicks and "whoa, girls" and proceeds to slowly clop her way down the beach at her pace and on the path she chooses.

I respect that.

There's a coolish breeze coming off the water, but the sun is hot, and I start to sweat. At first, I blame the fact that I'm still clad head to toe in black, but I also suspect that my body doesn't deal well with guilt.

I hold the reins with one hand and use the hem of my shirt to wipe my brow. The maneuver draws a curious glance from Luce.

"That's an interesting outfit for a hot summer day. I don't think I've ever seen you all in black before."

I can't read her tone. There's nothing in it that hints to whether her comment is entirely about my clothing or if she suspects this is not my first introduction to her horse.

"Yeah, well, it's been fifteen years. Maybe I've changed?"

She tilts her head ever so slightly, her eyes never leaving mine. "Maybe you have."

"So . . . uh . . . do you always take two horses out for a walk?"

I watch her body language, looking for clues, but she gives away nothing.

"Sometimes." She draws out the word. "But today was a special circumstance. Westley here"—she pets the black-and-white horse she's riding—"got out this morning and took off. I've been out here looking for him all day."

Shit.

I think a small part of me was hoping that Poppy's prank didn't play out the way that she hoped it would. That maybe Luce was never going to enter the pageant in the first place and that what happened this morning wasn't as mean or as terrible as it came off in my head.

"So I guess you missed the pageant sign-up?"

She nods. "Funny how that happened. But I've decided to take it as a sign from the universe that it wasn't meant for me this year. I mean, it's not like I'd even have a shot at winning anyway."

"What are you talking about? Of course you would."

Luce was always one of the final five.

Luce side-eyes me as if I've lost my head. "Come on, Sloan. I'd make it into the top three at best. But the crown was never going to come anywhere near my head."

"It might have."

Luce rolls her eyes. "I know it's been a minute since you've lived here, but there's no way you've forgotten how things go. The crown always belongs to the gorgeous cheerleader." She eyes my blond hair. "Maybe, once in a while, it ends up on the equally gorgeous but unassuming girl next door, but only after a life-transforming trip to Lois."

I self-consciously tuck a stray strand behind my ear but stop as I suddenly pick up on her meaning. "This isn't . . . It wasn't for—"

"It's fine, Sloan," Luce interrupts. "You and I both know there's a mold here in Carson's Cove. You can't help that you fit into it, just as I can't help that I don't. It is what it is."

I open my mouth to argue but find I have nothing to say because Luce is right. There is a mold to this place. Young. Attractive. Flawed only in a way that still makes you likable. If you don't fit into it, you're assigned another role. Outsider. Trouble. Mean girl.

"So why enter, then?" It's the piece that still doesn't quite fit.

Luce pulls on her reins, and her horse comes to a stop. Buttercup does the same without a command. I watch Luce inhale, then pause, as if she's choosing her next words. "Because I am a freaking force to be reckoned with," she finally says. "But nobody around this place cares. I had this dream of getting up on that stage and making it to the question round, and when the emcee asked me why I wanted to be named Ms. Lobsterfest, I'd tell them about my farm. How I'm driving real change. Sustainable practices. Low environmental impacts. I could show people in this town how smart and accomplished I am. And for once, the right things would be celebrated. But today has been a gross reminder of how stuck this place is. It's the same shit, over and over and over again. So maybe it's time I learn my lesson and be grateful that at least I don't have to put on a dress."

I have loved Carson's Cove for as long as I can remember. Spencer Woods was the boyfriend I aspired to fall in love with, and Poppy Bensen was the best friend I aspired to find. But now that I'm here, living through the makeovers and the pageants, I'm starting to rethink everything.

"Your farm sounds pretty great."

Luce nods but doesn't smile. "It's incredible up there. You should really come and see it sometime. . . . If you haven't already."

I forgot in the last few moments what we did to Luce this morning. But now the guilt returns in a fast and furious wave. I open my mouth, still uncertain if I'm going to explain what happened or just skip to straight-up groveling, but Luce clicks her tongue, and her horse heads away from the water toward the big patches of beach grass in front of Sloan's house.

I do the same, but Buttercup doesn't move. "Come on, girl." I kick. I tug the reins. I whisper sweet nothings into her big brown ears. It's futile. The animal won't budge an inch.

With nowhere to go, Luce's accusations start to seep in, and I think back to the *Carson's Cove* episodes, especially the early ones.

Poppy and Sloan weren't exactly nice to Luce. They hid her

cheer uniform so that Poppy could take Luce's place at the top of the pyramid, which ultimately secured her spot both literally and metaphorically at the top. They spread truthful but private rumors about Luce's sex life so that Chad Michaels would break up with her and get back together with Poppy. It all felt so justified as I watched it at the time. Sloan and Poppy were who I aspired to be. I wanted them to win. Come out on top. I guess I never really thought about the cost.

The horse snorts.

"Yeah, I know." I stroke the hairs of Buttercup's mane. "I'm going to make it up to her, I promise."

The horse swats its tail, but then turns and follows Luce toward the house.

"Hey. Wait up," I call.

Luce pulls on her reins, slowing her horse so I can catch up.

I draw a deep breath in an attempt to get it all out at once.

"I have two things I need to tell you. The first is that I was the one who let your animals out this morning. Well, technically, it was Poppy, but I was her accomplice. And I will admit I didn't know what was happening until after the fact, but I had a feeling she wasn't up to anything good, and I didn't try to stop her."

Luce doesn't say anything for a full minute. She just stares at the reins in her hands, and it's absolutely excruciating.

Finally, she looks up. "I know."

"You do? How?"

She raises her eyebrows and snorts. "Seriously? The majority of the angst in my life can be traced back to the two of you, as history tends to repeat itself in this place. Also, you realize you are dressed like a Navy SEAL. Or at least what Sloan Edwards thinks a Navy SEAL should look like."

I stare down at my entirely black outfit.

"If you knew, then why did you offer me a ride?"

Luce shrugs. "At first, it was fun making you sweat. Both figuratively and literally. But also, I'm tired of being your enemy, Sloan. I figured if you and Poppy were going to continue acting like mean girls, I was going to make my own choice and take the high road. I hoped at least one of you would come around, and if you didn't, I'd at least sleep better at night."

I'm tired of this too. I may not actually be Sloan, but I would hope that she'd want this feud to end as well.

"So what's the other thing?" Luce interrupts my thoughts.

My throat goes dry with the realization that I'm only halfway done with my confession.

"I signed you up for the pageant."

Luce stops her horse. "What?"

"I put your name down. Poppy said you wanted to compete. If you don't want to do it, I can tell her it was me. I just wanted you to have the chance to try."

"Why did you do that?"

I attempt to wrangle all of the stray thoughts from the last few days that led me to write down her name.

"I think, like you, I'm ready for this place to be different. All that stuff we did to you back in high school was wrong, and I'm sorry it's taken me so long to see it that way. I know I should have stopped Poppy this morning. I know there are probably a million other things I could also do. I really am sorry about your animals." I stroke Buttercup's neck.

Luce takes a deep breath, as if processing all of it.

She looks over. "Don't sweat it. We're good, Sloan."

I get an unexpected swell of emotion at her words, and for a moment, I think I might even cry.

"So, can we start fresh? I really would love to come out and visit your farm. I have had literal dreams about your goat cheese."

Luce doesn't look at me but nods. "I'd like that."

Buttercup snorts as if she too approves.

We ride the rest of the way to Sloan's beach house without saying much more.

When we reach the back deck, I dismount and offer to get some water for the horses. By the time I come back out with a water pitcher and glasses, the horses have already found a rain barrel and are drinking their fill.

I hold up the pitcher to Luce. "I'm sorry I don't have much more to offer you than water. I'm unfortunately out of wine."

Luce raises a brow. "You drink now?"

I nod. "I'd give up my firstborn for a Pinot Grigio."

She smiles. "I can't help you out there, but I may be able to do better."

She reaches into one of her horse's packs and pulls out a large wine bottle. "You know about the cheese, but I did not tell you about my other new hobby. I have a big wild strawberry patch at the back of my property. The berries are small, but they make a pretty potent wine."

I hand her the glasses. She pours, and each of us take one of Sloan's lawn chairs.

"Cheers." We clink glasses, and as I bring the glass to my lips, my eyes drift to the blue cottage next door, its windows closed and dark.

"Still into him, huh?"

Luce's question startles me.

"Is that surprising?"

She tilts her head to the side. "I guess not, but I kind of thought I saw something with Fletch the other night."

Heat floods my cheeks. "No. We're barely friends. And completely wrong for each other. Why would you even think that?"

She shrugs. "Just a vibe."

"Are you?" I ask.

She scrunches her nose. "Into Fletch?"

"No. Spencer. Or Fletch too, I guess. Either?"

Luce laughs. A hard, single *ha*. "That's a hard no on both."

I'm still piecing together what I thought I knew in the context of our conversation a few moments ago.

"I just thought about the other night, in the islands, and how you and Spencer . . . in high school . . ."

She puts her hand on my arm. "Before we completely start over, I think I should confess something. I wasn't really into him back then either. I think I just saw the opportunity to finally have something you wanted. I wanted to be the chosen one for once.

"Okay." She holds out her glass. "Enough talking. Let's have a drink. To new beginnings."

I cheers it with mine. "To new beginnings."

My wine goes down in a single gulp. I hold up my now empty glass, which Luce promptly refills.

"Wow!" I tell her. "You aren't kidding around. This is delicious!"

She tips her glass and takes a sip. "Yeah, it's good. But I was serious earlier. Go easy. This stuff is potent."

20

JOSH

am starting to get the hang of this again. Running my own bar. The place is even busier than it was last night. I had to hire one of the regulars, Barry McFly, to bounce the door. Seth and the Hungry Dingos now have a bass, keyboard, and drum. They don't sound half-bad. Or if they do, no one cares, because the dance floor in front of the stage is twice the size that it was last night.

I was missing Brynn's help until Sherry showed up. I didn't even have to ask. She slipped under the bar and started serving without a single comment. Not that there's all that much time to talk. I think everyone in town is here.

I stop serving long enough to appreciate all of my hard work, and my eyes land on a pale-pink cowboy hat weaving its way through the crowd. Although I can't see the person's face, I somehow know who it is even before she looks up.

"Howdy, partner." Brynn attempts to tip the brim but tugs too hard, and it ends up on the floor.

"Where did you find that?"

She turns a slow 360, tipping over slightly as she gets stuck in her twist. "I think her name was Jennifer. Or maybe Deb. But there was definitely a Jennifer involved."

She smiles, and I immediately see it. The sheen to her eyes. The sleepy smile.

"Brynn, are you drunk?"

She stumbles forward and places her elbows on the bar. "I'm not Brynn, remember? I'm Sloan."

She splays her arms, and I catch sight of the bottle in her bag.

"What is that?" I point to her purse.

"That's my purse wine."

"Did you drink all of it?"

She pulls it out and slams it hard onto the bar top. "Yup. It tastes like summer. Luce made it. We're friends now. Turns out I'm the jerk and not her. And I'm still thirsty. I could really go for a beer."

I pull a glass from the stack, fill it, and give it to her. She takes a drink and winces. "Is this tequila?"

"It's water."

She hands it back to me. "Well, I ordered tequila."

I leave it on the counter between us. "I think you may need a few more of these first."

She sticks out her tongue. "Don't kill my vibe, Fletch."

I'm not Fletch.

"It's Josh. And I'm trying to make sure you don't do something you'll regret in the morning."

She smiles slowly, the glass pressed to her lips. "Like what?"

I might be imagining it, but I swear I see her eyes flick to the apartment upstairs.

My mouth dries. And before I can compose the kind of answer to that question that won't leave both of us regretting something, there's a sharp whistle from the other side of the bar. Sherry makes eye contact and then jerks her head to the line of people waiting to order beer. When I turn back to check on Brynn, all I see is the stupid hat on her head again, heading for the dance floor.

I lose track of time, caught in the rhythm of popping caps and pouring shots. I keep my eye out for Brynn. The hat, although ridiculous, makes it easy to spot her dancing in the crowd.

Someone orders a margarita. And in the distraction of cutting limes and shaking ice, I lose her until I hear whistling. And cat-calling. And my stomach drops like a rock.

She's on the stage. Arms in the air. Sundress riding up her thighs. Head thrown back as she shakes in time to the music.

She looks good. And sexy. And I know that half the bar would agree with me.

"Get it together, Fletch. You're getting that everywhere."

I tear my eyes from Brynn to look at Sherry, who is nodding at the crushed limes in my hand. Her eyes follow mine back to the stage, where Brynn is now joined by two dancing dudes and a bass-playing Dingo vying for her attention.

Sherry shakes her head. "Better go get your girl."

I know she means it as a passing comment, but her words hit me hard.

My girl.

Brynn was just my roommate for so long. Then somehow, in the mess of being here, we became friends. Tonight, that word doesn't feel quite right anymore. But is she my girl?

I'm up and over the bar before I let myself answer that question.

The crowd parts enough for me to reach the stage. I hold my hand out to her.

"Come on, Brynn. It's time to go home."

She shakes her head. "I'm Sloan, remember? And Sloan wants to party."

I hold it out again. "I'm about to flip you over my shoulder and carry you out of here. Is that what you want?"

She smiles and keeps dancing. "Kind of."

I reach for her hand, but she's surprisingly fast. "Gotta move quicker than that to keep up with me, Fletcher Scott."

She twirls. And as she does, her foot slips, and she pitches sideways.

There's a terrifying moment when I realize she's about to fall. But my arms move automatically. Reaching out, they catch her before she hits the cement floor. When she's steady and safe again in my arms, I brush back the hair from her eyes. Gone is the easy smile. What remains is shock and fear.

"You okay?" I press my lips to her ear so she can hear me above the music.

She lays her head against my chest. "I think I just need some air."

I start to walk toward the front door.

"No." Her arms tighten around my neck. "Can we go to our spot?"

"How are you feeling?"

Brynn is sitting on top of the air vent, eyes closed, legs outstretched, leaning back on her elbows with her fourth glass of water clutched in her hands. She opens her eyes as I step off the fire escape and onto the roof.

"Everything is still spinny when I close my eyes, but otherwise, I'm good."

Sherry declared last call when I was up here the first time, getting Brynn settled. I went down to help her, but she shooed me back upstairs, claiming that she and Barry had it under control.

Then she told me that I could repay her by getting an early start on the cleanup in the morning.

Brynn holds up her water glass as if cheersing me, then tips it back for a long sip. "You are a most excellent bartender, Joshua Emilio Estevez Bishop. Has anyone ever told you that?"

I take a seat beside her. "Just my mom. But she's one of those kind and encouraging types. I never know if she's lying or loving me unconditionally."

Brynn snort-laughs, but then schools her face into a more serious expression. "Do you think she's worried about you? I keep wondering what's happening back home. Like . . . is life just carrying on without us? The fact that the dates are the same here as they are at home makes me think yes, and in that case, do you believe anyone even notices we're missing?"

They're the same questions I've been asking myself all week. "My boss will have noticed for sure. But people quit and ghost on their shifts at the bar all the time, so I doubt he's done anything about it aside from leaving me some angry voicemails. As for my mom . . . she actually called the night Sheldon showed up at our place, but it was late, so I never called her back. I'm kind of worried she thinks I'm avoiding her."

Brynn's nose crinkles. "Why would you be avoiding her?"

It's hard to explain. "Her message was about my dad's bar. It's up for auction again. She wants me to buy it. Thinks it's important for it to stay in our family."

Brynn cocks her head to the side. "What do you think?"

I pause for a second, collecting my thoughts. "I agree it's important . . . I just don't know if I'm the right guy to . . ." I can't even finish the sentence.

Brynn's hand covers mine. Her fingers are warm and soft as she squeezes. "You are really good at what you do, Josh. I have had way too much wine to try and lie to you right now." She hiccups as if backing up her point. "You have this way with people. You create a space that people want to be in. And I was watching you earlier tonight and you look like you love being behind the bar."

I can't deny that. "I do. And as much as it pains me to say it out loud, it's been fun to pretend to be Fletch and work on the Bronze. It's helped me figure a few things out, but . . ." I shake my head, clearing away any ideas that may have been forming. "It doesn't matter. Even if I wanted to do it, I don't know how we'll make it back home in time. The auction is Friday, June twenty-first."

Brynn frowns as she works the date out in her head. "That's the night of the pageant."

"Yeah. Bit of a rough coincidence."

Brynn gets quiet. And to be honest, I need a moment too as the reality fully sinks in.

We sit for a while, staring at the stars. The roar of the waves hitting the shore lulls us both into a serene state.

"I like it up here," Brynn finally says, leaning forward to look down at the street below. "It's so pretty. From this distance, it's still the Carson's Cove of my television screen."

It's an interesting comment.

"Are you implying the one down there isn't?"

She touches her finger to her nose. "You're very perceptive, Joshua Alan Jackson Bishop. Has anyone ever told you that?"

She hiccups, and I leave it as a rhetorical question.

"It's not that it's different," she continues. "It's just that being here, I'm seeing things that I never noticed before. Things still work out exactly as they're supposed to . . . but it's really just for a select few. Everyone else suffers the consequences."

She drops her head so it's resting on my shoulder. I hate how good it feels. How much I want it there. Brynn has been nothing but clear from day one: Her goal is Spencer, and I'm probably the furthest thing you can get from the guy. And yet. Fuck. I didn't want this to happen, but I ache to pull her into my lap. To kiss her. To fix every fucking thing that's making her feel anything less than.

"Hey, Josh." She lifts her head to look at me. "You hurt my feelings."

My stomach bottoms out. "What? When?"

She drops her head, her voice low. "You didn't like my hair?"

It takes me a second to figure out what she's talking about. Yesterday.

"I didn't say . . . I didn't mean . . . I like your hair. You look good. I just thought you looked good before, that's all."

"Oh." Her mouth forms a perfect circle, and I have to tear my eyes away.

"I guess I should take a lesson from Spencer, huh? He always seems to know what to say."

She shrugs. "He always has. Spencer is perfect."

The words hit hard.

Her gaze drops to her hands. "But I don't know if I want perfect anymore."

I turn her words over and over in my head, not wanting to ask what she means. I like that for this moment, I can live in a world where she wants a guy like me over one like him.

Before I know what is happening, she's kissing me. Her hands are in my hair, and she's sliding into my lap. Her tongue is in my mouth, and I'm thinking about how good it all feels and how I want to do this more.

Until reality clicks in.

She's drunk.

"Hey." I lift her off and set her down beside me. "This is not a good idea. I think it's probably best if I take you home."

"Oh . . . okay."

She's hurt. This time I don't need her to point it out. But before I can explain that it's not that I don't want this, and that I'm not entirely sure if *she* really wants this, she's on her feet.

"No worries, Josh. It's totally fine. I get it. No hard feelings."

She heads toward the fire escape, teetering a bit as she walks. I get up to go after her, because stairs and Brynn are probably not a good combo right now, but before I can reach her, she stops, stands rigidly still, and then makes an eerily slow 180-degree turn to face me. She opens her mouth as if she's about to speak. But before anything comes out, she whips back around and bends at the waist.

What does come out is all of the wine she ingested earlier, bringing with it what looks like the bowtie pasta she ate for dinner.

There are two more encores. And a complete reprisal of the third act when I finally get her down to the apartment.

Eventually, she passes out next to my toilet.

I rub her back, attempt a ponytail in her hair, and then carry her to my bed, tucking her in with water and a trash can.

"I'm sorry," she mumbles as I rearrange the covers around her. "I am regretting all of my life choices tonight."

Her eyes drop briefly to my lips, and I wonder if our kiss makes that list of regrets.

"Hey." I wipe a very sweaty strand of her bangs from her forehead. "The only regret you should have tonight is maybe the purse wine."

She moans what sounds like an "Mmm hmmm" and then tucks herself into a tiny ball. She's a clammy shade of white. Definitely sweating. Her hair is wild, and she smells a little like barf.

And fuck, I think I really like her.

21

BRYNN

'm in another beautiful dream.

I'm lying in the grass, sunlight streaming on my face, listening to the sounds of the ocean waves in the distance. Somehow I know I'm in Carson's Cove. Maybe because I can sense him lying beside me, our feet tangled together.

I can hear the even rush of his breath and feel the heat from his body. Everything feels easy. Exactly as it's supposed to be. As I turn my face to him, I inhale. He smells like cedar and sunsets. Like happiness. Like home. Like a woodsy lumberja—

"Josh?"

My eyes fly open at the same time as his. I scramble away, but our legs are intertwined. My body heaves itself off the bed, but without legs to stand on, the resulting motion is more of a log roll onto the floor.

"Gosh forking darn it!"

I hit the floor hard, my forearms taking the brunt of my fall.

I press my hands to the mattress, hoisting myself back up. Josh rolls gracefully out of the bed, body shirtless and hair perfectly tousled.

"Morning." He stretches and lazily scratches the back of his head. "How are you feeling?"

The moment the question leaves his lips, the throbbing headache hits. As do the spins and a rancid aftertaste in my abnormally dry mouth.

"What happened—" I don't even need to finish the sentence before the memories come flooding back.

My *Coyote Ugly* routine onstage.

The roof.

My water going down.

My pasta dinner coming back up.

"Oh my god." My hand goes to my mouth. "I am so sorry."

He runs his hands through his hair, and it causes his abs to contract.

I find myself counting. All eight of them.

I tear my eyes back to a safer body part. His face. Except all the hand-running has made his hair extra tousled and sexy, and now I'm picturing what Josh looks like post-sex, which immediately turns into what Josh looks like during sex. And that image is so provocatively filthy that I have to squeeze my eyes shut and count to ten.

One . . .

Two . . .

Thr—

"Listen, Brynn, about last night."

My eyes fly open in time to see him hesitate, and in that pause, a second memory surfaces. This one is the most mortifying of all.

I kissed Josh.

No. I mauled Josh.

Like a feral cat.

We were having a perfectly normal conversation. He shared intimate details about his fears about not getting home in time to buy his dad's bar back, and then I responded by climbing into his lap and sticking my tongue down his throat.

"Oh my god." I hold out my hand, halting whatever he was going to say next. "Okay. Listen. I had way too much to drink. I think it's best if we never mention the whole night again. Like, ever."

His eyebrows knit into a solid line. "Okay . . . I just thought . . ."

I don't want to hear it. I may have been drunk, but the memories are clear. I kissed him. He responded with a very polite "Thanks but no thanks." The last thing I want to do right now is rehash it all. Especially since he's not even the guy I should be kissing.

Speaking of the guy I should be kissing . . .

"Do you think he knows?" I peer between splayed fingers at Josh, who has crossed his arms over his chest.

"Who knows? About what?"

"Spencer. Do you think someone told him about my . . . performance last night?"

"I think you're good." Josh's tone is flat.

Relief floods my veins. "Well, at least that's one piece of good news."

He takes a tentative step forward. "I'm confused. I thought you weren't . . . ." There's a hesitancy to his tone.

"Weren't what?"

His arms drop to his sides. "Last night it seemed like you were maybe . . . reconsidering him?"

My head is pounding so hard that I'm finding it hard to think.

My brain is trying to list the reasons why I need to keep pursuing Spencer for Sloan, but my eyes keep wandering back to Josh.

Josh and his abs.

Josh and his kindness.

Josh and the ability he has to make me feel safe.

Josh and his low-slung sweatpants that expose his stupidly sexy hip dips.

Josh and the dark trail of hair that starts from his belly button and heads down, down, down.

No.

Eyes up, Brynn.

I shouldn't be imagining what it would be like to feel his hands all over my body. Or wondering if he tastes like he smells.

"Oh my god. I need to stop."

"Stop what?" He looks understandably confused.

"I didn't mean to say that part out loud."

What am I doing? Why can't I concentrate?

"I better go." I head for the door but stop before I hit the landing. Sherry and Barry are downstairs cleaning up from last night's party.

"I think I'll take the fire escape." I turn and head for the window.

"Why?"

Josh, still shirtless, steps toward me.

I avoid looking directly at him. "This town is too small. What if people see me leaving here? What will they think?"

"You're right. What would people think?"

My eyes fixate on the blank wall behind him, but I don't miss the hurt in his voice.

"I didn't mean it like that."

"No, you're right." He walks to the window and opens it.

"Spencer needs to end up with Sloan, or else we don't go home, right?" He steps to the side to let me out onto the fire escape. "It's still pretty early, so you should be good."

He turns and heads toward the bathroom before I get a chance to thank him for everything.

I manage to make it almost all the way back to Sloan's without anyone witnessing my walk of shame. Until I hit Sloan's street.

Spencer is on his front lawn in very tiny shorts, eyes closed in what looks like a very deep warrior one pose. I know I should be excited to see him, but I'm still in last night's dress and feeling terrible.

I attempt to sneak past, but the moment I do, his arms begin to windmill.

I panic, searching my surroundings for somewhere to hide, but there is no conveniently situated bush this time.

Spencer downward-dogs. Our eyes lock as he lifts his leg into three-legged dog, and he immediately straightens.

"Hey, Sloan! You're up early."

I adjust my wrinkled skirt and attempt to fluff out my bed-flattened hair with my fingers. "Yeah, um . . . I thought I'd go for a walk. It's such a lovely morning."

Spencer bends down, retrieves a white towel from his mat, and wipes his forehead. "I was actually hoping to run into you. I wanted to see if you felt like hanging out later. Maybe we could head to Pop's for a milkshake?"

Spencer moves the towel from his face to his neck, then tosses it over his shoulder. A thin sheen of sweat highlights the toned curves of his body. My eyes drop to his abs, but my body's response is a sour taste in the back of my throat that I can't seem to swallow away.

"Yeah, sure. That sounds like fun."

His face breaks into the most beautiful smile, the kind that, from the ages of thirteen through seventeen, would have made my stomach flip and my southern parts tingle. However, the only thing my stomach does this time is roil.

I practically sprint the rest of the way back to Sloan's house. I feel like I'm going to be sick. I'm sweaty and antsy, and my body feels off, which is silly because everything that I wanted to happen is happening. Spencer just asked me out again. His *Teen Beat* smoldering looks are aimed solely in my direction. *Carson's Cove* is set up to deliver on all of its promises. And yet . . .

I barely make it to Sloan's bathroom in time.

I repeat the events of last night, but this time, there's no Josh to hold my hair back.

When I'm certain there is nothing left in my stomach, I lean back and rest my head on the cool yellow tile as I reach out and flick the toilet handle with the toe of my sandal. The water whooshes, carrying away the contents of my stomach. I'm left with nothing but the pounding in my skull, which continues to grow louder and louder until it occurs to me that it may not be my head at all.

I consider staying in the bathroom, rationalizing that it's probably Poppy again and I'm not emotionally prepared to deal with her this morning. But the knocking persists. In this battle of wills, mine is weak, and I give up first, stumbling my way downstairs and flinging open the back door, mentally preparing for another lecture on my appearance.

But the person standing on the other side is someone else entirely.

"Sheldon?"

He's dressed like a UPS driver. Brown pants. Brown shirt. But as I read the gold embroidery, the letters are reversed: *USP.*

He steps inside the kitchen without invitation and begins to pace the six feet between the refrigerator and the stove.

"I've heard some very unsettling rumors."

My fingers start to tingle.

"Rumors? What rumors?"

He finally stops, and although his head is turned toward me, he avoids my eyes. "Oh, I don't know, that you were dancing with other men on a stage last night, drinking alcohol with your mortal enemy as if you two were the best of friends, and completely obliterating the perfect reputation of this town's most beloved resident?"

I feel a mix of agitation and relief. He doesn't know about Josh.

"Yes. I was hanging out with Luce yesterday. I don't know if we were ever mortal enemies, but we're definitely not now. And I don't know if I'd describe it as dancing with other men. It was more just dancing in proximity of other people."

Sheldon slowly shakes his head. "That is not part of our plan, Sloan. You and that poor excuse of a Fletch keep messing things up! Fixing up the Bronze, getting everyone in town drunk. You're not supposed to be running around changing things! I tried to send you a subtle message, but shutting down the power was clearly too vague of a hint, so now I'm here being very overt about what exactly needs to happen next."

"Wait! That was you who cut the lights?"

Sheldon throws up his hands. "You're missing the point. We had a plan and you're messing it up!"

I don't like his use of the word *we*. Especially since I feel like Sheldon's plan for Sloan may be deviating from mine.

"About that." I think about how to frame my next sentence without him freaking out. "Have you ever considered that Sloan has grown up a little these past years? She's thirty now. She's seen things. I mean, she has been on her own for a long time. Is it possible she's maybe changed—"

"No!" Sheldon slams his hand on the kitchen island so loudly that I jump. "She hasn't." He steps toward me, so close that I can count the flecks of yellow in his eyes. "She is still the sweet and lovable girl next door. She has finally come home, where she will take her place as Lobsterfest queen and, more importantly, queen of Spencer Woods's heart. They will end up together. Happily. Ever. After. No deviations. No funny business."

On some level, I understand Sheldon's need for this. I've been there. I spent three days straight in the same pair of gray sweatpants, on my second twenty-pack of nuggets, grasping at any reason for why things didn't turn out the way I wanted them to. As I watched rerun after rerun while going through my divorce, I looped both myself and Sloan into the same group of those that loved hard and lost.

But the last few days have shown me an error in my logic. I've assumed that there is only one way to that happily ever after: fall in love with the perfect boy and get him to love you back forever. Now I'm not so sure.

"What happens if she doesn't?"

Sheldon's eyebrows knit in confusion. "I don't understand."

"What happens if Sloan doesn't win the pageant? What happens if she and Spencer don't end up together?"

Sheldon shakes his head, his eyebrows doing the same thing as before. "That's simply not an option. She wins. They wind up together. If for some ludicrous reason it doesn't happen at the seventy-fifth annual Ms. Lobsterfest Pageant, then we try the seventy-sixth, then the seventy-seventh. I have all the time in the world."

But I don't.

More importantly, Josh doesn't either.

"Sheldon, I don't want to do this. I may have been on board when we first got here, but I'm not anymore, and Josh isn't either. We want to go home. Now. *Carson's Cove* is a television show. Sure, it didn't end the way we wanted it to, but it's not the end of the world. And that's why there is fanfic. You can dream up any ending you want."

"I don't think you get it." Sheldon straightens, his wiry body suddenly tall and looming. "You made a wish. That wish brought you here, and until you fulfill your purpose, there *is* no going home. I have been playing nice up until now. I have let you do things your way. But if you keep wasting this incredible opportunity, I will intervene and remind you that *Carson's Cove* isn't all about falling in love. It can get dark. Very dark."

I don't miss the threat in his tone.

"Message received."

I feel sick. Even worse than before.

"Good." Sheldon nods. "You should probably go get changed, then. I hear you have a date tonight."

22

BRYNN

By the time Spencer knocks on my door, I've rallied myself into a better headspace. I've gone full Sloan in a fresh outfit. My blond hair has been wrangled into beachy waves. I've meditated.

"Wow, Sloan. You look incredible." Spencer gives me the kind of look that I've been longing for since I got here. "My dad loaned me the boat tonight. I figured it would be fun to take it into town. What do you think?"

"I think it's perfect," I say with a renewed commitment to the plan.

The next few days are about three things, and only three things.

Win Spencer. Win pageant. Go home.

I take his hand and let him lead me down to the dock, where a fancy white speedboat is tied up and waiting.

I climb into the passenger seat. He turns the ignition key and the boat roars to life. There's a notable coolness in the air as we cruise out into the bay. The sky is a dull gray with dark clouds looming on the horizon. The wind has picked up. It's not much more than a slight breeze, but there's something different about it. A notable change in the texture, maybe? As if it's saying, *Something's coming.*

"It looks like it might rain." I glance around the boat to see if there is a cover, but there doesn't appear to be one.

Spencer taps on one of the round dials on the boat's dashboard. "It will probably blow past. It usually does."

As we pull up at the town docks, the weather seems bent on contradicting him. When Spencer jumps out to tie up the boat, I feel the first drops of rain on my bare shoulders.

"We may need to make a run for it." Spencer reaches down to pull me onto the dock. He looks around. "We can take cover in the gazebo for a few minutes. It's probably just a quick little summer rain shower."

He takes my hand and leads me up the gravel path that winds toward the park with the gazebo. When we reach the grass, the rain begins to fall harder, and we have to sprint the last thirty feet to avoid getting soaked. By the time we're under the gazebo, it's completely pouring.

"Wow!" says Spencer, watching the rain, which is now so thick that we can barely see Main Street. "I didn't see that coming. We may be stuck here longer than I thought." He turns to me. "But that's okay. I've got something important that I wanted to talk to you about anyway, and it feels right to do it here. A little like fate."

He takes my hand, and it reminds me so much of the perfect scene from the show's opening credits. Sloan and Spencer alone at the gazebo, holding hands and staring into each other's eyes, lips parted as if they are on the cusp of saying something that could change the course of their relationship forever.

It's romantic.

It's idyllic.

I shiver with the déjà vu.

"Are you cold?" Spencer's fingers trace the line of my collarbone.

"Just a little."

He curls his index finger under the strap of my sundress. "I'd give you my sweater, but I wouldn't want to ruin that pretty dress."

I smile weakly as he swallows, then draws a deep breath.

"Sloan, we've known each other since we were kids. And from the very first moment that I saw you on the beach, you captivated me with your sweet smile and unwavering spirit."

My stomach drops at the sudden realization that we're doing this here and now.

"You've grown into this tenacious young woman," he continues. "And whether fate held me back or our stars weren't yet aligned, it took until now for me to realize that my feelings for you have changed. . . ."

He tugs my hands so I have to step even closer.

The feeling in my stomach is less butterflies and more angry bees. My heart picks up speed but doesn't swoon, and the inside of my mouth tastes rancid as speckles of black begin to cloud my vision. I breathe and blink, and the perfect scene in front of me becomes a little like a Monet. I start to see the brushstrokes. The messy little flaws. And the picture-perfect beautiful bubble I was in a moment ago bursts.

Spencer's hands are sweaty and his breath smells like Doritos. More importantly, I realize with absolute clarity that I don't want this scene to happen.

Not today. Not at all.

And the moment I acknowledge it, the sky above us rumbles as if it wholeheartedly agrees or thinks me a fool. There's a crack of thunder so loud that I jump, pulling my hand from Spencer's as a bright flash of lightning hits the ground somewhere nearby on the beach.

It's a little too close.

It's perfect.

"I don't think we should be out here," I tell Spencer, who looks crestfallen, but still nods in agreement. "We can make a run for Pop's," I offer. "Wait the rest of it out with a cherry chip milkshake?"

Spencer points at the fudge shop. "If we cross Main Street, we can take cover under the shop awnings all the way to Pop's. But before we go, Sloan, I want to tell you that—"

I leap onto the grass before he can finish his sentence. The rain feels cool on my skin, and the wind, blowing stronger than it was a few moments ago, feels like a needed cleanse. A reset.

We sprint all the way to the sidewalk, and there's another low rumble, followed by a flash of bright lightning just as we take cover under the red-and-white awning. My chest burns from the sudden burst of cardio. I'm soaked down to my underwear, as is Spencer, whose white T-shirt is noticeably see-through and clinging to his rain-soaked chest. He runs his hands through his hair, slicking it back save for a single lock that falls over his blue eyes as they fixate on me. I'm living out four years of teenage fantasies all at once.

"Where to next?" I peek my head out onto the sidewalk in a desperate attempt to find our next source of cover and almost collide with a large green-and-white golf umbrella.

"Whoa!" The umbrella lifts to reveal a very dry Luce underneath. "Hey, you two. What's going on?"

"We got caught in the rain," I explain, very happy to see Luce's face. "We're heading over to Pop's for a milkshake. Why don't you come with us?"

Luce shakes her head. "Pop closed his place up. He's worried the storm is going to turn into something more. The only place in town that's open is the Bronze. Apparently, there's karaoke in there tonight. My horses like to be out in the pasture when it's stormy like this. It stresses them out to be inside, and it stresses me out to think about them getting soaking wet in the dark, so I'm heading over there now to distract myself. Why don't you guys come with me?"

No, not the Bronze.

As desperate as I am not to be alone with Spencer right now, the only thing that would make tonight even more complicated is throwing Josh into the mix.

"I guess we could." Spencer looks at me. "Or we could head back to my place? In case it gets really bad and the power goes out?"

I know what happens in Carson's Cove when the power goes out.

"The Bronze sounds great!" I say, despite my brain flashing through all the different ways tonight could end in a catastrophic clusterfuck.

Spencer shrugs. "Sounds good. It's been awhile since I've sung karaoke."

Luce lifts up her umbrella to make room for us to join her under it. We head back out into the rain toward the Bronze, where the off-key sound of someone butchering Shania Twain can be heard from half a block out.

When we finally do get inside, I hold out hope that this whole plan will fall apart because the place is so crammed from everyone driven in by the storm that there is barely standing room, but then Spencer points to a single unoccupied table.

"There! Over by the stage."

There are three empty seats.

Of course there are.

"Luce, why don't you take this one?" I nudge her into the middle seat, but our telepathy isn't quite where it needs to be yet. A moment after we all sit down, she jumps up with a "I guess I might as well go grab us a round of drinks" and heads to the bar, leaving Spencer and me alone.

I catch a break when the music is so loud that you can't carry a conversation, and then a second one when the bar is so busy that I can only see tiny glimpses of Josh if I really crane my neck.

I start to think that maybe tonight won't be as bad as I thought.

Then the music stops.

"Hey, folks!" The voice of the emcee booms through the speaker system. "Thanks for sheltering with us. We're going to take a quick break as we set up for the next few performers. Hold tight and get to know your neighbor for a few moments. We'll be right back."

Spencer reaches across our table for my hand. "Listen, Sloan. There's something I want to tell you and I don't want to wait any longer."

I jump to my feet. "Can you hold out a few more minutes? I'm still pretty soaked from the rain. I'm going to go dry off a bit." I point in the vague direction of the bathroom. "I'll be right back."

I don't wait for him to answer before ducking into the crowd and weaving my way toward the restrooms. I intentionally follow a path that takes me out of the line of sight of the bar, but as I turn the corner toward the bathroom, I'm cut off by a keg being wheeled by on a dolly.

"Whoa, sorry about that." Josh swerves and then stops, his face registering a look of surprise when he notices that his obstacle is me. "Brynn, hey. I was hoping you'd come tonight."

His voice is soft and his eyes are so kind. I get the urge to run away again, but this time I want to grab his hand and take him with me.

"I wanted to make sure we were good," he continues. "I didn't like the way we left things this morning, and I . . ."

His gaze flicks to something over my shoulder.

"Did you come here with Spencer?"

I nod, my cheeks heating. "Yes. I need to talk to you about that. Sheldon came by and—"

There's a loud mic screech.

I turn in the direction of the sound. It's coming from the stage. The crowd is so dense that I can barely see the bar, let alone our table, which makes me wonder how Josh knew I came here with—

My blood runs cold.

Oh, now I've fudged up.

Of all the catastrophes I envisioned tonight, I missed one.

The most obvious one.

I watch with that kind of detached horror you feel when you know something very wrong is about to happen and yet can't find the will to do anything but watch. The emcee takes center stage as the lights dim.

"Please welcome to the stage our very own Spencer Woods."

23

JOSH

"Oh my god." Brynn's hands cover her face. "No, no, no, no, no. Please, no."

I'm confused, my eyes following Brynn's to the stage. "What's happening? What's wrong?"

Brynn doesn't answer. She just stares, horrified, as Spencer takes the mic from the emcee, addressing the crowd with a seemingly humble smile.

"There's someone very special here with me tonight." Spencer runs his hand through his hair, dropping his eyes to the stage for a moment before acknowledging the crowd again. "And I haven't quite found the right words to tell her how I feel."

"No," Brynn moans into her hands. "Anything but this."

Spencer smiles. "But I think I've found the perfect way to tell her exactly what is going on in my heart . . . using the immortal words of James Blunt."

The opening bars of a song tinkle through the speaker system, and Spencer begins to sing. His tone matches the falsetto of

James Blunt almost perfectly. His eyes close with emotion as he sings about the beauty of the girl he'll never have.

"Karaoke serenade, eh?" My jealousy of the situation is squelched only by the fact that Brynn looks like she's going to vomit. "Why the face? I thought you loved grand gestures."

Spencer begins to walk forward, and the crowd between him and Brynn parts almost perfectly down the middle. I grab for the keg to move it out of the way, but Brynn reaches for me, stopping just short of grabbing my wrist.

"Don't leave me," she says between clenched teeth. "Please."

Spencer begins to sway in time to the music as the emotion in his voice intensifies.

"Hold on," I tell her, an idea forming.

"Traitor," she hisses back.

But her voice is drowned out by Spencer, who is now trying to harmonize with the track's backup vocals as the song transitions to the instrumental interlude.

I duck under the bar as the song hits the final chorus, and Spencer begins to improvise his own vocals.

When he finally reaches Brynn, he stretches out his hand. It's unclear if it's his final pose until he flexes his fingers, beckoning her to place her hand in his.

I can see the pleading in her eyes as he hits a final high note, and the song comes to an end. "Sloan," he says into the microphone. "I just wanted to tell you that I—"

I reach up and clang the bell above the bar, hard and fast.

The *ding ding ding* drowns out Spencer's voice, and the curious eyes of the crowd suddenly shift to me.

"Evening, everyone." My plan was half-baked up until this point. Now I'm improvising. "I . . . uh . . . just wanted to say thanks for making it out tonight despite the weather we're having. And to show my appreciation, I'm buying a round of hurricanes—on the house."

The tone in the bar shifts from pin-drop silence to a roar of whoops and cheers.

Spencer's song is long forgotten as the crowd rushes the bar. Candid love declarations are no match for artificial passion fruit and rum.

Sherry presses in beside me, her arm reaching for a tall glass as she eyes the growing crowd. "She better be worth it," she mutters under her breath.

I already know she is.

The next hour passes in a blur of tiny paper umbrellas.

We run low on rum, but every time we think we're out, another bottle somehow appears. Another strange coincidence in a town that seems full of them.

As the karaoke wraps up, the emcee puts on a playlist, and the dance floor fills almost immediately. Brynn and Luce jump up onstage, and as they do, Brynn catches my eye. She smiles and takes a notable step away from the edge, as if to say, *I'm good, I won't be falling into your arms tonight,* but it's followed by a moment where she holds my gaze just a little too long as she raises her hands above her head, her body moving to the music, and it makes me think that maybe she wouldn't mind too much if she did.

"You did that." Sherry pulls my attention off Brynn and onto a group of men, arms around one another in a huddle, belting out the chorus of "Sweet Caroline" on the dance floor.

"I'm sorry about the free drinks. I'll work it off."

Sherry shakes her head. "I know you will. You've been working your butt off all week."

She reaches into the fridge, pulls out two bottles of Bud, pops the cap off one, and hands it to me.

"Who is this for?" I glance around the empty bar, but there's no one waiting for it. Everyone is dancing.

Sherry holds out the second Bud and clinks it with mine. "The beer is for you. We're taking a break. The storm seems to have missed us, and that deserves a cheers." She takes a sip that's followed by a long, appreciative sigh. "And I wasn't talking about the drinks before. I was talking about this place. It's never quite been like . . ." She doesn't finish the sentence.

"Like what?"

Her eyes scan the stage, the dance floor, the tables. "Like a community. Everyone together. Or at least it hasn't for a while."

That was the thing my dad loved most about Buddy's. It didn't matter who you were or what you did, you could come and be a part of something. God, I've missed that place. I thought the hole inside me these last couple of years was from losing him, but I think part of it was from losing Buddy's too. My dad is gone, but Buddy's is not—and I'm finally willing to admit that I want it back.

Sherry tosses her empty beer bottle into the trash can. "You should ring that." She nods at the bell hanging above the bar. "It's closing time, and we should take a break in the weather as a sign to send these bozos home."

I wait until the end of the song to ring the bell.

There are a few disappointed faces when, instead of announcing another round of free drinks, I yell, "That's all for tonight, folks. Get home to bed and then come back tomorrow. If you need a safe way home, come and talk to me. Otherwise, good night." The crowd groans in protest but slowly makes its way out of the bar.

Brynn and Luce are the last of the dancers to jump from the

stage. They walk, arms linked, back to their table, where they pull a slumped-over, brooding Spencer to his feet, and the three of them make their way toward the bathroom. As they pass, Spencer points a finger at me. "You, sir, ruined my big finale."

I dip my head, feeling a little bit of sympathy for the guy. "Sorry about that, man."

He and Luce continue on to the bathroom, but Brynn changes directions, coming over to the bar, where she pulls out a stool and sits down.

"Good night?" I fill a pint glass with water and hand it to her.

She takes it and draws a long sip. "The best. I haven't danced that much in my life. I don't know if you were watching me out there, but I was pulling out some pretty sweet moves."

"I might have caught a few."

She nods at the stacks of glassware waiting to be put through the dishwasher. "You were busy."

I stack another glass on the pile. "Turns out this town likes to drink."

Brynn taps her temple with her index finger. "Yet another *Carson's Cove* tidbit I can tuck away for some undetermined future purpose." She leans forward over the bar. "When we get back, we should really look for one of those bar trivia nights. One that's dedicated to *Carson's Cove*. I was a force to be reckoned with before we got here, but now I think we could clean up."

My face must reflect my gut's sudden jolt of unease because Brynn's smile disappears. She tilts her head, her eyes studying me. "You okay?"

"Yeah." I shake my head in an attempt to dismiss the bad thoughts. "Just thinking about home."

Brynn leans forward again and places her hand on top of mine. "We will get back, Josh. I promise."

She squeezes my hand before letting go and sitting back in her seat. I load another tray of glassware and push it into the dishwasher. "Yeah, but not by Friday."

Brynn stares down at her half-empty water glass. "I've been thinking about that too. What if we got home on Sunday? Or even Saturday? Is there any possibility that the bar will still be up for sale?"

I shake my head, having already considered every possible scenario. "Probably not. It's an auction. They'll price it low to guarantee a sale, and then it will go to the highest bidder. I guess there's always a chance that person will sell to me later, or that they'll try to open it and things won't work out again, but that could take years, and as much as I want Buddy's back, I wouldn't want to wish that experience on anyone."

Brynn opens her mouth, as if she's about to say something else, but stops as Luce and Spencer reappear from the bathroom.

"Hey, you two." Luce's voice is slightly slurred as she slides onto the stool next to Brynn. "Looks like the rain's let up. I'm going to see if I can sweet-talk someone into giving me a ride back to my farm so I can check on my babies."

"I've got us a way home," Spencer yells from across the bar. "We can drop you, Luce, if you come now." He opens the front door and waits.

"You're not taking your car, right?" I call after him.

Spencer waves me off. "Of course not. Let's go, ladies." He disappears out the front door.

Luce nudges Brynn with her arm. "You ready?"

Brynn looks from me to Luce. "Actually, I think I'll catch up with you guys tomorrow."

Luce leans in close and whispers something into Brynn's ear.

Brynn, in return, turns a deep shade of red before swatting her away playfully.

"Night," Luce calls to me before following Spencer out.

Brynn busies herself by taking a long drink of water.

"You two seem to be getting on pretty well for archnemeses."

Brynn smiles into her cup. "I really like her."

"And him?" I ask, the jealousy from before bubbling up.

Brynn avoids my eyes. "No. But that's why I stayed to talk to—"

"Hey, Fletch." Sherry appears from the storeroom. "I'm going to head out in a moment." She bends down to pick up a knocked-over chair. "You'll take care of the cleanup?" She grabs two empty glasses from a table and places them on the bar.

"I got it," I tell her, knowing I'm still making up for my earlier free round. She nods, her eyes settling on Brynn.

"Tomorrow is fine if you're not able to get to it tonight." She winks, then bends down and picks up something from the floor.

"Jesus H," she curses, setting the object down on the bar. "Free drinks, and they still sneak in their own hooch. What is wrong with this town?" The object is a small silver flask.

Brynn slides down the bar toward it. "I think that might belong to Spencer," she says. "It's his LA kombucha."

Sherry picks up the flask, screws off the top, and sniffs. "Kombucha, huh? Is that what he's calling it? In my day, we called it straight-up moonshine. From the smell of it, I'm guessing this is at least a hundred and fifty proof." Sherry looks up at me. "He didn't drive home, did he?"

"No. I asked."

There's a gasp from Brynn. I turn and watch as all of the color drains from her face.

"What's wrong?"

She jumps out of her seat. "He didn't drive his car here. We took the boat." She looks directly at me, her eyes wide with panic. "Sheldon said things would get dark. But I didn't think he'd—"

She doesn't finish the sentence. She leaves it hanging as she turns and runs out the front door.

"Brynn, wait!" I call, hoisting myself up and over the bar to follow her.

"Fletcher!" Sherry calls out just as I reach the front door. "Be careful out there." Her sharp tone fades to a waver. "I don't want to see someone else get hurt again. But I especially don't want it to be you."

If she says anything else, I don't hear it as I run out the door.

I catch Brynn just as she reaches the beach.

"What's going on?"

"Out there!" She points to a speedboat that's trying to navigate the still-choppy waters. The shadows of two figures are visible in the moonlight. "I didn't think he'd take it this far. But now I'm not so sure. He won't hurt Spencer, but I'm worried about . . ."

She doesn't finish the sentence. She turns and cups her hands around her mouth.

"Luce! Spencer!" she screams into the night. But her voice is swallowed up by the waves—and a shriek as one of the bodies falls straight into the water.

24

BRYNN

'm paralyzed.

It's as if my feet are stuck in the sand. As if I'm watching the horror unfold on my television screen and not in the dark waters in front of me.

Beside me, Josh kicks off both shoes and then reaches for his belt. It isn't until he's down to nothing but his T-shirt and boxers that I even realize what is happening.

He's going in.

He's going after her.

"You can't go in there!" I call as Josh runs into the water, but my warning is drowned out by the wind. I'm helpless as I watch Josh make even strokes out into the bay, where Spencer and the boat are still making circles.

Josh reaches the spot where Luce went under. He waves down Spencer, who finally brings the boat to a stop.

I stop breathing completely as Josh dives beneath the waves, and I only resume with a few shallow breaths when I catch a glimpse of white as Josh surfaces before diving under the water again.

My heart is in my throat, hammering hard. It's almost impossible to breathe.

Please find her. Please be careful.

It's an excruciating minute before there's another break on the surface of the water.

This time, the flash of white stays. I squint and make out a second body. Luce.

Spencer reaches down and pulls her from the water. Josh climbs out next, his body disappearing from my view as he lifts himself up and over the gunwale of the boat.

I don't draw another full breath until he reappears at the wheel a few moments later, and the sound of the roaring engine cuts across the water.

The boat makes its way back to the shore through the choppy water. The entire time, my eyes never leave Josh's face. His dark hair is almost black with rain, and his brows are drawn low in a determined expression as he pulls the boat up to the dock.

I don't even realize a crowd has formed behind me on the beach until there's a collective gasp as Spencer steps onto the dock and holds out his hand to help Luce, who follows him on shaky legs.

She looks tired and scared, but otherwise okay.

I feel so relieved that I almost throw up and have to close my eyes until the nausea subsides as the adrenaline drains from my body.

Voices from the crowd swim around my head.

"Did you see that?"

"Spencer pulled her out."

"He's a hero."

"He saved her."

"What was she doing out there?"

"It's Luce, you know how Luce is."

"Who was driving?"

"I think it was Fletcher."

"Well, that's not surprising."

I want to scream every single profanity that has been on the tip of my tongue this week. I want to scream about how screwed up this place is. About how screwed up we all are for just accepting it.

Are you all blind? I want to take each and every person standing here by the shoulders and shake. *Spencer did nothing. Luce is a victim. It was Josh who saved her.*

Josh!

Where is Josh?

My eyes scan the dock, the boat, even the beach.

But there's no Josh.

There's just Spencer, his arm around Luce, walking her toward another small crowd of people on the dock, who cover them with blankets.

I run from the beach toward the boat, my mind flipping between second-guessing the memories of the last few moments and inventing horrifying what-ifs.

What if he fell back in? What if he never got out in the first place? Did I actually see him get into the boat? Am I sure he was driving?

My eyes scan the water for snippets of white.

The ocean is nothing but black swells of water.

Just as I reach the boat, I hear a low moan coming from inside it, and I stop.

I peer down inside, making out an arm. A head. Two legs. A

chest that fills with cold sea air and then contracts. Up and down. Up and down.

My body floods with a feeling of relief. Of something more.

"You're okay." I jump inside and sink down next to him. My cheek falls to his chest, just to make sure it's not a trick of the dark.

He's breathing.

His heart is beating a strong and steady *lub-dub, lub-dub.*

Wet arms encircle my body, pressing me closer.

"How is she?" Josh's voice is raspy and shallow, as if he swallowed the sea.

"She's going to be okay, I think. There are lots of people with her now to help. But what about you?" My eyes grope his body in the dark, searching for cuts, bruises, blood, answers.

"Just a little wet." He coughs, and I press my body away to give him room, but his hands tighten, and he pulls me back in.

We lie there in the dark.

Not speaking.

Not moving.

Just holding each other.

I listen as his breathing changes from shallow gasps to slow, even inhales and exhales.

A cold breeze blows off the ocean. It runs up my arms, and I involuntarily shiver.

"Are you cold?" He loosens his grip to rub my arms.

"Don't worry about me," I tell him. "I'm supposed to be taking care of you."

He tightens his arms again. "We take care of each other."

My head has finally stopped reeling enough to fully process what just happened. "You went in after her. You didn't even think."

He rolls his head toward the direction of the Bronze. "They were my responsibility. I served them. I should have been paying more attention—"

"No." My hands press to his cheeks, holding his head so I can look straight into his eyes. "Everything that goes wrong isn't your fault. If there's someone to blame here, it should be me. I wished us here. I went along with Sheldon's plan. I convinced myself that the only way I was going to feel good again was if Spencer fell in love with me. All you did was help me. Even if you disagreed."

Saying it out loud makes me see the last few days for exactly what they were: a stupid plan fueled by a selfish person. I derailed Josh's life, and now my stupid wish nearly ruined his future.

"Hey." He pushes a lock of hair from my forehead, the sand stuck to his skin lightly scratching me.

"I just didn't want to be hurt again. And he seemed safe. He didn't make me feel at all." Emotion swells in my chest. "But when you were out in the water, I realized losing you would feel way worse than anything else I could imagine. Because being around you is the best feeling I can imagine. And—" Tears begin to fall. Giant raindrops coat my cheeks. They tumble out of me as the full weight of what could have happened hits like a rogue wave.

"Hey." Josh pulls me into his chest again. "I'm okay. We're all okay. It's going to be fine."

"I was so scared, Josh." My chest starts to heave.

Josh strokes my back. "I know. But I'm not going anywhere, I promise."

This time, it's him who shivers.

"We should get you inside." I get to my feet and hold my hand out to help him. He takes it. And when he's standing again, he doesn't let go, and I don't either.

The wind picks up as we walk back to the bar. It's cold, but my hand is hot. It feels like fire is curling up my arm and running down my chest to my stomach, where it fills me with a burning heat.

He pauses at the threshold to Fletch's room. It's a silent question. *Do you want to come in?*

I step inside first. "We need to get you out of those wet clothes."

His eyes find mine as he steps toward me. I press my palm to his chest and wait. He covers my hand with his, and I feel the beat of his heart through the wetness of his T-shirt.

A drip of water trickles from my temple to my cheek to my chin, then falls onto my chest. Josh presses it with his thumb, then drags it along the line of my collarbone until the wetness seeps into my skin.

My knees buckle, and I shiver.

But it's not the cold that's undoing me this time.

My entire body is on fire. I close my eyes to savor the feeling.

The next drop trickles down the bridge of my nose and then falls. I can feel Josh's gaze following it as it slides between my breasts.

His hands grip my waist. The pads of his thumbs brush the ridges of my hip bones. Although his touch is feathery soft, it grounds me.

I know exactly what I'm about to do.

I know exactly what I want as I rise up onto my toes.

Our lips crash together, hard and hungry. My hips press to his as he pulls me close. Tight. Firm. Like he'll never let go.

When he parts my lips with his tongue, it's as if he's repeating

back to me exactly what I'm thinking. This is good. This is right. This is the way it's all supposed to be.

Not Fletch and Sloan.

Not pretending.

Us.

My fingers find their way under Josh's wet shirt to the abs I've been coveting from afar. I slide my hands up his chest until the material of his shirt stops me.

He laughs with a "Need a little help?," then lifts it off in one smooth motion.

I have this desire to run my hands over every inch of his skin. To suck and taste. But he reaches for the hem of my top, and before I can say "Take it off," it's joining his in a wet puddle on the floor.

"You've made the next part easy." I nod at his absence of pants and the wet boxers straining to hold in his erection.

"Then let's do you first." He walks me back till the backs of my knees hit the corner of the mattress, then kisses me until I fall onto the bed.

He slides the rest of my dress off in a single fluid motion and smiles at my nearly naked body. "Now we're even."

He leans in, reaching behind me to undo my bra. He plants a soft kiss just below my ear as he slips it off and tosses it somewhere out of view. His fingers trace the curve of my collarbone, then dip low between my breasts. His thumb drags across my chest until it circles my nipple.

I close my eyes and moan, then let out a soft *ahhhhh* as his thumb is replaced with his tongue. He repeats the whole experience on the other side. All the while, a deep ache builds between my legs. I have completely abandoned any further rational thought, too caught up in the contrasting sensations of the rough pad of his thumb and the wetness of his mouth.

His body shifts, and I immediately notice the absence of heat, but I am too distracted by his tongue, which has abandoned my breast to head south. His fingers tickle as they run along the elastic of my underwear, then curl and tug until they're around my ankles. The tip of his nose traces a long line from my ankle to my knee, up my inner thigh to my hip bone, where his tongue takes over as it drags all the way to my belly button.

My fingers grip the bedsheets. "You've barely touched me, and I'm almost there."

He laughs. The heat of his breath on my skin only furthers my point. "We're just getting started."

His fingers find my entrance, and as he drags his index finger through my wetness, my hips drive off the bed.

"Holy Moses." My abs contract, lifting my shoulders off the bed.

"Am I okay to keep going?" he asks.

"I cannot be held responsible for my reaction if you stop. Please continue."

Josh does not continue. He presses a knee between my legs and meets my lips with a hard, hungry kiss. He doesn't relent until my head falls back, landing on the pillow. This time, when his finger finds my folds, it's to part them, and the next sensation is the long, slow lick of his tongue.

"Oh my god, Josh." I'm very aware of how loud I'm yelling his name. He does it again, over and over, until I lose count of all the Joshes I have screamed out to the universe. When he inserts a finger, then two, and starts to move in and out, I lose complete control of anything and everything coming out of my mouth. I try to swear. I definitely moan. And when the pressure builds to the point that I can no longer take it, I let out a long, loud *ahhhhh* as I get a euphoric rush that fizzles through my body.

I barely notice when he crawls up and lies beside me. "How was that?"

My arm flops onto his chest. "Ask me again in a minute when my soul returns to my body."

I could fall asleep happy. Curl up in a ball, close my eyes, and dream of a naked Josh. But although Josh is lying comfortably beside me, one part of him is still very much awake.

"I need about thirty more seconds to recover, then I will be good to go." I reach beneath his boxers and stroke him, my thumb brushing over his soft, velvety tip. It twitches in my hand. Now it's his turn to moan.

I continue to stroke him, loving how hard he is from just the touch of my fingers, hearing the noises he's making and knowing it's me that's causing them. Then a worrying thought surfaces.

"Question for you. Do you have a condom?"

Josh's hazy, sleepy eyes grow wide.

"No," I moan. "This is Carson's Cove. Sex before marriage ranks right up there with underage drinking in the actions-have-consequences storylines."

Josh reaches into the nightstand and pulls out a strip of condoms. A very long strip of condoms.

"I get the impression my man Fletch is smarter than people give him credit for. He has this place figured out." He pulls one off the strip and rips the packaging with his teeth. He removes his boxers and rolls the condom on, then takes my head between his hands to kiss me. It's sweet and slow, and my stomach fills with a thousand happy butterflies.

He grabs my hips and flips me onto my back in a single smooth motion. His lips meet mine as he rubs himself, right where I need him, getting me wetter and wetter.

He presses in with the tip, giving me a moment to adjust, then starts to thrust in slowly—taking his time, inch by inch. My hips have other plans. They drive up from the bed. He laughs, says, "I thought I was holding back there, but I can't argue with that," then fills me completely.

He leans forward, maintaining a slow, steady pace. My hands roam over his back, his chest, and his shoulders. All of the places I've been able to look at but never touch. The sensation builds again. My arms drop to the mattress as I think of nothing but how good he feels. How close I am to the edge.

He picks up speed, going harder and faster, and just when I think I'm about to fall, he slows and shifts position.

"I'm not quite ready for this to be over," he whispers. He licks the tender spot behind my ear, and I shiver. He picks up speed again. But this new position has his hips in line with my clit. The new sensation is too much; my moans turn to *ahs* with every thrust. He presses up onto his hands, opening the space between us and using it to bring his thumb to my clit. He makes slow circles until I can't hold out any longer. "I think I'm going to come again."

He picks up the pace, and I get lost in the rhythm, trying my best to make this feeling last as long as possible. Until I can't. I yell, "I'm coming." Or maybe he does. Either way, I go off like a rocket. My head gets light, and everything blurs into a white haze.

Eventually, I come down. Back to the bed. Back to him.

He slips out of bed only for a moment to dispose of the condom, and when he returns, he holds out his arms until I nestle against his chest.

As I lie there, listening to him breathe softly, the puffy cloud of euphoria that I've been flying on starts to thin. I begin to fall.

The weight of everything that happened tonight drags me downward.

I brought this perfect man into an absolute mess.

I nearly got him killed.

We have no foreseeable way of getting back home unless I give Sheldon the ending he wants. That means choosing Spencer and not Josh.

We've found no evidence of another loophole. Even if one exists, the odds aren't good that we'll find it before this Friday.

Josh won't get the chance to buy back his father's bar. He'll lose his dream because of me.

I tilt my head up, kissing Josh's jawbone softly, savoring the way his stubble scratches my lips. I try to memorize how good it feels to lie here in his arms. How he smells. How safe I feel. How happy.

There's no easy way out of this.

Which means I need to do it the hard way.

25

JOSH

I awaken to the smell of strawberries.

Soft snores come from below my chin from the woman nuzzled in the crook of my arm, leg draped across me like a starfish.

I lay in silence, trying not to disturb her. I'm happy she's here and that last night wasn't just a hallucination brought on from ingesting too much seawater—until our peace is interrupted by a crashing sound from the bar below us.

Brynn's snores stop abruptly as she lifts her head. She tilts her face to mine, a confused ridge forming deep between her eyebrows.

"Josh?"

"Hey."

Her expression clears as she takes in her surroundings.

"How are you feeling? Any aftereffects of the—" Her thought is cut off by a second crash.

Brynn whips her head toward the door. "What is happening down there?"

The sound happens again, but this time, it's more of a piercing screech that morphs into something far more recognizable. The opening notes of a song.

"Someone's turned on the karaoke machine." I crane my neck away from my pillow to hear a little better. "What song is that?"

Brynn groans, snuggling further into the nook of my arm. "It's the opening credits for *Carson's Cove.*" She reaches for the nightstand. "Who in their right mind would be down there at the ungodly hour of"—she picks up the clock and reads it—"ten forty-five?"

Her answer comes in the form of a voice.

A singing voice.

She freezes, her hand still hovering over the nightstand.

"Sheldon," we both say at the same time.

From there, it's a quick scramble. I pull on my boxers and toss Brynn her sundress. In a matter of seconds, we're dressed. Brynn beats me to the door, but before she opens it, she hesitates, slowing her motions. She turns the handle so as not to make a sound, cracking the door open only an inch.

I peer over her shoulder at the bar downstairs.

Sheldon is on the stage, microphone in hand, eyes focused on Fletcher's apartment door as if he's waiting for us.

Brynn shuts the door and presses her back to it, blocking my way. "Wait. There's something I need to talk to you about first."

She opens her mouth, but the song from downstairs stops and is replaced by Sheldon's booming voice.

"I know you're up there, Sloan. Come down here. All I want to do is talk."

Brynn closes her eyes for a moment. When she opens them again, she turns swiftly, opens the door, and strides down the stairs. I follow close behind, the entire time watching the stage, where Sheldon stands eerily still.

"We have a saying here in Carson's Cove." His voice booms through the microphone, its ominous tone not helped by the echo of the empty warehouse. "Fool me once, shame on you. Fool me twice, shame on you again. We have gone over this, Sloan. How many times do I have to repeat myself? I'm starting to get angry." He begins to pace back and forth across the stage. "We had a deal."

My stomach drops. "What is he talking about?"

She shakes her head. "I wouldn't call it a deal. It was more like a straight-up threat."

Sheldon stops. "And you saw what happened when you completely ignored it."

Brynn steps toward him. "So that *was* you? With Luce in the boat. You made that happen?"

Closing his eyes, Sheldon runs his free hand through his already disheveled hair. "I warned you that things would get ugly." He throws his arm down as his eyes fly open and grow wide while they fixate directly on me. "I would really hate for them to get even uglier."

"Don't you dare, Sheld—" Brynn steps toward the stage, but I grab her arm and pull her behind me.

"Smothers. Tell me what's going on."

Her hand finds mine, and as our fingers lace together, Sheldon growls into the microphone.

"You." Sheldon points his finger straight at my chest with such fervor that I swear I can feel it. "You are not one to take a hint, are you? I tried to be subtle with a well-timed power outage or two, but you managed to screw up being the screw-up!" He shakes his head, the volume of his voice dropping to speaking level. "I should have been more careful. I should never have let you come here. That was my bad. I got impatient." He continues to pace the stage until he once again stops midstride; this time, his finger is aimed at Brynn. "But you—" He glares. "I expected more from you. It's one thing that you interfered with my ending for Luce last night. But spending the night with him—" He thrusts his hand in my direction so violently that the microphone shrieks. "Sloan doesn't belong with Fletcher Scott."

I open my mouth to argue. To tell him that Sloan may not belong with Fletcher Scott, but Brynn belongs with me.

Brynn, however, steps forward before I can speak. "You know what? You're right."

My stomach bottoms out.

"I screwed up big-time," Brynn continues. "You had a plan for this place, and I messed it all up. I don't know what I was thinking."

I'm lost.

Brynn and I haven't had the chance to talk about what happened between us last night, but I thought we were on the same page. No more denying it. No more Spencer. We were going to figure this out together.

"We made a mess of your plans," Brynn says. "And I'm very sorry for that, and I want to make it up to you."

She holds her hand out to him as if talking to a small child. "Let's go talk. Just the two of us. I know how we can make everything right."

Sheldon sets down the mic, his eyes shifting from Brynn to me.

As he crouches down to jump from the stage, I reach for Brynn's hand. To get her out of here. To run. To do anything but stay here and comply with this sicko. But Brynn shakes me off.

"You still want to go home, right?" she asks through clenched teeth, her eyes fixated on Sheldon.

"Of course, but—"

"June twenty-first," she whispers. "I'll get you home in time. I promise. Trust me, okay?"

"I trust you, but what are you—"

She shakes her head. "I need to go take care of this. But meet me tonight. Seven o'clock. At our spot?"

Sheldon finally reaches us. Brynn points to the door and beckons Sheldon to follow her. I watch as they leave together.

"Are you sure about this?" I yell, just as the door is closing.

There's a moment when I think I'm too late. But then Brynn's head reappears around the corner.

"I'm sure," she says. "I'm going to fix everything."

26

BRYNN

"Five . . . Six . . . Five. *Six*. Seven. Eight."

"Isn't She Lovely" croons through the speaker for the 347th time.

My cheeks hurt from smiling.

My arms hurt from the incessant, repetitive *port de bras* that Poppy keeps yelling about in a fake French accent as we are trying—and failing—to get this opening pageant number to the level "that is expected for a town celebrating seventy-five years of tradition."

Her words, not mine.

This is all part of my deal with Sheldon. Follow his plan. No opinions. No objections. No funny business.

"Heels like this should be illegal," Luce whispers as she chassés around me. "I considered taking them off, but with the looks Poppy keeps giving me, I feel oddly comforted by having two weapons strapped to my feet."

Poppy shoots Luce a seething glare, as if she can tell from the other side of the stage that we're talking about her.

One of the other contestants gets confused and thinks she is the object of Poppy's wrath. She freezes in terror mid-chaîné turn, and the contestants behind her pile up like crashing dominoes.

There are sequins flying everywhere. A few screams. Some crying.

I sit down on one of the crates covered in decorative sparkly lobsters, welcoming the temporary break as everyone gets back on their feet.

Luce plops down beside me, removing one of her shoes. "Forget what I said. These things need to come off. I forgot being a beauty queen was so painful. I'm gonna need a whole lotta wine tomorrow. The sequins of my dress cut my underarms so badly that I have to hold my arms in a permanent port de bras." She mocks Poppy's French accent. "I can't believe you signed me up for this."

My head whips toward her. "You told me you wanted to enter."

She laughs, knocking me with her elbow. "That was a joke. And yes, I enjoy willfully submitting to torture." She leans back on her elbows and sighs. I find myself scanning her face, looking for any signs of last night's trauma. She catches me doing it and rolls her eyes.

"I told you, I'm absolutely fine."

She's caught me doing this twice already. "Are you sure?"

She nods. "I'm a little tired and very embarrassed. I made a really stupid call."

She did. And so did Spencer. And in typical *Carson's Cove* fashion, the town has woken up as if nothing major happened. Even Main Street, with its perfect flower boxes, looks as if the events of last night's storm are a distant memory.

"Ladies!" Poppy claps her hands. "Let's take five. A few of you need some touch-ups." She circles her face with her hand.

"Sloan." She holds up her arm and beckons me with her fingers. "Come. I need to discuss something with you."

I get to my feet with a groan.

Luce nudges one of her heels with her bare toe. "Just holler if you need backup. I got you."

I laugh until I catch sight of Poppy watching us, and her expression makes me want to ask Luce if she doesn't mind coming with me—just in case.

As I cross the stage, Poppy disappears into the wing. I follow her, and when I get close enough to talk, she grabs me by the wrist and pulls me into a dark corner.

"Why are you all, like, buddy-buddy with her?" Poppy's tone is clipped.

I know exactly who she's referring to, but try to play cool. "Who? Luce?"

"Uh, yes, Luce. I keep catching the two of you whispering."

"We're just talking—"

"No." Poppy shakes her head. "We're not going there. It's not Luce and Sloan. It's Poppy and Sloan. It's always been Poppy and Sloan and it will always be Poppy and Sloan. Right?"

I open my mouth to argue, but the curtain of the wing begins to move and a man steps out from behind it.

Sheldon.

He has a black headset on and is carrying a clipboard as if he's a stagehand.

I hate this.

All of it.

But a deal is a deal.

And I'm a woman of my word.

"Got it," I tell Poppy. "BFFs. Forever."

Poppy smiles, throwing her arms around me. "Love you,

babe!" When she pulls away, she lowers her voice. "Okay, so the other reason I called you over here is to give you this." She drags me into a dressing room, where there is a rolling rack with a single suit bag hanging from it. She unzips it slowly, revealing a floor-length gown in a deep midnight blue.

"I think you should wear this as your evening wear," she says as I pull the gown fully out of the bag.

It's a simple strapless mermaid silhouette. The material has tiny crystals sewn in that shimmer with any movement.

"You wore this when you won," I tell her, touched by her thoughtfulness.

"Exactly," she confirms. "It's a miracle dress. It sucks you in at all the right places." She pokes the soft folds of my stomach with her finger. "And it does a decent job of lifting the girls, but I strongly suggest you get a push-up bra. And maybe skip dinner tonight? You're broader than I am, and you don't want to look stuffed into the thing." She smiles, squeezing my arm. "It's amazing, right? It will look perfect with the crown."

"It's beautiful." I nod, placing the gown back on the rack.

"Well, it's made for a queen." She lowers her voice. "But a true queen needs to look the part even when she's not out on that stage. You know? Dress for the job you want and all?" She gestures to my disheveled hair and wrinkled dress from yesterday. "Maybe you should go home? Freshen up a bit? Then you can come back more like that picture-perfect girl we all love."

She gives me an air kiss and heads back onto the stage.

I attempt and fail to smooth the creases from my outfit. Poppy was not wrong in her assessment that I could definitely use a shower and some clothes that aren't from yesterday. The pageant practice breaks for lunch, and I slip out the front door of the town hall, heading down Main Street toward Sloan's

house. I pass the docks and beach. Both are so serenely picturesque that had last night not been imprinted so firmly on my
memories, I could probably convince myself that it never even
happened.

It was one of the worst and then best nights of my life.

My heart hurts from all of the emotional whiplash.

I still ache now, knowing that there's only going to be more.

I've made a deal with the metaphorical and potentially even
literal devil, but that deal is going to give Josh his dream.

My walk-and-sulk is interrupted as Bob the mailman steps into
my path. "Morning, Sloan." He tips his imaginary hat. "Lovely
day for a walk, isn't it?"

I nod and smile as we do that weird dance where we both step
to the left and then to the right, still blocking each other's path
until I concede and cross the street.

As I hit the sidewalk, the grocer steps out from behind a giant
pile of oranges. "Hi, Sloan," he calls as the spray from his hose
forces me back into the street.

"Hey, Sloan!" Two small children circle around me on their
bikes.

"Morning, Sloan."

"Howdy, Sloan."

"There's our girl."

My stomach clenches into a tight knot.

This town is getting friendly, but this is next-level, start-of-a-
horror-film weird.

I look around, suddenly more aware of my surroundings.

There are what feels like an abnormal number of people span-
ning this block. All outside. All sneaking glances at me and smiling.

My senses tingle with a warning. Something is up.

I reverse directions and head toward the shore, thinking the beach may be less populated. However, Doc Martin is blocking my path.

"Not that way, little lady." Doc physically turns me by the shoulders, then steers me back into the middle of the street and over to a folding chair, where I'm forced to sit.

I look around at the sea of faces watching me, watching them, and unease grips my chest.

My thoughts are startled by a sound: a blaring of trumpets that make my blood curdle. The sound builds, becoming louder and louder as the pieces of exactly what is happening fall into place.

Oh god.

I desperately hope that I'm interpreting all of this wrong and that what is about to happen isn't about to happen.

Then a Beyoncé-like voice comes in, and I know without any doubt that I am Carson's Cove's latest victim.

It's a flash mob.

They come out of every nook and cranny. Out from behind flowerpots, parked cars, and even a sewer grate. Doc Martin, Lois, even elderly Pop. They're gyrating. They're port de bras-ing as what sounds like a knockoff, watered-down, censored-for-prime-time-television version of Queen Bey's "Crazy in Love" is blasted from speakers that seem to be all over town.

Then the tubas come. A low *buh-bum* that shakes me all the way to the core.

Then the trumpets.

The drums.

It's the entire Carson's Cove High marching band.

And leading them—blond hair shining in the sun—is the former man of my dreams.

He's a great dancer.

They're all great dancers, actually.

There are lifts.

There are splits.

Everyone looks like they've spent years training on Broadway.

I'm still trapped. I can't go. I can't leave. All I can do is watch as Spencer dances his way toward me.

"Hey, Sloan." Spencer walks perfectly in time to the music. "I've been trying to find a way to tell you that I'm crazy about you. Ever since we shared that magical kiss the other night, I can't get you out of my head. And I have an important question to ask you."

My heart stops completely.

Tiny black specks linger at the corners of my vision. They start to close in as he drops to one knee.

Oh. My. God.

I am certain that I'm seconds away from fainting. Or throwing up. It's fifty-fifty at this point.

But he doesn't pull out a little black box.

Someone tosses him a brown paper bag.

The little black specks clear away enough that I can watch him pull out a sweater.

No, it's a jacket.

Maroon and gold with a #18 stitched onto the leather sleeve. His basketball jacket from high school.

"I was hoping I could give you this. I should have done it years ago, and I'm sorry, but I'm hoping you'll accept it now."

My icy heart melts just enough to see the sweetness in his gesture. He clearly went to a lot of trouble here.

His hopeful eyes look up at me. They match the ocean perfectly, and as I hesitate, they flick from me to the crowd surrounding us.

They're frozen in their final pose. One hand on their hip, the other raised triumphantly above their heads, punching the sky.

Everyone is watching us. Smiling. So hopeful. Doc. Pop. Lois. Even Poppy and the rest of the pageant contestants.

All of Carson's Cove appears to be here.

Including Josh.

He's at the back. On the sidewalk out front of the Bronze, next to Sherry. Neither appeared to have been part of the dancing.

Of all the eyes in the crowd watching me, it's his I feel the most.

Waiting.

Josh is the one I want. I have no doubts. In fact, I have feelings that are so deep and serious that I need time alone to sort through and truly unpack them. But the tiny hairs on my arms stand on end as another gaze falls on me.

Sheldon is still in his pageant crew headset. Dressed all in black. And although he says nothing, his eyes communicate everything: *This is what you wanted.*

My heart actually aches as I meet Spencer's eyes.

"I would love to wear your jacket," I tell him, taking it from his hands.

The crowd cheers as I slip it on, the sleeves cracked and the wool scratchy.

Spencer picks me up and spins me in a circle.

I'm dizzy and nauseous as he sets me down.

I catch sight of Luce on the sidewalk as my vision stabilizes. She doesn't look gleefully joyous like everyone else, or confused and sad like Josh. She just looks curious.

The crowd begins to disperse, and my eyes drift back to the spot in front of the Bronze, wondering how much of my plan I can communicate to Josh with just my eyes.

But the front stoop is empty.

And Josh is gone.

27

JOSH

I slam the door to the Bronze behind me, but it doesn't close with a satisfying bang. There's a soft thud, followed by a "Jesus H. Christmas, are you trying to kill me?"

I whip around to find Sherry glaring at me.

"Sorry." My anger dissipates for a moment of guilt. "I thought you stayed out there with them."

Sherry rolls her eyes. "Those bozos? There's a reason I've kept this place a dump for so many years. Up until this past week, it's kept a nice distance between me and the riffraff."

"Sorry I ruined that."

She rolls her eyes. "I was being dramatic. I can deal with the riffraff as long as they are buying seven-dollar pints." She passes me, heading to the bar, but stops, opening her mouth, as if choosing her next words carefully.

"Listen, I wasn't going to say anything, but I'm getting the sense you need to hear it. Whatever has gotten into you the last little while, I like it. I've been waiting for a long time for you to grow up and stop wandering around this town like you don't know your ass from your head, and frankly, I was starting to lose hope. This place has really turned around. And that was entirely due to your sudden change in attitude. Whatever has happened, keep it up."

I'm a little lost at how I should respond here, as I'm pretty sure the personality changes she's referencing are due to the fact that I'm an entirely different person than her nephew, Fletch, but I decide to take her comment for what it is.

"Thanks, Sherry. The last few years have been rough. Finally seeing things go right has been good for me too."

She raises a brow. "Rough how?"

I didn't exactly think my comment through before I made it. I assumed that, like in every other conversation these past two weeks, Sherry would rip a few insults and move on. But she sits down on a barstool and beckons me to join her. I formulate the best way to tell her the rest as I take a seat.

"Well . . . while I was out in the world . . . finding myself for all those years . . . I became very close to a man. He was like a father figure to me. And he got very ill and left me his bar to run, and I couldn't do it. I couldn't get customers through the door. I couldn't pay the staff, and eventually, I had to sell the place so I didn't go completely bankrupt."

Sherry doesn't immediately say anything. She abandons her seat, ducks under the bar, and fetches two glasses and her best Scotch. She pours us each one and slides mine across the bar. "Sometimes in life, the universe kicks us in the ass, and there's not a whole lot we can do to stop it." She takes a long swig of her drink and then sets it down. "But it's only a loss if we don't learn something from it. So, what was it?"

It's not a rhetorical question. She pins me with her stare, sipping her Scotch as she waits for my answer.

I'm not sure. Losing my dad's bar was such a terrible time in my life that I try not to think about it. It's all a blur, with all my memories defined as before Buddy's or after.

"I guess I learned that live music is always a draw. That kara-oke night worked really well too and—"

"No." Sherry sets her glass down with a hard clink. "What did you learn about yourself?"

I have to really think. When Buddy's was going under, all I could think about was that my dad would have never let it hap-pen. I tried everything, and I did everything, and at the end of it, it still wasn't enough, and it hurt to put everything I had on the line and still come up short. With the Bronze, things were differ-ent. There were no expectations for me or Fletch. We started from the bottom, and with the pressure gone and the distance, I was able to do things differently.

"I guess I learned that I'm actually really good at running a bar like this one. That, yeah, there were some pretty crappy cir-cumstances the first time around. And I guess there's always a risk that things can go wrong again, and it will be out of my con-trol, but all of the good times still make it worth it."

Sherry doesn't say anything, but her lips curve upward—on Sherry's terms, I'd call it a smile.

"I like that. And I'm going to butt into your life one more time this morning, seeing as I'm on a bit of a roll." She lowers her voice. "You know that compliment I gave you earlier about know-ing your ass from your head?"

I snort. "That was a compliment?"

"You know damn well it was. Now I'd like to see you take the same initiative with that girl."

She means Brynn.

I shake my head. "That's not the same thing."

Sherry crosses her arms and huffs. "I am a few good years away from going senile, and my eyesight is just fine. I see the way you look at her and the way she looks at you. I've been behind this bar for over thirty years. I've learned a lot more about the world than how to pour a stiff drink. She likes you. You like her. You're telling me she isn't worth the risk?"

"It's a little bit more complicated than that. Plus, she's out there with Spencer. Maybe that's the guy she needs."

Sherry narrows her eyes. "And you're in here, sulking, doing absolutely nothing about it." Sherry pokes a bony finger right between my ribs. "You just told me you learned something from failing. But from what I can see, you've rolled over and played dead. Given yourself a pat on the back and said, *The best man has won*. But I don't think he's the best man, and I don't think you think that either. There's nothing he can offer her that you can't. But there's one thing he did do that you didn't."

"Coordinate a flash mob?" I offer sarcastically.

Sherry doesn't laugh. "Yes."

"She hated that. It's one of her worst—"

"Not the dancing." Sherry cuts me off. "The fact that he told her exactly how he felt. He left no questions on the table. No doubts. We've all been scorned by past lovers. God only knows I never learned my lesson, and as much as we shouldn't, we carry the emotional baggage with us far longer than we should. If you really like that girl, tell her. Leave no doubts in her mind. Fight for her, because although you think it hurts to try and fail, it hurts a hell of a lot worse when you walk away and then realize when it's too late that she was the love of your life."

Sherry's words hit hard.

She's right.

About all of it.

What I feel about Brynn.

That if I don't do something, she will end up with Spencer or someone else that comes along.

"Okay." I get to my feet, a plan beginning to formulate in my head. "I need to do a few things before seven, but I haven't finished stocking the beer fridge and someone needs to be here at six to let the Hungry Dingos in to set up. Is there any chance you can . . . ?"

She rolls her eyes, waving me off. "Yes. Fine. Go find love. I got it."

I give her a kiss on the cheek. She cups my face with her hand before giving it a light slap.

"You're not going to plan a flash mob, right? Just to be clear, that part was metaphorical."

Nope. If I'm going to win Brynn, I need to do it my way.

"Yeah, I have something completely different in mind."

28

BRYNN

He knocks on Sloan's kitchen door precisely at 6:00 P.M., just as planned.

"Uber Eats," he says, laughing as I swing the door open. "Get it?" He holds up the white box. "Like the night we met and—"

"I get it."

He steps inside, and I immediately kick the door closed. I'm far less enthused about what's waiting for me inside the box compared to that night several days ago.

"So how exactly will this work?"

Sheldon was surprisingly agreeable when I proposed he let Josh go home tonight. I was prepared to beg, plead, and offer up my firstborn, but Sheldon just smiled when I suggested it, seeming rather pleased with the whole idea.

"It works the exact same way the original cake did. You make a wish, you blow out the candle, and when Josh Bishop wakes up tomorrow morning, he will be warm and cozy in his very own bed. Easy peasy lemon squeezy."

Which will give him plenty of time to get up north and buy his dad's bar back.

"Will he remember what happened?"

Sheldon hesitates ever so slightly as he sets the box down on the counter. "He should remember everything. There's no reason why he wouldn't, but wishes can be finicky things. I can make no guarantees."

Josh might not decide to go up north if he doesn't remember. And if he doesn't buy his dad's bar back, this whole plan is a waste. Not to mention he'll have no recollection of the time we spent together here.

"Relax." Sheldon's voice is eerily calm. "It will all work out exactly as it's supposed to. Have you forgotten where you are?"

I haven't forgotten. How can I? The place where everything ends up as it's meant to be—or at least I once thought so.

Sheldon opens the lid of the box. The cake is identical to the original one from back home and from the window of Bake a Wish. Same white icing. Same rainbow sprinkles. Even the birthday candle nestled in its center is the same. It's adorably innocent-looking, considering its power.

Sheldon pulls a lighter from his back pocket. He flicks his thumb, igniting an orange flame that flickers eerily in front of his face before he holds it up to the candle. I step in close and inhale, but he pulls the cake away.

"Uh, uh, uh. I'm not leaving any room for funny business. I want to hear your wish out loud."

I had anticipated this. Although I would have happily taken negligence on Sheldon's part to wish both Josh and me home tonight, the plan felt a little too easy.

"Fine. But before I do, I want to make sure we are clear on our agreement."

Sheldon crosses his arms over his chest. "Go on."

"I will wish Josh to go home tonight, and in exchange, I will stay here and give Sloan the ending she deserves."

Sheldon's lips curl into a slow smile. "That's the deal."

There's something in his smile that bugs me. I don't know if it's because it doesn't quite match the look in his eyes or because maybe I've lost my faith in this place.

"To be clear, I win the pageant, Sloan and Spencer fall in love, and then I go home too just like our original agreement, right?"

His smile falters. It's the tiniest twitch.

"What aren't you telling me, Sheldon?"

He holds up his palms. "I'm not hiding anything. Our agreement is very straightforward. Sloan gets her happy ending, to be with Spencer . . . forever."

All at once, I see the fatal flaw in my plan. Sheldon's loophole. Why this all felt a little too easy.

"So I'll never be able to go home?"

Sheldon drops his hands with a feigned dramatic sigh. "Is that really such a bad thing?"

My blood cools to the temperature of ice. I've been played. Hoodwinked. Right from the very beginning.

"Was that your plan all along? To keep us here indefinitely?"

Sheldon makes no effort to hide his rolling eyes. "What else do you want? I've basically handed you the perfect life: a town full of charm and whimsy and an overabundance of seasonally appropriate festivals. Idyllic weather—"

"Yeah," I interrupt, "unless you count the occasional hurricane."

Sheldon waves me off with the back of his hand.

I close my eyes and picture my future: life in Carson's Cove with Spencer, laid out so perfectly that I can see every detail.

Weekly date nights to Pop's for milkshakes. A wedding at the ga-zebo with everyone in town in attendance. Growing old together. Happy. Easy.

Never seeing Josh again.

This terrible thought grows and grows until it consumes every-thing else.

There is nothing stopping me from abandoning this whole agreement with Sheldon right now.

I could easily and enthusiastically tell him to shove his plan up the one place in Carson's Cove where the sun doesn't regularly shine.

I could go back to Josh. Explain everything. Live like we have been these last few days. He'd have the Bronze; I could hang out with Luce. We could be happy.

But in the deepest corners of my heart, I know that Sheldon will never stop trying to tear us apart. And even if, by some mir-acle, we evade Sheldon's plans, if Josh stays here, he will never get the chance to buy his father's bar back, and he'll never see his mom again.

In either scenario, my fate is sealed.

It has been since the moment I made that first wish.

But Josh's doesn't have to be.

"How do I know you'll keep your word?"

Sheldon slides the cake toward me again. "This is no ordinary dessert. It's got the magic of Carson's Cove baked right into it. It's bigger than you and me. It's made of whimsy and suspension of belief, that same television magic that keeps you glued to your television each week. Once you make your wish, your contract is set. There's nothing you or I can do to change it."

His words make my stomach sink.

"You win, Sheldon." I close my eyes. "I wish that Josh Bishop will wake up safe and happy in his own bed back in Toronto tomorrow morning, and I'll agree to stay and give Sloan Edwards the ending she deserves . . . no matter how long it takes."

I open my eyes and look at Sheldon. "Is that good enough for you?"

He lifts the cake up to me. "Let's make it official."

29

JOSH

was worried she wouldn't come.

Especially after Spencer swooped in yet again with something over the top, and Brynn chose him.

But she appears at the top of the ladder, right on time, and as she steps onto the roof, the string lights reflect in her eyes, making them sparkle.

"Oh my god. It's so beautiful." Brynn spins in a slow circle, checking out my best attempt at a romantic gesture. I've cleaned up the beer bottles and hung a few of the extra lights from downstairs. In the twilight, they give the roof an almost ethereal feel.

"I can't believe you did this." As her arms fall to her sides, her expression changes. Her brows draw together as she visibly swallows. My stomach bottoms out completely as she averts her eyes and says, "I need to talk to you about something—"

I hold up my hand. "Before you tell me whatever it is you need to tell me, I have something I want to say first. Please." I hold out my hand. An invitation to sit. Brynn walks tentatively over to the vent and perches on the edge, watching me the entire time.

I draw a deep breath.

"I can't sing. My dancing is even worse. Really, what you're looking at here"—I point to the lights—"is my capacity for grand gestures. I'm never going to be the kind of guy that always has some epically perfect monologue with all of the right words. I'm terrible at planning dates. I didn't think observatories were something you could actually visit. I'm still not sure how they work. I'm the kind of guy who likes a pretty spot that's quiet where you can easily talk." I gesture to the view of the ocean. "I don't pack picnics, but I'm usually pretty reliable with a cold beer. My point is . . ." I close my eyes and breathe for a moment before continuing. "I'm never going to be Spencer. And I am okay with that. He may be your dream guy. And I won't blame you if at the end of this *pick me, choose me, love me* speech, you choose him, but I think you'd be making a huge mistake. Because even though he's perfect at a lot of things, I don't think he can love you better than I can, because I do, Brynn. I love you."

I know as the words leave my mouth that they're true. That although I've said them to other people before, I've never meant them in quite this way.

Her mouth falls open, but she doesn't say a word.

"I don't have a whole lot I can promise you at this moment," I continue. "I can't even promise you I can get us home, but I can say that you're it for me. And I want to be it for you."

I end it there, satisfied that I've left no doubts. Hoping it's enough.

She stands, her face still unreadable. "For a guy who claims he can't deliver an epic monologue, that was pretty perfect." She takes a step toward me. "I'm so sorry, Josh."

My stomach bottoms out completely.

"It's okay, I get it."

"No. No, that's not what I'm saying." She shakes her head. "I'm sorry I didn't tell you what I was planning to do. I can't imagine how you must feel after watching that whole scene this morning. I didn't know it was going to happen. I wanted to talk to you first." She moves until she's right in front of me. Toe to toe. "I made a deal with Sheldon."

My body goes completely still.

"When you wake up tomorrow, you'll be back home. You'll be able to bid on your dad's bar and get your happily ever after."

The elation only lasts for half a second.

"What about you?" As the question leaves my mouth, she looks up.

Her eyes have a sheen that she's trying to get rid of by blinking. I know the answer even before she speaks.

"I am going to stay. I've agreed to give Sloan the ending she deserves."

I feel like I'm falling. Like the ground I was standing on only seconds ago has suddenly shifted, knocking me straight on my ass.

"Okay . . . but this is just temporary, right? So, what? You stay, kiss him or whatever, and then you can come home?"

She shakes her head, and with every turn, something inside me twists tighter and tighter.

"Sloan's happy ending is to be with Spencer forever, so . . ." Her voice breaks. "It's the only way he'd agree to let you leave."

I pick apart her words, trying to find some other way to interpret what she just said.

"I don't care about that. I'm not leaving without you. We don't split up. We stick together, remember?"

"I remember." A single tear slips down her cheek. "And I knew you'd say that, because that's the kind of guy you are, Josh. You're sweet and caring, and you're loyal, and you've done nothing but put me first since we got here, despite the fact that it was my wish and my actions that got us into this mess. But now I'm going to make it right. You need to have your bar. I know you care about it. It's your dream. I've seen you at the Bronze, looking comfortable and so fudging happy, with that little glimmer of pride in your eye. But you deserve to have that with a place that is all yours."

No. This isn't the answer.

"We can talk to Sheldon. Negotiate."

She shakes her head. "It's too late. It's done. I've made another wish. There was one of those stupid cakes. There's no going back, even if I changed my mind. And I haven't."

I pause and look at her. And the truth sets in. "How long do I have?"

She closes her eyes. It causes more tears to fall. She reaches up and wipes them with the back of her hand. "Until midnight."

That's it? That's only hours. There has to be another way.

"There's nothing we can do?"

She shakes her head. Her arms reach for me, then stop in mid-air. As they drop back to her sides, she looks up at me, a strained line of worry between her eyebrows. "Can you forgive me for making the decision without you?"

Her voice wobbles on the last few words as her eyes cut left, breaking contact.

I draw her in, tucking the top of her head under my chin, wrapping my arms around her with the thought that maybe if I don't let go, I won't need to leave. "You're already forgiven. But if we only have a few hours, I don't want to waste another second."

30

BRYNN

His arms come around me as if he can sense the turmoil inside my head. Although I'm doing the right thing, it feels so wrong. It's like Pilates, physiotherapy, or saying no to a second slice of Billy Miner ice cream pie. My mind has very rational, solid reasons why Josh needs to go home. But my body feels otherwise.

He bends down and kisses me softly on the lips. All of the noise, all of the worrying thoughts in my head stop—and the only thing left is him.

The softness of his lips.

The ticklish way his fingers skim up my arms.

The way I feel right now. Like this is exactly how it's supposed to be. His soft, comforting kisses to my temple trail down my neck, and I feel the need between us shift from the desire to be close and to comfort to something else entirely.

I take him by the hand, and he follows with no protest. No further explanation needed.

We walk in silence down the fire escape, to the window to

Fletch's room, and to the bed, where Josh reaches for the hem of my sweatshirt and lifts it off easily.

Immediately his lips are on my neck.

My fingers seek out his shirt. I repeat his maneuver with far less finesse, seeing as Josh is much taller than I am.

He picks me up. I wrap my legs around him as he carries me to the end of the bed and sits.

Josh dips his head and kisses me lightly behind the ear.

"I just wish we had more time." His hands bring my body along as he leans back, and I kiss him, long and hard, until I find myself needing more.

I reach for the button of his jeans and spend far too many precious moments trying to get them open, only to realize that his pants have a button fly.

"Where does Fletch buy his clothing? Time is of the essence here. This is the modern man's equivalent of a chastity belt."

Josh laughs and moves to help me, slipping the remaining three buttons open with ease. He slides his jeans down his hips, then follows with his boxers. In less than the amount of time it takes me to scoot up onto the bed, he's naked.

I reach out and stroke him, my thumb making a lingering loop of his velvety soft tip.

"Mmmmm," Josh moans, and the sound of his voice reverberates all the way to my core.

I want . . . no . . . I *need* to make him moan like that again.

But Josh is nudging me onto my back and undoing my bra with an easy flick of his fingers. And then his mouth is on my nipples, and I start to lose myself with every swirl of his tongue.

I whimper.

I feel like I'm melting into the mattress, and the only thing that's tethering me to reality is Josh's tongue and the way it sends an almost electric pulse through my entire body.

His hand finds the waistband of my jeans. He has none of the same issues I had, and before I can say "Touch me everywhere," my pants are a heap on the floor.

Josh's hands skim along my naked thighs. His thumbs hook the thin waistband of my underwear, and I lift my hips to help him slide them from my legs. His hands find my skin again, and suddenly, it feels like they're everywhere. And I want them everywhere.

We kiss for a few moments, Josh's chest pressing against my breasts, his erection hard on my stomach. His mouth pecks chastely along my jaw. Then, without warning, his tongue plunges into my mouth, his hand finds my nipple, and his thumb resumes those slow, tantalizing circles that I've decided are my new favorite thing.

"This okay?" he asks, breaking our kiss.

It's a thousand million times better than okay, but all I can manage is a quick, breathy *mmmm hmmm*. But it's enough for Josh to replace his hand with his mouth, which frees up his thumb to travel down . . .

Down . . .

Down my body to the spot in between my legs that has been patiently waiting. His finger finds the pool of moisture that's gathered at my entrance. He circles twice, then runs his fingers up my slit. I gasp, the sensation driving my hips off the bed.

I can feel him smiling against my breast as he repeats it twice more.

"Good?" he asks.

"Yes, but . . ." I can't find the words to finish my sentence.

Every time I get close, Josh's hand does another circle, and I lose my train of thought. On top of that, I'm not certain what I actually want to happen. This aching repetitive bliss is driving me mad, but with every stroke, I want him more, and *ahhhhh.*

His thumb settles on my clit, joining his tongue in the same slow, circular rhythm.

Yes. This. This is what I want. Each swirl drives me closer to undone. I feel the pressure build between my legs. A moan escapes my lips, then another as Josh pushes a finger inside me.

I moan so loudly that I'm grateful the bar is closed tonight. The friction between my legs makes me feel like I'm on the upward climb of a roller coaster, inching closer to the thrill to come.

He picks up the rhythm, and his teeth scrape against the sensitive skin of my nipple. He sucks hard, and the sensation drives me fucking wild. He adds a second finger, and the pressure explodes, sending waves of hot pleasure through me. My body clenches around his fingers as his lips move back to mine and kiss me tenderly. He moves to rest beside me, and I miss him almost immediately. As if he can sense it, he intertwines his fingers with mine.

"So does Fletch have any more—"

Josh rolls off the bed before I finish my sentence. He finds his pants and pulls out a foil packet. He walks back to the bed and leans in to press a sweet kiss to my lips before climbing back beside me. I stroke his cheek, feeling him hard against my stomach.

He lifts his hips to roll the condom on, then pushes onto his knees to straddle my legs. My knees fall open as he angles himself at my entrance.

And I get this overwhelming need to feel him inside me. He pushes in slowly, giving me time for my body to adjust. He leans down and brings his lips to mine. Our kiss is long and deep, and

I moan into his mouth as his hips start to pick up their rhythm and that delicious friction builds between my legs again.

"You feel so good," he whispers as his pace builds. Fletch's bed squeaks beneath us, and I worry it may fall apart, but the rest of my thoughts flutter away as a new one occurs.

"Hey, Josh."

Josh stops at the sound of his name.

"I think I want to go on top. To ride you."

His face breaks into a wide smile as he slides his arms under my shoulders, and before I know what's happening, he's rolling onto his back and pulling so I end up on top of him.

"That was impressive."

He reaches up and cups my cheek. "Tell me what else you want."

I feel stupid saying what I want out loud. So instead, I begin to rock, enjoying this new position, the way I can control the rhythm and the pressure.

It feels so good, but there's something missing.

"That thing that you do with your thumb on my clit."

Josh drags his thumb through my wetness and begins a slow circle.

"Is this what you want?"

"Yes." *Oh, yes.*

I arch my back and let myself float to that happy place where my brain is hyper-concentrated on the insane pressure building between my legs and how it feels like every molecule in my body is on edge, waiting for sweet release.

Then I feel it.

A little spark.

Right there.

But then Josh shifts, and the sensation is gone again. I moan and take his hand in mine, moving his fingers exactly where I want them. "Here, a little harder."

Josh does what I ask, resuming the circles with perfect pressure.

The little spark is back, and now it's exploding like a firecracker, spreading waves of pleasure through my body.

"I'm coming," I tell him, too lost in the feeling to comprehend anything more than that he is moaning too. His hand finds my hip and pulls, so I'm grinding even deeper.

There's a thin sheen of sweat over his chest, and his breathing is labored and ragged.

Whenever I think he can't get any sexier, I get proven wrong.

I collapse onto the bed beside him. He pulls me to his chest, to the little Brynn-shaped nook where I fit just right. He places a kiss on top of my head, and we lie there in silence until his breath slows and takes on a steady rhythm.

I lie there in the dark, listening to him sleep, trying to memorize what it feels like to lie next to him. His smell. The heat of his body. The protective way his arms wrap around me.

I start to drift to that state that's halfway between reality and dreams. I know that our time together is limited, but there's nowhere else I'd rather be than asleep in his arms.

I turn my head and press my forehead to his.

"Don't forget," I whisper. "When you go back. Don't forget me, okay?"

He doesn't answer.

I listen to his breaths until everything goes black.

31

BRYNN

The bed is cold when I awake. The covers must have fallen onto the ground sometime in the night, leaving my naked body exposed.

I'm alone.

There's no sleeping body next to me. Not even an indent in the mattress. No evidence that Josh was ever here. The empty condom wrapper on the nightstand is my only solace, proof that I didn't dream up the perfect man. It's a reminder that he was under my metaphorical nose and actual roof for months, but I was too preoccupied with my own cluster of a life to notice. I needed to drag us both to an alternate reality to see it.

My jeans are still in their heap on the floor. I pull them on, but when I reach for my T-shirt, I instead grab his. As I pull it over my head, I inhale the last fumes of his smell. And then I debate crawling back into bed for a good ugly cry. But I can't.

Today, I'm not mopey, glass-half-empty Brynn, who just said goodbye to the love of her life.

No, today I am Sloan Edwards. Carson's Cove's beloved wall-flower. About to become a beautiful swan.

And I have a pageant to win.

Sherry is already behind the bar when I descend. She gives me a funny look when she spots me coming down the steps, but if she's curious about why I'm coming out of Fletcher's room at eight-thirty in the morning, she doesn't say anything. She continues drying glasses with her bar rag, humming what sounds like an old Alanis Morissette song under her breath.

"Good morning, Sherry," I say in my best Sloan voice. "Fletch asked me to tell you that he had to leave town unexpectedly. He's not sure when he's going to be back, and he wanted to apologize for leaving you hanging."

She sighs, visibly annoyed. "That kid. Where's he gone off to this time?"

I shake my head. "I'm not quite sure," I lie. "It's because of me. I got myself into a bit of a mess. And . . . well . . . he's helping me work through the consequences. He's a really good person, honestly. He wouldn't have—"

Sherry holds up her hand. "I don't need the lecture. I know he's a good kid. A few years ago, I'd tell you you're full of it, but he's changed. He's a good egg. And if you say he's helping out a friend, that's all I need."

It's a small relief but a welcome one. "Thank you, Sherry. And if you ever need a hand, I'm happy to—"

Sherry stops me again, this time with a loud snort. "Honey, I've seen you in action. Thanks, but I think I'll be okay."

She goes back to wiping down the bar as I head outside and walk to Sloan's to put on a Poppy-approved sundress, then head toward the town hall for the last pageant practice.

It's yet another beautiful, sunny day in Carson's Cove, but it feels different.

Josh is gone.

It might just be a trick of the light, but Carson's Cove looks different too. The paint on the door to the grocery store is chipped. Its color is more of a dull rust than a bright red. There are cracks in the sidewalk with tiny green weeds peeking through. The flowers in the curb boxes are wilting. They look how I feel. Sad. Uninspired. Homesick.

I don't have time to mope though. I push open the front doors of the town hall. Every unmarried female between the ages of sixteen and thirty seems to be in some stage of pageant preparedness. Every available space is filled with sparkling evening gowns, string bikinis, hairspray, Red Bull, and duct tape. There's even a Kirkland Signature box of plastic wrap.

I don't want to know what it's used for.

Poppy has us run through the opening number so many times that I start to lose count.

My feet are achy and raw from my too-high heels. It feels like I've come full circle. But there is no more Josh to pick me up and carry me home, both literally and figuratively.

So I channel all of it into earning the crown.

My cheeks ache from smiling. My stomach hurts from sucking in.

But it works.

I glide with the grace of a non-plastic swan.

I port de bras and *pas de basque* and chassé with an ease that makes Sandra Bullock look like an amateur.

I am pageant ready.

"Okay, ladies," Poppy calls through her megaphone. "We have

finished rehearsals. You will be ready to go on at seven P.M. sharp. Am I clear?"

There's a low murmuring of agreement from the contestants.

Luce appears at my elbow; she uses me for balance as she removes her heels. "Good god, that feels good. I have no idea why I'm still wearing these puppies. It's not like anyone can see me in the back."

Poppy moved Luce's spot in the opening number to the far back corner, far away from my front-and-center position. Not only did it put poor Luce out of the judges' sight line, but it also made it almost impossible for the two of us to talk today.

Luce unzips her purse a third of the way, just enough for me to see the bottle of strawberry wine concealed inside.

"Want to get ready with me?" she asks. "I brought just enough to ease the pre-pageant jitters."

"Heck yes," I tell her, grabbing the suit bag with my dress from the rack.

She grabs her bag, and the two of us find an empty bathroom on the third floor, where we plug in our curling irons and alternate taking swigs of her strawberry wine, the entire time talking and laughing about nothing in particular.

I like Luce.

She tells funny stories about her farm animals as we curl our hair.

She says out loud all of my feelings about pantyhose and strapless bras. She's a magician with a contour brush, but she doesn't make me feel like I need it. We're just having fun.

And it makes me feel that this is exactly what I've been missing. A friend. Someone who just gets me. Accepts me. Doesn't want to use me for anything but simple companionship. And although

I haven't directly hurt Luce in the same way Sloan has, I've still judged her from behind the safety of my television screen.

"Okay." Luce and her contour brush lean back. "You look amazing, but you need to tell me what the deal is with that face."

I debate the best way to explain. "I'm just sorry. For all of it. All those years . . ."

She holds up her hand. "Water under the bridge. We're good now, okay?"

I nod.

"I haven't seen your man around today. I thought he'd be by."

My heart thumps heavily in my chest. "He had to leave town for a bit."

"Spencer left?"

My mouth drops open as I realize my fuck-up. "I meant Josh. I mean Fletch. I thought you were asking . . ."

She knocks her shoulder into mine. "I think he's good for you. And I'm glad you're finally admitting it."

I swallow away the lump that's suddenly formed in the back of my throat. "Shall we get dressed?"

Luce rolls to her feet.

I unzip the bag with Poppy's dress. It's even more beautiful in the late afternoon light. I twist the hanger, letting the crystals catch the sun. When I hear a gasp, I think it's Luce looking at it in awe until I turn and see her face.

"What's wrong?"

She holds up the red material of her dress in her hands.

It takes a moment for me to see what she's looking at. What I thought was a slit in her sequined dress is actually a sizable rip.

"Oh my gosh. What happened?"

She sinks down onto her knees, the dress still cradled in her hands. "I shouldn't have gotten my hopes up. I should have known better."

"Should have known what?" I ask, still confused. "What happened to the dress?"

When she looks up, her eyes are glossy. "What do you think? This place never changes. It's like living the same Groundhog Day over and over and over again. I should have been used to it by now, but no matter how often it happens, it still hurts."

I begin to piece together what has happened. "No," I tell her. "We can fix this. Let me go downstairs and talk to Poppy. Maybe someone brought a backup."

Luce holds up the dress, making the rip even more apparent. "Don't waste your breath. . . . Let's take this as a sign from the universe that I'm not meant for that stage. . . ."

"You are." I place my hand over hers and squeeze. "Give me ten minutes. I'll figure something out, I promise."

I find Poppy backstage, yelling at one of the crew members about the awkward hanging angle of the giant sparkling lobster meant to be the backdrop for the show. "Hey," I call to her. "We have a bit of a problem."

As Poppy turns, the crew member uses the moment to scurry away.

"What?" she barks, holding up her hands.

"Luce's dress is ripped—"

"Yes, I know that—" Poppy interrupts.

"What do you mean, you know? How?"

Poppy grabs my arm, pulling me into one of the wings.

"Come on, Sloan." She covers the mic of her headset with her hand. "She's your biggest competition. If she makes it to the evening round, you're screwed. I was helping you."

My stomach drops.

"You ruined Luce's dress on purpose? Poppy, that's terrible."

She waves me off with a flick of her wrist. "It's not terrible. Maybe a little predictable—unimaginative, even—but I couldn't let her win the thing."

"Why not?"

"Because this is the year Sloan Edwards, golden girl of Carson's Cove, finally gets her crown. The year she wins Spencer's heart. It's what everyone wants, obviously! So I just . . . helped it along a little bit." Poppy presses her finger to the earphone of her headset. "Are we done here? There's a crisis with the seating."

Stunned, I slowly walk back to the bathroom. Luce looks up as I walk in, her eyes big and hopeful, until I shake my head. "I'm sorry."

She shrugs slowly with a resigned sigh. "It's fine. I'll be fine. Here." She tosses her dress into the sink. "Let me help you zip yours up."

All of a sudden, all of the feelings I've been repressing all day bubble to the surface.

"No."

Luce looks confused at the force behind the single word.

"No," I repeat. "I'm not wearing this dress."

I'm not wearing the dress, and I'm not winning the pageant.

I pick up Poppy's sparkling blue evening gown. "You're going to wear it."

Luce shakes her head, confused. "You want me to wear your dress? Sloan, that's not right."

But it is.

Luce is right about everything.

This town is still stuck. It will never change unless it's forced to. The least I can do is take the first baby step.

"I want you to wear it, and I want you to win. You deserve this, Luce."

She takes the dress from my hands. As its weight leaves my arms, the lingering weight of my actions isn't lost.

"Are you sure?" She holds the dress up to her body. I can already tell that it's going to fit her perfectly. A Carson's Cove miracle.

"Absolutely sure."

She raises an eyebrow. "Poppy is going to flip her lid. You know that, right?"

"Yup." A slow smile spreads across my lips. "She's going to lose her freaking bananas."

An idea occurs. One that Poppy is probably going to hate even more than our last-minute dress swap.

I check my watch. We have exactly two hours until the pageant.

"Hey, Luce? I'm gonna need your help again with my hair."

32

BRYNN

The town hall of Carson's Cove is packed.

Every metal folding chair in the roomy multipurpose hall is filled with a familiar face. There are characters from seasons past, extras, guests that made a one-time appearance, and all the familiar regulars: Pop, Lois, Doc Martin. The gang's all here.

Backstage is equally buzzing with excitement as all twenty-three Ms. Lobsterfest hopefuls in our matching seventy-fifth-anniversary T-shirts get ready for our opening number.

"You ready?" Luce nudges me with her hip, sneaking a peek through my secret crack in the curtain.

"Ready as I'll ever be," I tell her back. I pick up a lock of her freshly dyed pink tips. "You look amazing. I have a feeling the crown is yours."

She rolls her eyes. "I appreciate the optimism. I'm just glad I have a fair shot." She nods at my hair, which is still up in curlers under a silk scarf. "You ready to take those out? We're about to go on."

My eyes scan backstage for Poppy. She's on the opposite side of the stage, engrossed in a conversation with Sheldon. Both of their backs are to us.

I nod. "Let's do it."

Luce undoes my hair. As each dark-brown curled lock comes out of its roller, I feel more and more like me.

Luce places the final curler onto the dressing table, then leans forward, squeezing my shoulders and meeting my eyes in the mirror. "Much better," she says with a smile.

She picks up a can of hairspray and gives me a final spritz as a booming voice echoes through the speaker system: "Good evening, ladies and gentlemen."

As the voice lays out the night's events and snacking and flash photography rules, Luce and I take our places in a sea of excited contestants. My stomach begins to bubble with nerves, as if I'm only now realizing that I actually have to go out there and compete in a pageant.

The emcee's voice echoes through the hall. "Please put your hands together and welcome this year's Ms. Lobsterfest contestants to the stage."

The cheesy elevator pop music pumps through the speakers. It's the same tune we rehearsed to all week. I take one last deep breath, push all the remaining nerves as far down into my gut as they will go, and do exactly what I've been doing since I stepped into Sloan's life—I force myself to smile.

When I step onto the stage, the lights are so blinding that the audience turns into one black blob with the occasional camera flash or eyeglass glimmer. Not being able to see anyone is kind of soothing.

Even though my brain is working on its lowest function, my feet go through the motions of the opening number completely of their own accord. I guess Poppy knew exactly what she was doing when she made us practice it over and over and over again.

The whole routine is a haze. I feel like I'm moving through Jell-O until Sloan's name is called, and it snaps me back to reality so hard that it feels like I have whiplash.

The announcer turns to me and smiles. "Welcome, contestant number eight: Sloan Edwards. Sloan loves the beach, growing organic herbs, and designing fashionable and sustainable sundresses. Please give a round of applause for Sloan."

I walk to the X, just like Poppy taught us. Shoulders back to show off my boobs. Jaw jutting forward to avoid the double chin. Mouth open slightly to make my face longer and leaner than it is.

This part is also well practiced.

Putting on my brave face.

My *I'm totally fine* look. The mask I've been wearing for the last four years. The one that hides the broken heart that, although mended, still sports ugly scars.

I'm met with roaring applause.

Cheers. Shouts. Whistles.

"Ladies and gentlemen, your Ms. Lobsterfest contestants. Let's give them one last round of applause before they head off to change for the evening gown and interview rounds. Thank you, ladies."

We exit the stage in a rush of half-naked bodies, shedding lobster-embellished T-shirts for silk and sequins.

Luce slides on the blue gown. It fits as if it were made for her.

"You look like a princess."

She smooths the bodice with the palms of her hands. "Amend that to warrior princess, and I'll take it."

She eyes my red shorts and lobster shirt. "You're absolutely sure you want to do this?"

I nod. "Never been more sure of anything in my life."

Luce laughs, but her smile drops as her eyes shift to something over my shoulder.

"What the heck, Sloan?"

I turn to see Poppy glaring at Luce.

"Why is *she* wearing my dress?"

Poppy is in her own evening wear: a velvet body-hugging mermaid gown in such a deep shade of green that it's almost black. Her hair is slicked back into a sleek ponytail, leaving not a single wisp to hide the look of utter disdain on her otherwise beautiful face.

"As I told you earlier, Luce's dress is ripped." I step forward, placing myself between them. "You had other things to worry about, so I came up with a solution. I think she looks beautiful."

Poppy shakes her head. "No. Absolutely not. She cannot go out there in it. Take it off, now!" Poppy lunges. Her lacquered red nails look like talons as she grabs for the dress, almost as if she intends to rip it off Luce right here and now.

Luce, who ditched her heels earlier in favor of elegant flat sandals, has an agility not achievable in Poppy's four-inch stilettos. Poppy's hands grasp nothing but air as Luce ducks behind a crate of plastic lobsters, just as the emcee's voice booms through the speakers. "And now, please welcome to the stage contestant number three: Ms. Lucille Cho."

Luce's eyes meet mine. I mouth a silent *Go!* while stepping in front of Poppy, arms outstretched, as if I'm fully prepared for her to drop her right shoulder and take me out with a diving tackle so she can chase Luce off the stage.

She doesn't.

Instead, she turns the full force of her heated laser gaze on me. "You witch!"

There's venom in her tone, and I'm surprised by how little it affects me. "It was the right thing to do, Poppy. You should have never ruined her dress. Even if you did it for me."

Poppy swats my hands away. "Since when do you care about Luce?"

I hold up my hands again, this time in more of a gesture of defeat. "I am turning over a new leaf."

"Well, turn it back."

There's a loud smattering of laughter coming from the audience. It halts our conversation. It's a reminder that Luce is on the stage answering her question.

And from the sound of the crowd, she's killing it.

Poppy stamps her foot. The crack of her heel is so loud that I'm surprised it doesn't snap off.

"You've screwed everything up. You know that, right?"

I nod, knowing the repercussions are even worse than what Poppy's implying.

She throws out her arm—a wild gesture in Luce's direction. "Just so we're clear, without a dress, there is no way in hell I am ever letting you out on that stage. Luce is going to win."

"I am okay with that." As the words come out, I know they are true. I am okay if Sloan never wins the crown—tonight or ever. Even if it means she never gets her supposed happily ever after.

She didn't win fifteen years ago. It wasn't the perfect ending everyone wanted, but she went on to do amazing things. Moved to Paris. Started her business. I have a feeling Sloan—I—will be okay this time too. Even if we're not following the plan.

"Can I ask you something though?" I step toward Poppy, lowering my hands. The dress drama tonight sparked a thought about that season finale. A loose end that was never cleared up.

"Fifteen years ago, my dress. That was you too, wasn't it?"

Poppy crosses her arms over her chest. "Guess you'll never know."

Guess I won't. And I don't need to. I'm done with Poppy either way.

There's a round of roaring applause from the audience, the loudest I've heard all night. Poppy and I both turn and watch as Luce exits to the opposite side of the stage. Poppy adjusts her headset and glares at me one last time before turning her heel and heading in the opposite direction.

I'm alone when the emcee calls Sloan's name. I debate, attempting to send him some hand signal to let him know that I've disqualified myself, but as I step toward the wing and catch sight of the audience, I realize that this may be my last opportunity to step out on this stage.

And I have something to say.

The announcer calls for Sloan Edwards again. In a split second, I make a decision. I sprint onto center stage before Poppy or anyone else can stop me.

The lights again blind me as I stumble toward the man with the microphone and try to remember precisely what I'm supposed to do. Find the X. Chest out. Smile.

My head is still swimming with everything that has happened.

An uncomfortable silence settles over the crowd as they take in that I'm still in lobster-wear.

I turn to the emcee. "I am ready for my question, sir."

He hesitates for a moment, then repeats the same question he's asked every contestant this evening. "If you could tell this town one thing on the seventy-fifth anniversary of Ms. Lobsterfest, what would it be?"

There's probably a correct answer here, something to do with peace on earth, but there's more I want to tell this town.

"I thought I wanted a life where everything turned out exactly as it was supposed to. Where your best friend always stayed your best friend, and the feelings of the boy next door never wavered. Where you stand up in front of the entire town and prove that you're finally a woman worthy of love.

"But here's the thing: I've spent the last few weeks falling for the wrong boy. And finding a kindred spirit in the friend who was supposed to be my enemy. I spent a disproportionate amount of time in a bar and had more fun than I can ever remember.

"The point is, nothing at all played out like it was supposed to, and it made me realize something. . . .

"I want messy days that make me appreciate the really good ones, and I don't so much mind that feeling of hitting rock bottom because it makes me appreciate that I'm a tough-ass bitch capable of crawling out of it. Divorce, despair, having my entire life pulled out from under me and tossed into a new dimension— I can take it.

"I am okay to wake up every morning and know that there aren't guarantees in life, but that there is adventure. That there are new beginnings. That I need to love hard for whatever time I'm given because life can throw curveballs at any moment, and sometimes those curveballs are wild.

"So if I'm giving advice—and I really shouldn't be, considering the current state of my life—it would be to take a good hard look around at this town that hasn't seemed to change in the last fifteen years and ask yourself, is this safe and predictable life worth it? Because I think you're missing out on getting to know some great people and experiencing some wild endings. Thank you, and good night."

With that, I drop the mic, turn on my heel, and proudly exit stage left.

There's nothing but silence—literal crickets in the audience. But as I enter the wing, another nagging thought surfaces that I need to get out.

I sprint back to my spot on the stage and pick up the mic still on the floor. "One last thing while we're all gathered. Sloan Edwards has run a sundress empire for the last fifteen years. She doesn't need a crown to tell her she's smart, driven, talented, or worthy of anything. While thinking about everything I just said, you might want to consider nixing this pageant. It's gross. Good night for real this time."

This time, I exit the stage out of the left wing.

I don't stop when Poppy attempts to corner me backstage with an *Are you fudging kidding me, Sloan?* Or when Sheldon calls my name as I exit through the back door.

I run down Main Street, unsure where I'm headed until I turn down the bar's back alley and find the fire escape.

With each rung, I breathe a little deeper. Like a weight is slowly being lifted from my chest. I climb. Higher and higher. Until I can see the stars.

33

BRYNN

The roof is empty.

There are no signs that anyone has been up here at all, except for an empty Moosehead bottle tipped on its side, likely left here from the other night.

I think a small part of me secretly hoped I'd climb these steps and find Josh waiting, somehow teleported back by the magic of Carson's Cove.

I really have to find another show.

"Hey—"

My heart triple-skips at the sound of a man's voice, but steadies as I turn to see a familiar blond step from the fire escape onto the roof. He's wearing khakis and a flannel. The man of my dreams. But I don't want my dreams anymore. I want reality.

"Listen, Spencer—"

He holds up his hand. "Before you say anything, there's something I want to tell you."

I brace for yet another love declaration.

"I heard what you said back there, and I think it was incredible."

Surprised is not quite the right word for my reaction. "You do?"

He nods, his blue eyes bright despite the darkness. "Yes. This town has been so stuck. It's the reason I left and why I stayed away for so long. I haven't been able to put into words what was wrong. But you did. It was amazing."

I'm still caught off guard by what he's saying. He and this town are so entwined that it's hard to separate them.

"Well, thanks."

He takes a tentative step forward. "You don't love me, do you?"

The vulnerability in his voice makes my heart clench. "I'm sorry, Spencer, I don't."

He nods as if this is the answer he was expecting.

"Did you ever?"

I think about his question. "You were the perfect guy all through my teenage years and, in a very special way, my first love. I've been working through those feelings, among others, these last few weeks, and I was sending you some mixed signals, so I apologize for that."

He nods. "I think I may have been caught up in the past too. Being back here has done funny things to my head." He takes a step closer. "I still want to stay friends. Get to know you again."

I know I speak for both Sloan and myself when I say, "I'd really like that too."

He points at the air vent. "Want to sit for a bit?" It's the same spot where I sat with Josh. I join Spencer, looking out over the town.

"I wonder if the rest of this place will ever change."

Spencer looks over at me. "I think it has. I mean, you saw what happened tonight."

I stare at him, confused. "You mean my speech at the pageant?"

He shakes his head. "No, at the crowning."

My heart does a little flip. "What happened?"

Spencer smiles. "Well, after Luce won, Poppy threw a fit. She admitted to fixing the pageant for years with Lois, and the two of them were stripped of their duties indefinitely. There was even talk about getting rid of the pageant completely. You were right, it's kind of a dated concept. Why do you look so surprised?"

"I guess I didn't expect things to turn out that way."

Spencer tilts his head. "Me neither, but I think it all turned out for the best. Luce finally got her crown. Poppy got what was coming to her. And you are exactly where you should be."

"What do you mean?"

Spencer looks at me thoughtfully. "You always loved Carson's Cove. I think it shocked a lot of people when you moved away and never looked back. I think everyone expected you to waltz into town and be that same girl—but you're not. It's obvious that you still love this place. But you're right, it really does need to change. And now you're forcing people to take a hard look at what it has become. And I think Carson's Cove and all the people in it are going to be different—better—after tonight, and that's because of you."

I still don't know how all of this works, or if there is a real Sloan out there who's lived this life that Spencer just described, but I'd like to think that there is and that she'd be proud of everything that's happened here tonight. That it's exactly what she'd want.

Spencer checks his watch. "It's almost midnight. I think I'm going to head home. Do you want me to walk you?"

I shake my head. "I think I'm going to sit for a little longer. I'll catch up with you tomorrow."

Spencer leaves.

I consider going back to Sloan's, but as I climb down the steps, I pass Fletch's window. The bed calls to me. I shed my clothes and climb in, pulling the sheets up over my head.

It still smells like Josh.

As I close my eyes, a single tear trickles down my cheek. My thoughts settle, leaving me with just one.

I miss him.

And with the choices I made today, the odds are that I will never see him again.

34

BRYNN

There's nothing but darkness when I open my eyes.

I can't breathe.

My legs. I can't move them.

Am I injured? Am I paralyzed?

Am I . . . bundled up like a burrito?

I roll my head to the left out of habit, expecting to see the view of the beach from Sloan's bedroom window. But I'm not looking at the beach.

I'm staring at bright-red block letters that spell . . . Netflix?

I blink. Shake my head to clear the brain fog.

I'm wrapped in my fuzzy blue blanket.

On my couch.

My couch back home in Toronto.

"What the actual fuck?"

I can swear.

"Fuck!

"Shit!

"Damn!"

I can voice all my profanities as loudly and as filthily as I want.

And I utter them with abandon as I maneuver my arms out of the fuzzy blue straitjacket, but by the time I am completely free, I'm 100 percent certain I am in my living room and on my couch back in Toronto.

But how did I get here?

My last memories are of my conversation on the roof with Spencer. Then climbing into Fletch's bed.

I run to the full-length mirror next to the front door. I'm still wearing my black lululemon leggings and tank. The ones I went to sleep in on my thirtieth birthday.

Could I have been sleeping? This entire time?

My face is marked with indentations from the cable-knit pattern on my throw pillow.

I sink down, my back pressed to the wall, until I crumble to the floor. I feel like I've been hit. My soul is battered and bruised because everything I felt, everything I went through, was fake? A hallucination? I don't even know.

My eyes flick to the first room down the hall.

Josh's room.

If Carson's Cove never happened, then we didn't either.

My heart clenches. The pain is so sharp that I wonder if I've just felt it break—as if the term *heartbreak* isn't just something made up by Hollywood romantic comedies. It's a real medical condition, and I just experienced it.

No.

You can't dream up entire days in the type of vivid detail that leaves memories imprinted on your brain forever.

There must be another explanation.

My phone.

I scramble to my feet and search the living room until I remember I lost my phone at the bar.

I find my laptop, and as the home screen appears, I have to stare at the date in the corner for a moment to fully process.

It's June 22.

I've been gone for a week.

My eyes land on the coffee table, where the wedge of white cake is still sitting uneaten on a plate. The candle with its singed black wick still in it.

It happened. All of it.

"Josh!" I call, making my way down the hall to the door of his room. "Josh, are you there?"

I bring my fist to the door, but as my hand hits the paint, the door swings open with the force of my knock.

His room is dark.

And empty.

I glance around for clues. His dresser drawers are pulled open, as is his bedside table. It's as if he left in a hurry.

Then it clicks.

"The auction."

Relief washes over me. He made it back too. He's on his way up north. Wait! No, the auction would have been yesterday.

With no phone to call him with, I sit back down on the couch, resigning myself to waiting until he returns home. The Netflix still of *Carson's Cove* is still on my television screen.

I last exactly thirty-two seconds before I decide I hate this plan.

I can't wait for him to come to me. I need to go to him.

I get changed as fast as humanly possible.

I skip running a brush through my hair and return to my laptop and Google. Josh grew up in Orillia, Ontario, and the bar's name is Buddy's. The town is small, and I find an old Facebook page with the address.

I fling open my front door with the heart of a woman ready to get her man, but I halt at the sight of a male body blocking my path.

Holding a bakery box.

"Fuck. No." I point a very stern finger at Sheldon. "Did you hear what I just did? I swore at you. And I will think about you every time a profanity leaves my lips from now until the end of time."

Sheldon holds up the box. It's red. The words *Tim Hortons Doughnuts* are written in familiar script across the front. "This is a peace offering. There are two Boston creams, a honey cruller, and a maple dip. No funny business, I promise."

He moves to step inside, but I block him. "Forgive me if I refrain. What exactly are you doing here? Reminding me that I broke your perfect *Carson's Cove*?"

He pauses before answering. "Maybe. Or maybe you fixed it?" He holds up the doughnuts again. "I came to explain. Can I have five minutes?" He opens the box, pulls out a Boston cream, and takes a bite. "See. My intentions are noble."

I step aside slowly. "You have two. I have somewhere to be."

He sits down on my couch and stares for a moment at the television screen. "It was my happy place too, *Carson's Cove*," he says to me. "Five beautiful years. They were the best of my life. I was relevant. People recognized me. There was a whole website dedicated to me. It even had a newsletter."

He takes a wistful bite of his doughnut.

"But then it ended, and everyone moved on to bigger and better, and I was left stuck. It was supposed to be my big break.

Working on *Carson's Cove* should have propelled me to teen drama fame, but I never got credit for my parts. I couldn't get another job. My own happy ending never happened."

My ice heart melts, just a fraction, because I can relate to the feeling—just not the whole altering-reality-to-deal-with-it.

"But your speech made me think," he continues, "that I've been stuck in the past, and it's high time I moved on with my life too."

Suddenly the last twenty-four hours make a lot more sense.

"So that's why I'm home? You changed your mind?"

Sheldon, however, shakes his head. "I wasn't lying when I told you the magic was bigger than me. You got home because you fulfilled your wish. You gave Sloan the ending she deserves."

A happily independent woman with a true best friend, running her sundress empire and drinking strawberry wine and dancing on the weekends.

She may be a fictional character, but it makes me feel better to know that maybe somewhere in some parallel slip in time, she's living her best life.

"So you just came here to clear the air between us?" I ask Sheldon.

He stands. "Am I forgiven?"

He holds his arms out for a hug. I pick up the doughnut box and shove it into his hands. "You're back in the real world, buddy. You want my forgiveness? You need to earn it."

I walk to the front door and hold it open. Sheldon sulks past me, and as he steps onto the front stoop, I notice a bright-red Mini Cooper in the street.

"Wait!" I call after him.

He turns.

"Is that your car?" I point at the Mini.

His face reddens. "Technically . . . no."

I hold out my hand. "If you give me the keys right now, I'll consider it a significant step toward reconciliation."

His face lights up as he reaches into his pocket and then tosses them to me. "Where are we going?"

"*I* am going. This is a solo mission."

I run across the street and climb into the familiar front seat.

"Can you at least drop me off at the subway?" Sheldon calls as I pull a U-turn.

"Sorry," I shout at him through the open window. "No time. I'm going to get my happily ever after."

35

BRYNN

t's lunch by the time I make it to Orillia, thanks to Toronto traffic and the slew of Torontonians heading north to cottage
country.

The town is busy by the time I cruise in.

It's been a couple of years since I've been here, and as I navigate the Mini down the main street, I'm struck by how much it
reminds me of Carson's Cove. The quaint independent store-
fronts and historic buildings boast that small-town, picturesque
vibe that I've always loved.

It takes me two tries to find the side street where Buddy's is
located, then a full twenty minutes to find parking. I'm so preoccupied with logistics that I don't fully notice the butterflies in my
stomach, which have multiplied exponentially, until I'm standing
in front of the blue-painted bar door, twisting the knob, and finding it unlocked.

"Hello," I call as I push it open.

The place is quiet. It smells a little musty, as if the doors have
been closed for a while. The floor is deep-brown carpet. The

chairs and tables are stained dark wood. It's dated, for sure, but it has a homey feel. Especially the bar. It's made of a beautiful wood. Intricate designs are etched into the shelves. Its U shape reminds me of the Bronze. I can perfectly picture Josh behind it, a white bar towel tossed over his shoulder as he pulls a beer from the tap.

"Hey, sorry. We're closed," says a voice.

It freezes me in place.

"I'm tight with the bartender. We crossed a space-time continuum together. It's bonded us in weird and wonderful ways."

"Brynn?"

My thoughts scatter as I turn a slow 180 degrees to face him. All of the things I wanted to say are forgotten as I lock eyes with a man I'd cross a hundred dimensions to find.

"You changed your hair."

I pick up a lock of hair between my fingers and drop it. "The blond never felt like me. I think my soul is a brunette."

He takes a step closer. "It looks so different." He shakes his head. "Good, I mean. Beautiful." He runs both his hands through his hair and lets them drop. "Sorry. I'm still learning."

"So am I."

I take a step toward him, then another, then one more, till there's nothing but a breath between us. I'm almost afraid to touch him, worried that he'll burst like a bubble. A beautiful illusion.

He moves first, his fingers traveling up my arm, lightly skating upon the surface until he cups my chin.

"You made it back." His thumb brushes my cheek, and I fight the urge to close my eyes, wanting to soak in every single second with him.

"It's a really long story," I tell him. "But I'll spoil the ending. Sloan doesn't end up with Spencer."

Josh's hand stills. "An unexpected twist?"

"Turns out they work best as old friends. She's got too much going on. Luce. A sundress empire to run. She's only in town for a short while before she's off to see the world."

Josh smiles. "I like that ending."

I nod. "I do too. But tell me, what about *your* happily ever after?"

Josh takes a step back, his hand dropping from my cheek. "This place is going to take a lot of work. It needs some updating. New flooring. I kind of think it could use a band. I was thinking I could really use a partner."

I try to hide my smile. "I may know someone. She's pretty slick behind the bar. If you can steal her away from Applebee's, she might be perfect."

He steps toward me again, his arms coming around my shoulders as he pulls his head to mine. "I think she'll be perfect."

His lips travel from the bridge of my nose to my lips, where he plants a soft kiss.

"Hey, Josh." I pull back to say the magic four words that I traveled through time and space to tell him. "I fudging love you."

He laughs, pressing his lips to my forehead.

"I fudging love you too."

36

BRYNN

There's music coming from downstairs.

It has a thumping bass that reverberates up through the floorboards, tickling my socked feet. I abandon my project, an Instagram reel featuring the updated decor of the bar downstairs spliced with photos of the original Buddy's when it opened for the first time over forty years ago.

Although the new, updated Buddy's has been open for a few weeks, the official grand reopening isn't until this Friday, and I have been using every marketing tactic in my skill set to ensure that every single beer-loving human living in a fifty-kilometer radius knows about it.

After Josh and I reunited (and consummated our reunion on the wooden bar), we made the decision to move in together. It was mostly a symbolic gesture, seeing as we already shared an address, but the big, scary change came when we also decided to move up north so that Josh could be close to Buddy's.

Being a Northern Ontario bar wench was definitely not the

plan I'd had for my life. But I have been living here for almost four months, and if this place is not my happily-ever-after, it's most definitely my happily-for-now. I'm drawing an income from renting out my Toronto townhouse to a lovely lawyer and her labradoodles. Josh and I live very frugally above the bar, which means I'm able to work at my fully remote marketing job for only three days a week, leaving ample time for entertaining bar patrons with my bottle-flipping skills on the weekends. Josh and I joined a curling league and are enjoying the laid-back routine of living in this low-drama small town. I can't remember ever being this happy.

I shut down my computer and head downstairs.

Josh is behind the bar when I walk in. His arms are crossed over his chest, and he's staring at the stage, where a band is playing their audition set. One of the first things Josh did when he took over was pull out some booths and build a small stage in the corner of the bar. When Buddy's officially reopens, it will have live music every Thursday through Saturday, along with karaoke every Sunday and Wednesday night. Josh has promised to give me fair warning if he ever feels the urge to sing a love ballad.

"Hey," I call to Josh, who turns at the sound of my voice and watches me as I attempt to crawl under the counter with the grace of a newborn baby antelope. He holds out his arm when I make it through, and I tuck myself underneath. My favorite place on earth.

My former favorite place on earth, Carson's Cove, is still shrouded in mystery. I haven't been able to bring myself to watch an episode since we got home. The only glimpse of Sheldon I've gotten since I stole his car happened by accident as I was watching an episode of *Law & Order: SVU*. He played an obsessed cyber-stalker. I had to change the channel—that wound was still a little too fresh—but in the brief few moments before I recognized him without his bleached-blond hair, I did hear him deliver a few lines. Enough that I'm confident he'll get the credit he desperately wanted.

The band rolls into a new song. It's a cover of the Weeknd's "Blinding Lights."

I press up on my toes to get closer to Josh's ear. "They're no Seth and the Hungry Dingos, but they sound pretty good."

He plants a kiss on the top of my head and squeezes my ass. "You smell really good," he tells me. "What is that?"

"Cedar Lumberjack. I bought my own stick. I was tired of smelling like a field of flowers, and I feel like I can pull it off now that we live up here."

He buries his nose in my neck and kisses me softly behind my ear. A promise of what is to come later when we finally get upstairs.

The front door to the bar opens and a woman walks through. Her back is to us, and it takes a moment to place her until she turns around and I recognize Josh's mom. She walks toward us, and in her hands is a white sheet cake, decorated with green icing that spells out *May all of your dreams come true.* In the center is a single white candle. Its wick dances with a tiny orange flame. She sets it down on the bar in front of us. "I'm so proud of you, sweetheart," she says to Josh as she reaches out to squeeze my hand. "I thought you both deserve a celebration for all of the work you've put into the place, and the sweetest little bakery popped up just around the corner. Everything in the window looked delicious and I couldn't resist." She nudges the cake toward us. "I know it's not tradition, but why don't you make a wish?"

Josh turns and looks at me.

I inhale, my mind swimming with a million ideas for our next adventure.

"On three?" Josh asks, smiling as if he knows exactly what's going on in my head.

"One . . . two . . ."

We close our eyes, hold on to that feeling, and blow.

Acknowledgments

I was sitting pretty smug back in the spring of 2022 when I already had a great idea for Book #2 and a solid opening three chapters. Dangerous thoughts occurred: "The sophomore curse won't happen to me." "I'll do exactly what I did the first time, but better."

Then, of course, I was humbled.

Draft #1 of *Prime Time Romance* needed a major overhaul. The nice thing about having an editor is that when your manuscript hits rock bottom, you have someone sitting there beside you, ready to help you climb out of the deep hole you've fallen into. I had Emma Caruso, who not only provided a firm editing hand (i.e., a very bright flashlight if we're still using the hole analogy) but also a constant, motivating chant of "You can do it!" Eventually, I *did*, and the chant became an "I'm so proud of you." EC: I appreciate the tough love as much as I appreciate your constant and unabashed optimism.

Bibi Lewis, I'm convinced you're a shark disguised as a sparkly pink dolphin. I love how you've become a regular presence in my life. My day gets infinitely better with a Bibi phone call (especially ones made from remote weddings with no cell service because you cannot wait to share the good news). I appreciate your willingness to talk me through all the small things, strategize the big things, and be my sounding board for everything else in between.

To Whitney Frick and the Dial team, last year, when I wrote the acknowledgments for *This Spells Love,* I had only an inkling of the marketing/PR/strategy powerhouse that was The Dial Press team. Cindy Berman, Debbie Aroff, Madison Dettlinger, Melissa Folds, every time someone says "Wow! Dial knows how to launch a book," I think of you. There is something truly special happening at Dial and I am so grateful to be a small part of all the wonderful books you bring into this world.

To the wonderful team at Viking UK: Lydia Fried and Jasmin Lindenmeir. You have worked publishing miracles in the UK and I am incredibly grateful to be a Viking UK author.

Petra Braun, your beautiful works of art make my soul so happy. Thank you!

I often get asked, "How did you know how to write a book?" and my answer is always, "I didn't. Until I found the writing community." I have never met a group more willing to lift one another up, pass on knowledge and expertise, and celebrate every single tiny milestone (even if it's your 3,495th Instagram story on the same topic). I am forever appreciative of the expert eyeballs of Sarah T. Dubb, Mae Bennett, Ingrid Pierce, Jenny Lane, and Amanda Wilson, who helped find all the good in this manuscript and weed out the bad. Katie Gilbert, Aurora Palit, Jessica Joyce, Ambriel McIntyre, Ellie Palmer, Amy Buchanan, Scarlette Tame, and Maggie North, as well as The Boners and all the members of SF 2.0. Thank you for trusting me with your wonderful words and providing a safe space to share mine.

Hudson Lin, Shade LaPite, Lindo Forbes, Farah Heron, and the rest of Toronto Romance Writers: Thank you for the many nights and emotional support nachos that got me through my debut year.

Lavanya Lakshmi, my black heart has found a kindred spirit in yours. Thank you for talking me off a ledge multiple times (and, of course, the emotional support cocktails). Sarah Adams, Sarah Hogle, Karma Brown, Jen Deluca, Marissa Stapley, and BK Borison, I didn't have a chance to thank you for your kind words on and off the page with *This Spells Love.* I am forever grateful for your willingness to blurb an author you didn't know at the time. You are exactly what I mean when I talk about the generosity and kindness of the writing community.

To those who have read, reviewed, and shared their thoughts and posts for both *This Spells Love* and *Prime Time Romance:* I appreciate how much time it takes to review a book, create a beautiful post, or reach out with kind words. These happily-ever-afters could not happen without you and I am endlessly grateful.

Finally, to my family, friends, and neighbors, thank you for reading, texting, and winking covertly at school pickup to let me know you made it to the spicy scenes. I appreciate your page-by-page text updates, covert relocations of my books to the best tables in the bookstore, and every selfie when you spot my book out in the wild. Love you all. xo

Prime Time Romance

Kate Robb

Dial Delights

LOVE STORIES FOR THE OPEN-HEARTED

Prime Time Romance
Easter Egg Hunt

Unless I really missed the mark, you hopefully got a few *Dawson's Creek* vibes from the town of Carson's Cove. But *Prime Time Romance* was an homage to more than just *DC*. It was a nostalgic nod to all of the teen dramas that shaped my formative years. If you didn't catch them during your read (or get a funny inkling), here are the teen drama Easter eggs I planted, changing just enough details to not get sued.

1. **Carson's Cove:** The picturesque seaside town with tiny inlets perfect for a nighttime paddle (or row) is a definite nod to the picturesque New England town of Capeside.
2. **The Bronze:** *Buffy* fans, I know you caught this one! Sherry's bar was named after the Scooby Gang's favorite underage hangout. What a perfect place for Seth and the Hungry Dingos to play (a not-so-subtle nod to Seth Green's character, Oz, and his band, Dingoes Ate My Baby).
3. **The Ms. Lobsterfest Pageant:** You might be thinking I'm going back to the Creek with this one, but you'd be wrong

(partially wrong). The annual pageant was a staple for most TV dramas that wanted an excuse to pour their beautiful talent into a sparkling evening gown. (I'm looking at you, Ms. Mystic Falls and the *Vampire Diaries*.) But Ms. Lobsterfest was very much inspired by the Malibu Sands Miss Liberty pageant from *Saved by the Bell*. (Side note: Lisa Turtle and her red mini were robbed IMHO.)

4. **Poppy Bensen:** Cherry Bomb, Addison Montgomery, Chuckie. I love a redhead ready to stir up some shit. Although I definitely had *Riverdale*'s Cherry Bomb in my head as I was writing, I was channeling Brenda Walsh energy. The show *90210* was notorious for the "you are my best friend, but I will still stab you in the back" plotlines that were staples for '90s teen dramas. Bonus points if you caught the parallel backgrounds (both Poppy and her brother, Peter, and Brenda and Brandon were the new kids from Minnesota).

5. **Pop's Diner:** This fifties-themed location was inspired by Pop's in *Riverdale* but also the cult classic *Pleasantville*, which heavily inspired the plot of *Prime Time Romance*.

6. **The Alanis Morissette song playing in the diner:** Along with this Easter egg, you are getting a little history lesson. When *Dawson's Creek* originally aired, the producers wanted Alanis's "Hand in My Pocket" as the opening theme song but couldn't get the rights worked out. Then, when *DC* aired on Netflix internationally, they ran into international licensing issues and used "Run Like Mad" by Jann Arden outside the US. Jan and Alanis were my go-tos for unrequited love sing/sob sessions, and it gave me immense pleasure to give my fellow Canadians a nod.

7. **Forehead kisses and hair tucks:** You know how in *The Great Gatsby*, the grass is green and the ceiling looks like a wed-

ding cake, and your high school teacher insisted it was symbolism? Well, the forehead kisses and hair tucks are my symbolism. I may have overdone it with the forehead kisses, but that was Pacey Witter's signature move, and I think it's the perfect way to show true and genuine love and care. Spencer, on the other hand, loved to tuck Sloan's hair behind her ear, and I used this to show that a) it's an overused and cliché move, just like our boy Spencer; b) it's kind of annoying, especially as hands are greasy; and c) it's superficial. If you love someone, just let their hair do its own thing.

8. **Character Names:** All of my characters had unique combos of the best (and worst) characters from prime time television. Poppy's boyfriend "Chad Michaels"—I had to reference Chad Michael Murray somewhere! Poppy's surname is a nod to *Pretty Little Liars'* Ashley Benson. Little Chuck (our bouncer) is a reference to the iconic Chuck Bass. I feel like there are even more that crept their way from my subconscious to the page. Bonus points if you can spot them!

Who Was Your TV Boyfriend?

Teen dramas played a big part in my coming-of-age experience. In addition to setting unrealistic expectations for my high school experience, they also helped shape the expectations of what I should expect in a good partner. Although these dramas tended to skew to toxic and even harmful examples of what love should look like, there were also a few gems. Here is my list of late '90s/ early 2000s TV drama boyfriends who made me believe in love:

1. **Pacey Witter (*Dawson's Creek*):** I know, you're totally shocked. I will admit that, along with most of the world, I began my *DC* journey very much in the camp of Team Dawson.* I fully blame the Tamara Jacobs storyline for this early error in judgment, but the moment Andie McPhee arrived in the Creek, I was firmly on the Pacey train. Charming and

---

*Although I definitely threw some shade at Dawson Leery the character, I do want to share my eternal love and admiration for JVB the man. *Don't Trust the B* is a masterpiece. You are brilliant. Your TikTok gives me life. Fuck fire ants!

self-deprecating, sweet and loyal, and good god, those kisses in the rain. Pacey Witter will always be my top slot (unless we move into adult dramas, then Peter Bishop knocks him out, but you can see a theme here: Joshua Jackson forever).

2. **Ryan Atwood (*The O.C.*):** Now, I know the correct answer here is probably Seth Cohen and his undying love for Summer, but I was a Ryan girl. Maybe it's the bad boy persona—I just want to smother him in love until I change him. But blond, brooding Ryan was my man.

3. **Logan Huntzberger (*Gilmore Girls*):** I may have opened the can of worms with Ryan Atwood, but now I am hurling the can across the room, leaving a long trail of worm guts behind me. I know, I know, the internet loves Jess. My reasonable adult brain sees his floppy hair and arms full of books and acknowledges you know what you are talking about. But my teenage brain, with its unformed frontal lobe, had a thing for blond bad boys (see above). I was a sucker for the "hot guy wants her and wants her bad," and that was Logan's whole thing. Also, Rory changed him (he became a better boyfriend—it can happen!).

Bake a Wish—Possibly Magical Birthday Cake

THE CAKE

2⅓ cups cake flour

2¼ tsps baking powder

¾ tsp salt

¾ cup softened unsalted butter

1½ cups white granulated sugar

1 cup buttermilk

3 eggs

2 tsps vanilla extract

Vanilla Icing

¾ cups softened unsalted butter

3 cups icing sugar

⅓ cup full-fat milk

1 teaspoon pure vanilla extract

1 pinch of salt

Directions

FOR THE CAKE

* Preheat oven to 350°F.
* Cut two 8-inch rounds of parchment paper and line the bottom of two 8-inch pans.
* Spray both the pan and the paper with nonstick spray.
* In a separate bowl, whisk together the flour, baking powder, and salt.
* Place the butter and sugar in a separate bowl and beat using a hand mixer or Kitchen Aid mixer-like contraption (mine is named Tina Sparkle).
* Beat on medium speed until very soft and light (4–5 minutes).
* Reduce the beater speed to low and beat in the buttermilk and eggs, followed by the vanilla.
* Add in your dry ingredients, using as few beater spins as possible. (Fun fact: I actually took Baking Arts 101 at George Brown College, and one of the only things I remember is that the more you mix flour, the more you activate the glutens and the tougher/chewier it gets. Therefore, lots of kneading if you're making bread, but as little as possible for fluffy baked goods.)
* Pour the batter into the cake pans.
* Bake the cakes for 30–35 minutes (double-check by sticking a toothpick into the middle and ensuring it comes out clean).
* Make sure the cakes are completely cool (this is always my downfall).

FOR THE ICING

* Get out Tina Sparkle again (or whatever awesome name you've given your mixer).

* Cream the butter on medium for about 2 minutes.
* Turn the speed down to low and add icing sugar, milk, vanilla, and salt.
* Crank that baby up to high and let her/him/them go to town for another 2 minutes.
* Taste-a-roo: If the icing is too thick, add some more milk. If the opposite is happening, add a little more sugar.

DECORATE

* Once the layers are cool, you can frost your cake. Feel free to add a surprise to the center layer.
* Decorate with sprinkles!
* Enjoy, and don't forget to make a wish.

KATE ROBB is the author of *This Spells Love*. She dated a lot of duds in her twenties (along with a few gems), and they've all provided excellent fodder for writing weird and wild romantic comedies. She lives just outside of Toronto, Canada, where she spends her free time pretending she's not a hockey mom while whispering "hustle" under her breath from the stands and concealing Pinot Grigio in her YETI mug. She hates owls, the word "whilst," and wearing shorts, and she aspires to one day be able to wear four-inch heels again.

katerobbwrites.com

About the Type

This book was set in Baskerville, a typeface designed by John Baskerville (1706–75), an amateur printer and typefounder, and cut for him by John Handy in 1750. The type became popular again when the Lanston Monotype Corporation of London revived the classic roman face in 1923. The Mergenthaler Linotype Company in England and the United States cut a version of Baskerville in 1931, making it one of the most widely used typefaces today.